# THE
# SORCERER'S
# CIRCLE

Also by Michael Siverling

*The Sterling Inheritance*

# THE
# SORCERER'S
# CIRCLE

*Michael Siverling*

THOMAS DUNNE BOOKS
ST. MARTIN'S MINOTAUR
NEW YORK

This is a work of fiction. All of the characters, organizations, and events portrayed in this novel are either products of the author's imagination or are used fictitiously.

THOMAS DUNNE BOOKS.
An imprint of St. Martin's Press.

www.thomasdunnebooks.com
www.minotaurbooks.com

Library of Congress Cataloging-in-Publication Data

Siverling, Michael.
    The sorcerer's circle / Michael Siverling.—1st ed.
        p. cm.
    Sequel to: The Sterling Inheritance
    ISBN-13: 978-0-312-36192-1
    ISBN-10: 0-312-36192-0
    1. Family-owned business enterprises—Fiction. 2. Parent and adult child—Fiction. 3. Satanism—Fiction. 4. Private investigators—Fiction. 5. Mothers and sons—Fiction. I. Title.

PS3619.I95  S67  2006
813'.6—dc22

                                                                2006046595

First Edition: December 2006

10  9  8  7  6  5  4  3  2  1

For Tom Wilde

# ACKNOWLEDGMENTS

Once again, I owe an incalculable debt to the people who made this book possible:

Penny Rudolph, wonderful writer and wonderful friend, who looked after me.

Sorche Fairbank, agent extraordinaire, who made it all happen despite me.

Ruth Cavin, who always manages to beat a better story out of me.

India Cooper, who does a wonderful job saving me from me.

Alan and Shawnie, for putting up with me.

Denise and Nicole, just for being with me.

And, of course, Mom.

# THE
# SORCERER'S
# CIRCLE

# CHAPTER ONE

The blade of the knife came scything toward my face as I threw up my left arm for a block. I had twisted my body around, trying to clamp my right hand down on the arm that held the blade when I suddenly got jerked back and down, slamming into the ground flat on my back. Before I knew it, I felt the knife slash along my throat. I was dead. Again.

I would have been, too, if the knife hadn't been a hard rubber practice blade. As I lay on the workout mat, trying to catch my breath, I reminded myself that the reason I was being subjected to this torturous workout now was because just over a month ago I'd been badly cut by a real edged weapon. According to my boss, getting stabbed was simply not acceptable. "Okay, Junior," I heard, "get up. We ain't done yet."

With effort, I raised my head and looked around. It was bad enough to get thrown around like a rag doll, but to have an audience like this made it infinitely worse. I was the object of scrutiny by seven eyes: The first two were bright blue and belonged to Timothy O'Toole, my chief torturer at the moment, who for the last three hours had been beating the living daylights out of me under the guise of testing my fitness in the arena of unarmed combat. I was disgusted to see that there wasn't a drop of sweat to be found anywhere on his barrel-chested, muscular fifty-something-year-old body. The second set was the dark Asian eyes of James Bui, who examined my every move with clinical scrutiny. He'd already put me through my paces this morning at the cold and foggy outdoor firearms range where I had to demonstrate my shooting ability ad nauseam.

But it was the last three eyes that I looked to in the hope of being able to call an end to my current torment. "How about it, boss?" I managed to croak. "Have I had enough?"

Victoria Wilder, the silver-haired, steely-eyed owner of the Midnight Investigation Agency, regarded me with a cool, dispassionate gaze. The woman who gave me employment, she had given birth to me as well. Sitting next to her was the owner of the odd eye of the group—Beowulf, a former River City police canine who had lost his other eye in the line of duty. He just looked at me and yawned, indifferent to my plight. Without taking her eyes off me, Mom said, "Gentlemen?"

Jim Bui shrugged. "The boy did okay this morning, but I'd like it better if he'd trade in that damn antique revolver and start carrying something more efficient."

"And he's as soggy as a bag of wet potato chips," Tim O'Toole added. "He needs to get his butt back in shape. Other than that, he's okay."

"Very well," Mom said airily. Turning her attention to me, she said, "Congratulations, kiddo. You're now officially back in the working world. Do get up off your back, Jason. It's undignified."

"Your wish is my command," I groaned. It took me a couple of tries, but I managed to pull myself to my feet. O'Toole held the rubber practice knife out to me. "One last thing," he said. "Let's go through the universal knife defense maneuver."

"Oh, hell, no," I groaned. "I know that one. You just want

to slam me on the mat again. Forget it. I got your point already, so to speak."

The man I'd known all my life as Uncle Timmy smiled. "Really? And that point was?"

"That you should never, ever, ever get up close against a guy with a knife. I got it. Can I go home now? I've got a date tonight, and I'd rather not spend my evening in the emergency room."

"Again," Jim Bui added softly. I shot Uncle Jimmy a sour look. I'd had enough of hospitals to last a lifetime. "Actually," Jimmy continued, "the point O'Toole was trying to drive home was that you should always bring a gun to a knife fight."

I nodded in agreement. I'd lost count of how many times I'd been killed this afternoon, and my recent encounter with a sharp object left me with a skin-crawling feeling whenever I thought about it.

"Okay, boys, that's it for today," Mom announced. "Jason, I'll expect you back here bright and early tomorrow. So try to not exert yourself tonight."

Uncle Timmy looked at me with interest. "You've got a date? With a girl and everything?"

"Two, in fact," I replied. "A tall brunette and a short blonde."

From the corner of my eye, I saw Her Majesty Victoria smile with royal approval. "Good," she proclaimed. "It's about time you grew out of your bimbo-du-jour stage." She then gave me a quick wink and ascended the stairs, Beowulf trailing obediently behind. Timmy and Jimmy followed, with Uncle Timmy saying, "Well, I should head to the gym. I didn't get much of a workout today."

I waited until I heard the door leading to our basement-armory-storage-torture chamber shut, then I finally allowed myself to double over and press my hand to my right side, just over the spot where I'd been cut open. There were times during my recovery when I'd have sworn that the doctors stitched me shut while taking a couple of inches of skin in, like a tailor shortening a pair of pants. Before I submitted myself to the day's marathon of activity, I thought I was pretty much healed up, but off and on all day it felt like nerves in my side were being pulled apart and snapped like strings. I didn't dare show any signs of pain for fear that I'd be put back on light duty, which in my case meant being tied to the front desk and being the company receptionist. I'd done that gig for the last two weeks, allowing Paul Merlyn, our usual front man, to take an unscheduled vacation. At this point, I was on the verge of going plain stir-crazy.

I drew in a breath and straightened up, slowly. After a full day of strenuous abuse, I'd collected a lot of other sore areas of my body to keep the pain in my side company. I then noticed that I'd been left the chores of rolling up the padded floor mat and putting the practice weapons away. As usual. At least I'd already cleaned my handgun during the lunch break. Then all I had in front of me was the job of making myself presentable for the evening. *Which at this stage could take some doing,* I thought ruefully.

Unfortunately, I took a little too long cleaning up the basement. As I reached the back offices and got my jacket, I heard the front doorbell announce a visitor. It was well after five in the evening, the time when most normal businesses close. Then again, the Midnight Investigation Agency has never been what you'd call normal.

I had been left alone, the office deserted long ago. I was sorely tempted, along with being just plain sore, not to answer the door, but I'd been raised and trained to never turn away visitors—at least until I found out who they were and what they wanted. I sighed, ran my hands through my still sweat-soaked hair, and went to check the back room security monitors. I turned on the screen and saw a single visitor at the front door: a man, dressed all in black with long white hair and a matching beard. His face was shrouded by the brim of a dark hat and a pair of dark glasses, which struck me as unusual seeing as how it was already dark out this early December evening. I keyed the intercom switch. "May I help you?"

The man seemed to start. "Ah. Hello. I wasn't sure anyone was in. Are you still open?"

I tried to keep a disappointed tone out of my voice as I asked, "Are you here on business, sir?"

"Yes. I was told to come here. The police suggested it."

"The police?"

"Yes. They said that you were the only ones who could help me."

Now I was suspicious. It was a pure and simple truth that the River City Police Department had no acknowledged use for the Midnight Agency. This no doubt stemmed from the fact that we were a hell of a lot better at our jobs than the police were at theirs. Not surprising, really, as my mother, Jimmy, and Timmy used to be detectives on the force, along with my father. It was Dad's death that caused Mom and my surrogate uncles to quit the department and start up their own private investigation shop. Since then, the Midnight Agency has become known far and wide as the best PI outfit around.

My suspicions were fueled by the fact that our little detective agency had recently made the police look like a bunch of incompetents when we managed not only to solve a homicide and clear an innocent person but also to crack a case that had been unsolved for over twenty years. After those recent escapades, the only thing I'd expect to come from the River City police would be a ticking package on our doorstep.

Be all that as it may, I was still left with an unbidden guest, and Her Majesty Victoria had very strict rules in regard to company. "Just a moment, sir," I said through the intercom. "I'll be right there."

As I walked through the first-floor offices, I was hoping I could see what this gentleman's problem was and still be in time for my date. I unlocked the heavy outer door and greeted my guest. "Good evening, sir. My name is Jason Wilder. How may I help you?"

My visitor smiled, revealing a set of bright, perfect teeth. From the wide brim of his hat to his long coat, worn over his shoulders like a cape, to every other piece of apparently expensive clothing, he was dressed entirely in black, in stark contrast with his long hair and beard, both the color of snow. The only variation in his personal color scheme was a large and ornate gold ring on his left hand. If he took any notice of me in my jeans, sweatshirt, and Eau de Gunpowder cologne, he gave no sign. He removed his dark glasses while offering me a long, slender hand. His eyes, now revealed, were dark orbs beneath white brows.

"Ah. Mr. Wilder. Thank you for seeing me." As he took my hand, his grip suddenly increased in pressure, then released. "Ah. Ah, yes," he said in an undertone.

I stepped aside and ushered him in. "Right this way, sir." I led him through the reception area to the place we call the Throne Room, the dark-wood-paneled, richly appointed office where Queen Victoria holds court. I gestured for my guest to have a seat in one of the two high-backed leather chairs while I did a quick turn around the massive mahogany desk and eased into Mom's chair. He spent a moment looking around the office, from the grandfather clock to the gilt-framed portrait of my father above the fireplace mantel. I noticed that he was slightly taller than my own height of not quite six feet, and slender. As he seated himself, I asked, "Now, how can I help you, Mr . . . ?"

"I'm sorry," the man said in his rich baritone. "You've experienced some tragedy, I see."

The statement threw me off, at the same time sending an electric chill up my spine. "Tragedy is the family business," I said in response. "Speaking of which, what brings you here?"

He gave me a thin smile. "I'm sorry. I was sidetracked. And again, thank you for seeing me. My name is Elijah Messenger. Perhaps you've heard of me?"

"Sorry. Can't say that I have."

He looked disappointed. "Ah. I see. Well, Mr. Wilder, as I said before, the police suggested I come to your agency."

"Well, Mr. Messenger, if you need investigative work done, we are the best place in town. What exactly do you need, sir?"

"Mr. Wilder, I believe someone is going to kill me."

He said it with the same lack of expression as you'd say, *It's probably going to rain today*. "You mean," I said, "that you think someone is going to try to kill you?"

He shook his head slowly as he said, "No, sir. I mean that someone is going to kill me. And soon. Very soon."

I got that tingly spine-crawling feeling again, the kind you get when you just know something isn't right. "Mr. Messenger, tell me, how is it you know someone is going to kill you?"

"Mr. Wilder, please tell me first." He leaned forward and looked straight into my eyes. "Do you believe that there are those in this world who can see beyond the veil, so to speak?

Those who are gifted with senses denied to normal men, those who can see into the realm beyond?"

*No,* I wanted to answer, but I did believe I was now in the presence of a total whack job. So that was it, that feeling I had. It was my internal radar trying to tell me that I was close to someone afflicted with insanity. It certainly wasn't the first time this sort of thing had happened. People who are cursed with psychosis frequently seek out organizations like the police or the FBI and try to get their help with whatever demons are tormenting them. It was clear to me now that Mr. Messenger had already spun his tale to the local police, who then decided to send him on his way and off in our direction.

I'd have loved to find out who the comedian with a badge was, but at the moment I decided to settle for getting rid of my unwanted visitor. "Mr. Messenger, unless you can tell me who it is that wants to kill you, I don't see where my firm can help. I mean, has anyone threatened you?" *Anyone real?* I thought.

Messenger's dark, expressive eyes searched my own, as if he were looking for something on a far-off horizon. Finally he looked down and said softly, "Ah. Of course. I see." With a sigh, Elijah Messenger rose from the chair. "It's not your fault. There are so few who can really see, you know?"

Suddenly I felt sorry for him. As he stood to leave, I asked, "Mr. Messenger? Is there anyone you'd like me to call for you?"

He stopped, turned, and smiled, though sadly. "No," he said as he shook his head. "There's nothing anyone can do for me, I'm afraid. I, of all people, should know that some things are fated to be."

I escorted him to the front door and watched as he walked off into the amber-lit street. When he disappeared from view,

8

I shook my head. River City is full of reality-challenged people. Poor Elijah Messenger was just much better dressed than most.

I closed the door, certain I'd seen the last of him.

■

# CHAPTER TWO

I had to hurry home to my apartment to wash up and change for my date. I didn't get nearly enough time in the warm, soothing shower, but I was drawn out by the desire to see my tall brunette and my short blonde. My girlfriends. On the agenda for tonight's date was dinner and a movie. The dinner was at the apartment of the tall brunette, and the movie to follow was *Peter Pan,* shown on the television and complete with popcorn. The film was a recent favorite of the short blonde's, and I have to confess that I enjoyed it as much as she. Maybe more. Then again, she was only five years old.

In short order, I was snuggled on the couch between the two females. Jenny Chance, the taller of the two, a.k.a. Angelina's mother, was to my left, while little Angelina herself was tucked in on my right. We had just reached the last fight scene, where Hook was being chased across the lagoon by the crocodile, when Jenny clicked off the movie.

"Aw, Mom!"

"Now, Jason," Jenny responded to my protest, warmly but firmly. "You know it's past Angelina's bedtime. She should be asleep by now."

The little blonde and I looked at each other, then we both threw our heads to the side, snoring loudly. "Comedians,"

Jenny said. "I got a bunch of comedians on my couch. All right, you two. Playtime's over. It's sleepytime now."

Angelina threw her arms out to me. "Fly me!"

I stood up. "Okay, Tinker Bell, what's the magic formula?"

Angelina stood up on the couch, arms out wide. "Faith-Trust-Pixie-Dust!" she shouted quickly as she launched herself into space. I swear, the girl is fearless. I caught her in midleap and made a production of spinning her up and around as we caromed around the living room and down toward the hall. Because of the space constraints, I then had to throw her over my shoulder and dangle her upside down until I got her to her room, where I gave her one last lift toward the ceiling before I bounced her on the bed. All of which woke up all those abused body parts of mine and hurt like hell, but I wasn't going to let a little thing like pain keep me from showing the girl a good time.

"Again!" Angelina said instantly.

"Not tonight, sweetheart," Jenny said from the doorway. "You don't want to wear out your playmate. Now give Jason a kiss good night."

Angelina stood up on her bed, and she and I exchanged a noisy, comical kiss. "Good night, Tinker Bell."

"See you tomorrow?"

"I don't know, Tink. We'll see. Now get some sleep."

"I don't wanna. I'm not tired."

"Okay, all boys out of the room," Jenny announced. I made a production of looking around while Angelina laughed and thumped me on my chest. "You! You're a boy!"

"Oh, yeah. I forgot. Good night, baby."

As I turned away, Jenny whispered from the side of her mouth, "Stick around and stay awake. I'll remind you." To Angelina she said, "Okay, you. Jammies or nightie tonight?"

I slipped out of the room and padded down the hall in my stocking feet to the living room. Jenny's place was a small two-bedroom apartment on the inexpensive side, a place she mostly referred to as "the Hell Hole." I looked around at the cluster of clutter in the living room, most of which was my fault, as Angelina and I had played while Jenny fixed our pasta dinner. I was about to pick up some of the toys when one of the portrait photographs on the wall caught my attention. My favorite was the one that I first saw on Jenny's desk in her office at the Castle Theater: mother and daughter with their heads close together, Jenny's dark hair entwined with Angelina's pale blond, with two pair of the most beautiful blue eyes in the world looking back at you.

If you've gotten the impression that I'm kind of fond of them both, you're right.

I sat down on the couch, gazing at the picture, and as I did so, Elijah Messenger's words came back to me: *You've experienced some tragedy, I see.* I wondered what he would have made of Jenny Chance. In the short time since I met her, I had learned she'd lived through more tragedy than anyone else I knew. On the other hand, as Jenny herself would say it, she has the most wonderful daughter ever, and there's nothing in the world more important than that to her. Fortunately, thanks to a little help from Mom and me, she not only avoided being jailed for a murder she didn't commit, she was now on her way to becoming a relatively wealthy woman.

My own part in the Castle Theater affair ended with yours truly nearly being shishkabobbed, but finding Jenny and Angelina made it all worthwhile, although I'd be hard-pressed to define our relationship. I was bound and determined to take things slowly with Jenny, knowing she'd need time to come to terms with everything that had recently happened in her life.

So for now, the only subjects we discussed that ignited her passions were Angelina and the house Jenny would soon be able to afford for the two of them.

During my musings, I found that I had slipped into a supine position on the couch. It felt good to close my eyes. Just for a moment.

"Jason?"

I had a weird feeling, like my life was a movie and there was a bad splice in it. "Huh?" I heard myself mumble.

"Telephone. It's your mother."

"What?" I pushed myself upright on the couch, noticing that somewhere along the way a blanket had found its way over me. "What time is it?"

"It's a little after midnight. Here." Jenny handed me the telephone in time for me to hear my mother's voice say, "Just pour a bucket of cold water over him, dear. Then hit him with the bucket."

"It's me, Highness."

"Ah, Jason. Good morning, son. Would you please be so kind as to explain to me why I'm expecting to have a policeman calling upon me at home this morning?"

"What's that?"

Her Majesty Victoria suddenly changed gears, the way only she can. "The coppers, kiddo. Looks like someone named Messenger was found deceased. He had one of our business cards in his pocket."

"Messenger? Tall, skinny guy? White hair and beard?"

"If you say so. How soon can you get dressed and be here?"

"Soon. I'm dressed already," I said.

"Really?" I swear, she sounded disappointed. My brain must have been waking up in stages, because it suddenly hit me. "Whoa."

"What?" Mom asked.

"Messenger. I met him tonight. He said someone was going to kill him."

"Indeed? Well, it appears your Mr. Messenger was positively prescient. I'll expect you to tell me all about it. See you soon, love."

I clicked off the phone. "Damn. Where are my shoes? And why did you let me fall asleep?"

Jenny, now dressed in a warm and comfy-looking bathrobe, gave me a look that could only be described as scathing. "What do you mean I let you fall asleep? I did everything but douse you with water. An idea that's still looking good to me, by the way."

I got up and retrieved my shoes, feeling a chorus of aches and pains through my body that seemed to wake up as I did. "Funny. Sounds like you and Mom are starting to think alike. Wait. That's not funny. That's scary."

"What's going on?"

"A man came by the office earlier today. I mean yesterday. Right before I left to go home. Apparently he's been found dead. The police want to talk to me about it."

Her blue eyes flew wide. "Jason! Oh, my God."

I did a one-foot kangaroo hop as I slipped my first shoe on. "Welcome to my world."

I finished with my shoes and grabbed my beat-up old leather bomber jacket. "Hey, lady. How about a kiss? To keep me warm on the way home?"

And she did. A kiss that kindled a fire that could have kept me warm the whole winter long. Then she gently shoved me away, her full, lovely lips twitching a quick smile. "Out with you," she said. "And next time, try to stay awake a little longer. I haven't seen enough of you lately."

I smiled as I headed out the door and into a shockingly cold night, Jenny's words providing a warming bracer against the chill. My emerald-colored classic Mustang GTO, dubbed the Green Hornet, took me through the dark streets of River City in excellent time until I pulled up to the redbrick Victorian on Galleon Street. This place was both the palace of Her Highness Victoria Wilder and the operations center of the Midnight Investigation Agency. It had also been my home for most of my life, although now it was simply my own personal Fortress of Servitude.

As I parked, I saw that I was too late to give Mom a private recitation of events, judging by the gray Ford sedan that just about everyone in town could spot as an Official Undercover Police Vehicle. I jogged up the steps, unlocked the door and deactivated the alarms, and went through the reception area to the ornate door that leads to Mom's office. I stopped and knocked, although it would have been pointless to wait for a reply to enter; that door is as soundproof as they come.

Stepping into Mom's office is like stepping back in time to the turn of the last century. Servants in house livery wouldn't be out of place here. Her Majesty was dressed to receive company in a vibrant red kimono adorned with a golden dragon, her long silver hair unbound and falling loosely to her shoulders. Where Mom looked like the Queen of the Mysterious East, her visitor reminded me of nothing so much as a troll in a trench coat. The man was short and rounded, with a thatch of black hair plastered over a moon-shaped head whose only feature seemed to be the dark, horn-rimmed glasses there.

"Hi, Ma," I said as I entered.

Mom was poised to be poise itself. "Good morning, Jason.

This is Detective Nicholas Navarro. He would like to ask you a few questions."

Detective Navarro bobbed his head in greeting as he offered his badge and identification in lieu of a handshake. I nodded in return as he said in a light tenor voice, "Hello, Jason. I'm sorry to rouse you at this hour, but I understand you had a visitor here late yesterday?"

"If by visitor you mean Elijah Messenger, then yes."

"And would you talk about that with me now?"

"Sure."

"Good. You mind if I record this? Just to save us the time of me taking notes, really."

I suppressed a smile. Navarro was good. As a detective working a homicide, he could have just opened up with questions while sticking a tape recorder in my face, but he took a little time to warm up.

He turned his attention to Mom. "Ms. Wilder? Could I speak with Jason alone, please?"

"Certainly. Would you like some tea? I put the kettle on after I received your call."

"Oh, no, thanks. Ma'am." Navarro answered.

"Very well. Just make yourselves comfortable and I'll give you some privacy." As Mom headed for the reception area, she made a casual gesture of smoothing her hair above her ear, silently telling me that she'd be listening. I suppressed another grin. Concealed behind the genuine antiques in Mom's office are some of the most sophisticated electronic devices on the market.

Before Mom made it to the door, Navarro said, "Oh, one more thing. I'm expecting another officer to join me here."

"That's fine," Mom said warmly.

After the reception door shut, Detective Navarro fished around inside his baggy coat, coming up with a handheld voice recorder. "Go ahead and have a seat." I took off my jacket and settled into Mom's throne while Navarro spoke into his machine, identifying the date and time and the fact that he was interviewing one Jason Wilder. He then carefully placed the recorder on the desk, closer to me than to himself, and began by saying, "So, what can you tell me about your meeting with Elijah Messenger?"

"Not much. He showed up here around 5:30 this past evening. He told me that he thought someone was going to kill him."

"I see. Did he have an appointment?"

"No. He just showed up."

"Did he speak with anyone else here?"

"No. I was the only one here at the time."

"Did he say anything about who he was afraid might kill him? Or how?"

"No. Frankly, I thought he was a head case."

"Head case?"

"Yeah. Not quite sane. What happened to him?"

Navarro held up a hand. "Let me ask a few questions first, please. Then, if I can, I'll answer yours." *Sure,* I thought. *Tell me another one.* Speaking with detectives on a case is like playing poker for high stakes; they never reveal what's in their hand.

Navarro cleared his throat. "Can you tell me, to the best of your recollection, exactly what Elijah Messenger said to you earlier tonight?"

I leaned back in Mom's high-backed throne and thought. "Well, when he first came in, he just sort of looked at me and then told me I'd had some tragedy in my life and he was sorry."

"He did? You said you didn't know him. Didn't that seem odd?"

"Yeah. As I said, I thought he wasn't quite sane. Anyway,

then he told me that he believed that someone was going to kill him soon. Only he couldn't tell me who. Then he asked me if I believed in things that couldn't be seen, or something like that. Anyway, I told him that I didn't think I could help him. He left shortly after that."

"Okay," Navarro said slowly. "Can you think of anything else that he said? Anything that seemed unusual?"

"The whole thing seemed unusual. I felt sorry for him."

"Yet you didn't tell him to go to the police?"

"I did. He said he'd already been there and that someone told him to come here."

Detective Navarro reached across the desk and picked up his tape recorder. He quickly consulted his watch, spoke the time into the machine, and shut it off. Standing, he said, "Thank you, Mr. Wilder. Do you have a card? I may want to get back in touch with you."

I slipped one of my business cards out of my wallet and handed it to him. "That reminds me. My mother said something about Messenger being found with a business card of mine. The only problem with that is, I didn't give him one."

Detective Navarro shrugged, as if my information were old news. "Actually, your business card was not the only one discovered in Messenger's clothes. Which reminds me, who do you know in the River City Police Department?"

"Well, quite a few people," I started to say, only to be interrupted by a knock on the office door.

"That must be my colleague," Navarro said.

I stepped around Mom's desk and went to the door. "For instance," I said, "Patrolman Hector Morales is a good friend of mine. Also, I recently worked on a case with Detective Walter Dolman. He's a good guy."

I was opening the office door and speaking over my shoulder to Detective Navarro as I said, "Oh, and I worked with that pain in the ass Lori Banks," only to turn and damn near jump out of my skin at the sight of the beige-haired devil herself standing in the doorway.

"Well, screw you, too, Wilder," she said in greeting.

■

# CHAPTER THREE

For a quick, reflexive moment, I was tempted to slam the door in Lori Banks's face. Unfortunately, she pushed her way in past me, robbing me of the opportunity. "Hey, Navarro," Banks said in her high-pitched, nasal voice, "what's up?"

In the reception room beyond, I saw that Queen Victoria appeared highly amused. She flashed me a grin and then picked up the phone receiver on the desk to resume her eavesdropping. I rolled my eyes as I shut the door and turned to face my guests just as Detective Navarro was saying, "Sorry to drag you out tonight, Lori. Did you give a man named Elijah Messenger one of your business cards earlier today?"

Lori Banks screwed her face up in thought. She obviously had dressed herself in a hurry, throwing on some gray sweats with a beat-up fleece-lined denim jacket. Then again, this could be high chic for her. "Yeah," she said finally. "Some whack job came in to the front desk and said he wanted to report a murder. They called me down, and when I ask the guy who's the victim, he tells me it's gonna be him. Like I said, the guy was a whack."

"And you gave him your card?"

Banks threw a thumb over her shoulder at me. "Yeah, and Wilder's, too. I figured it was more up his alley than mine. So what happened? I just got the call to get up and get over here." Banks turned her head toward me, her muddy brown eyes suddenly lit with a smile. "I was hoping someone was calling me over here to arrest this guy."

"No, not at all," Navarro said quickly. "Elijah Messenger was found dead tonight."

Banks turned back to Navarro and whistled. "That so? Huh. Who'd have thought?"

"Well, apparently he did," I said. "He came over here and pretty much told me the same thing. Speaking of which, what's up with you sending Messenger over to see me, anyway?"

Banks shrugged again. "Like I said, the guy was a whack. Or at least he sure talked like one. When I told him I couldn't help him, he asked if there was anyone who could. It just happened I had one of your business cards from a month ago, when you were busy screwing up my case."

"Oh, you didn't need my help on that, Banks," I said. "You managed to screw that up all on your own."

Detective Navarro read the look on Lori Banks's face and took a quick step in between the two of us, but I wasn't quite done yet. "So let me get this straight, you gave that poor guy my name and sent him over here just to get rid of him? What the hell happened to protecting and serving the public?"

"Listen, you jerk," Banks shot back, "I tried to talk to him, but he wasn't making any sense. And what about you? He obviously made it over here before somebody killed him. So what was the matter? Didn't he have enough money to get your help?"

"Enough!" Navarro barked. He swiveled his round head back and forth between Banks and me. "Enough," he repeated quietly. "Detective Banks, please wait outside."

Lori Banks gave me one more glare then marched out the door. Navarro pulled it shut. "Mr. Wilder, I think it's likely that

I'll want to speak with you again, but for now my partner is waiting."

I forcibly calmed my breathing down, annoyed at how that damn Lori Banks made my blood boil. "I understand, sir. You're in the middle of the Golden Day."

Behind his glasses, I saw Detective Navarro's eyes widen slightly. "You know about that, eh?"

"The Golden Day" is an old homicide detective phrase. Statistically speaking, if murders aren't solved within the first twenty-four hours, the odds of finding a suspect drop dramatically. All homicide detectives know this and are ready to work straight around the clock from the moment they get the call.

"In that case," Navarro continued, "I'm sure you'll excuse me for now." He shook my hand, gave me a business card of his own, and then turned to go. Before he went out the door, though, he quickly turned and gave a brief nod in the direction of the fireplace, to the wall where Dad's portrait hung. I heard Mom exchange gracious pleasantries with the detective as she saw him out the front door, while I just stared at the painting of my father, Wild Bill Wilder, one of River City's finest detectives; for some reason, he seemed disappointed with me.

I was still looking up at Dad when Mom came in behind me. "So, you want to tell me what all this is about?"

I sighed. "It's about me apparently being one of the last people on earth a man named Elijah Messenger saw. Weren't you listening in?"

Mom walked around to her accustomed place while I dropped into one of the guest chairs. "Of course I was," she said reasonably. "I was just wondering if there was more to the story. Were you holding anything back from the good detective?"

"No. Nothing."

"I'm sorry to hear that," Mom said quietly. She leaned in, resting her chin on her tented fingers. "Because if what I'm hearing is correct," she continued, "a man came to us for help, and it sounds like we turned him away."

I felt myself start to sink into the chair. Her Highness wasn't employing the royal "we" in her speech; she's often said that anything any one of us does at the Midnight Agency reflects upon us all.

"Look," I said, "I'm feeling bad enough about this as it is. Believe me, if I'd thought for a second that Elijah Messenger was in danger from the real world, I'd have done something, but as much as I hate to agree with the disagreeable Lori Banks, she's right. The man appeared to be a lunatic."

"An apparent lunatic who made a tragically accurate prediction of his own demise," Mom said. "What's more, the police have evidently determined the case to be a homicide, although Nicholas was extremely stingy with his information."

"Nicholas? You mean Navarro? Yeah, he didn't drop a clue as to the where or the how, just gave us the who. You know him from your past life?"

"Only slightly. He wasn't in the Detective Bureau when Timothy and James and I quit the force."

Prompted by the murder of my father. I hopped off that train of thought just as Mom was opening the large carved wooden box on her desk that conceals the computer monitor. Her other hand retrieved the wireless keyboard out of the top drawer. Lady Victoria always avails herself of the best modern conveniences. She just doesn't like to see them cluttering up her office when they're not being used. "What are you doing?" I asked.

She activated a concealed switch under the desk, and I heard the faint whine of electronics springing to life. "I thought I'd do a little independent checking. I want to be ready in case the agency winds up in the papers over this. Also, my curiosity's piqued. I swear the name Elijah Messenger sounds familiar to me."

"What do you want me to do?"

"Go home, and take the morning off. I'll expect you back at the office after lunch." She placed her gold filigree reading glasses on the end of her aristocratic nose and shot me a look over the lenses. "Go on, beat it, kiddo. You look like hell."

"Aye, aye, Your Majesty." I fired off a salute, grabbed my jacket, and got going. When I got home to my apartment. I noticed a message light glowing on the phone. I hit the PLAY button and was rewarded with hearing Jenny's voice: "It's me. Call me when you get home."

I grabbed the phone and punched her number on the speed dial, smiling at the memory of my friend Roland Gibson telling me that having a woman's number programmed on your phone was the first sign of a committed relationship. (He added that he himself had never progressed to the next step.) Jenny picked up on the second ring.

"Hello, you," I said.

"Hey," came her sleepy reply. "Are you home?"

"Yeah. Just got in."

"Everything okay?"

"Sure. Just business as unusual. Price I pay for being a big-time detective."

"That's my Sherlock," she said around a yawn. "I just wanted to make sure you were all right. You said something about a dead man?"

"Yeah. Well, I'm not really involved."

"That's good. I worry about you, you know. Hey, can I buy you dinner tonight? I haven't had a big-girl date in a while."

"Just you and me? Oh, yeah. I love Angelina to pieces, but

a little quality time with her mom sounds real good to me right now."

She laughed in a low, throaty tone. "Me, too. Besides, Angelina got her date with you already. It's my turn. I'm going to look at some more houses today. I'll call you later about a time, okay?"

"Okay. And I promise not to fall asleep on you this time. 'Night, baby."

"Good night," she cooed as she hung up.

Just like that, I didn't feel tired anymore. No doubt about it, the woman had an effect on me. I cast my eyes around my living room, mentally debating between listening to music or watching a little television. Like Mom's office, my apartment was furnished with some beautiful antiques. In stark contrast, however, was the fact that all the classical stuff shared space overtly with my collection of twenty-first-century conveniences; gorgeous carved wood mated with ugly smooth black plastic. I elected to turn on the television with the sound down low so as not to disturb my neighbors, figuring that some brainless channel surfing should lull me into slumber.

I'm not sure how long I'd been sprawled out on my couch, letting the television numb my brain until I passed out. When I woke, I was dimly aware that the TV was now on a news channel. The predictably attractive female newscaster was saying something about the police while the caption behind her read BODY FOUND. I accidentally switched off the TV in my haste to crank the sound up, and by the time I found the station again all I heard was the newswoman saying, "—in the river. The authorities state that the man, whose identity is being withheld for now, appeared to have been stabbed to death and may have been involved in what police describe as a cult-like ritual that occurred sometime last night near the banks of the Americano River. We'll have more on that story as it comes in. And now, over to Jamie for the sports highlights."

I shut the television off and sat there for a while, wondering if what I just saw was the story on Elijah Messenger, hoping I was wrong, yet convinced I was right. I couldn't shake the feeling that I should have done something more for him. Now it was way too late for anyone to do anything. The most anyone left among the living can hope to accomplish for the dead is to exact a little revenge—and the only reason we do that is to make ourselves feel better.

Well, at least I could try to find out what the hell happened. My mother was checking her sources, and I thought that I might as well check some of mine. I reached over to the phone and punched in Roland Gibson's office number at the *River City Clarion*. Since the television news already had the story, I figured that one of the city's major newspapers couldn't be too far behind.

I waited until Roland's recorded greeting ran through its spiel, then said, "Wake up, Rollo. It's me, the guy who pretends to be your friend. Call up the other members of the Epic Hero Society and meet me at the crack of noon for breakfast at the phony European place you hate. Later."

With any luck, I'd have not one but three of my best friends there. Even if it turned out that I couldn't dig up any information about Elijah Messenger, at least I knew they'd do their best to try to make me feel better about the whole thing.

I shoved myself off the couch and went over to the curtains that lead to my miniature balcony, drawing them aside and looking up to the steel and concrete mountains of the city, now backlit by the glow of the predawn sun. It looked like it might turn out to be a beautiful day.

I found myself wondering what the killer of Elijah Messenger was doing right now.

# CHAPTER FOUR

$Y$ou have got to be the worst detective in the whole world."

Now, normally I suppose those words would have spurred a response, but this was the kind of abuse I was used to, seeing as how it came from one of my friends. I looked around our table in the faux country French cuisine restaurant known as Philippe's Bistro to see if there was a consensus among the other members of the Epic Hero Society. Robin Faye was seated to my left, and since I've always considered her the smartest one in our group, not to mention the most beautiful, I valued her opinion the most. Her golden brown eyes simply registered amusement at the moment. Hector Morales was to my right, but he was up to his mustache in his omelet and apparently couldn't be bothered to state his position. So I faced straight ahead to the guileless, boyish features of Roland Gibson and challenged him with "Oh, yeah?"

"Yeah," Roland asserted. "You suck. I mean, look at yourself! Do you even own a trench coat? Or a fedora?"

"I don't wear hats," I answered.

Roland nodded. "That's my point. You don't do anything right. You don't work out of a dingy office with a bottle of bourbon in the desk. You don't go around shooting people. And God knows you don't get beat up nearly enough."

Robin laid a gentle hand on my arm. "Personally, I think you get into way too much trouble. How's your side feeling?"

I patted her hand. "Fine. Mostly these days, it itches."

Roland pointed an accusing finger in my direction. "See? A real detective wouldn't have spent time in the hospital. You're supposed to just pour some high-octane booze on the wound, then light it up with your cigarette to cauterize it. You're such a wimp."

"Hey, it got infected. Besides, I don't smoke."

Roland threw up his hands. "I give up. I swear, I don't know why I bother to hang out with such a loser."

Hector finally came up for air and said, "So why we here, bro?"

"I called this meeting of the society for help. Abuse I could provide myself," I said as I stared at Roland.

Roland grinned as he took off his round, rimless glasses and said, "I always knew you were a self-abuser."

"Never mind the comedian," Robin said in her warm, lush voice. "Just let us know what we can do for you."

"Actually, it was Roland's help I was looking for."

Roland put his glasses back on and stated in a serious tone, "Well, if we regard the birds and the bees—"

"What do you know about a man named Elijah Messenger?"

Roland clapped his mouth shut in midsentence, shook his head, and dropped his voice, saying, "Elijah Messenger? The scam artist? The one they dragged out of the river last night with the perforated gut? Why? What's he to you?"

"He came to see me last night."

"Before he was killed?"

"No, afterward. Dumb-ass," Hector said helpfully from the sidelines.

Roland grinned. "Screw you, Morales." He rubbed his

hands together as he leaned in on the table. "You got a little premortem visit, eh? C'mon, spill it."

So I did. When I concluded, Roland rubbed his hands together again. "Oh, baby! I smell story. I take back all those awful truths I said about you. So what do you want from me?"

"Just give me what you can on whatever news the paper got. Not that there's anything I can do about it, mind you, but I'd like to know."

Hector frowned. "What about us? Robin and me?"

"As duly appointed coroner's deputy and city policeman, respectively, I'd never ask either of you to do anything to compromise your professional ethics. Whereas on the other hand, Roland has neither."

"Flatterer," Roland said.

Robin looked down at the table as she said softly, "Good. As a mater of fact, Elijah Messenger was brought into the morgue last night, but I wasn't assigned to work on him."

Hector shrugged. "Don't mean nothing to me. I'm on vice patrol now. So I'll be hanging with live hookers instead of stiffs dragged out of the river."

"Hookers?" Roland asked with evident interest. "Do you guys allow ride-alongs?"

I tried to bring Roland back to the subject. "What did you mean when you said Messenger was a scam artist?"

"Just what I said. He had some kind of phony psychic bit he did where he screwed little old ladies out of their money by claiming to talk to their dear departed."

"How do you know it was phony?" Robin asked. "Maybe those who have gone before can still speak to us."

Roland made a rude noise. "Don't you think that if anyone had the power to tell the future, they would choose to spend their time making a fortune at the racetrack? It's just a bunch of crap fed to the gullible, of which there is an endless supply. One born every minute, to quote the great W.C. Fields."

"Actually," I said. "I think the quote belongs to P.T. Barnum."

"Whatever," Roland said impatiently. "The fact remains, this Messenger guy was a con artist. I'm betting that he was done in by some disgruntled former customer who finally realized the guy didn't have any special powers."

"And yet," Robin said thoughtfully, "he seemed to know his own time was near. How sad that must have been."

"Yeah," I agreed. "I just can't help thinking there was something more I should have done for him."

"Not your fault, bro," Hector said. "Sounds like he tried to go to us cops first. Although it was his real bad luck to run into 'Pit Bull' Banks."

Roland narrowed his eyes at Hector. "So what about you, Hec?"

Hector just shrugged. "I was raised Catholic, man. We're supposed to believe in miracles."

I was about to make another attempt to finish my belated breakfast when my phone interrupted. The incoming number informed me it was Mom. "Greetings, Your Majesty," I said.

"Good afternoon, Jason. We have a developing situation here," she said.

"Developing situation" is one of our in-house phrases for "emergency." "I'm at Sixty-fifth and Mast Street," I advised. "I'll get there as soon as I can."

"Please do," Mom said, "but no need to collect a traffic ticket on the way. Come directly to my office when you arrive."

"Got it," I said as I snapped my phone shut. "That's it for me, kiddies. I'm back in the working world."

"Is everything okay with your mom?" Robin asked.

"Yeah. I think it's just an office kind of emergency. So much for my morning off."

Roland handed me the bill. "Here, you can take care of this on the way out. I'll make sure Robin and Hector leave a good tip."

"Thanks, cheap-ass. Just give me a call with anything you can dig up on Messenger, okay?"

"Sure thing. Then later I'll have Robin do your horoscope or something."

I was already in motion, weaving through the other tables at the restaurant, as I heard Robin say sweetly from behind me, "Oh, Roland, I see something in your future."

"Oh, yeah? What?"

"This!"

The smacking sound came a split second before Roland's "Ow!" and Hector's laughter.

I crawled through the midday urban traffic back to the office and found an expensive, late-model limousine parked in front. Waiting in it was a young male driver in a basic black business suit and dark glasses. It looked like the Midnight Agency had managed to snag another high-dollar client. Our receptionist, Paul Merlyn, was out to lunch, so I knocked on Mom's office door and let myself in.

Her Majesty was entertaining the River City Mayor himself—a relatively fit, middle-aged guy with salt-and-pepper hair, dressed in a well-tailored dark suit with pin-stripes. Mom was equally decked out for company in one of her flawlessly tailored business suits. On her lapel was her personal totem and our company logo, a jeweled, stylized eye with a clock in the center with its hands permanently set at twelve. Both Her Ladyship and the mayor rose as I entered. "Ah, here you are," Mom said. "Your Honor, may I present my son, Jason Wilder? Jason, this is Mayor Addison."

31

I automatically held out my hand to the mayor. He gave me a perfunctory grab-and-squeeze as he said, "Good to meet you," with a frown that silently said the opposite. "My pleasure, sir," I replied. I wondered what Mom had in mind for me that would concern the mayor. With my luck, she'd have me spying on his political opponents. At best, all I could hope for would be that they'd have some interesting vices.

"Mayor Addison came to us with a matter that requires discretion," Mom said. "I have given my personal assurance that our agency delivers nothing less."

Mayor Addison waved a dismissive hand. "No need to remind me, Vicki. You've more than proven yourself in the past."

I tried to keep my expression neutral. No kidding Mom could be discreet. If she ever did any work for the mayor before today, it was news to me. Mom continued, "His Honor is here on a matter related to the homicide of Elijah Messenger."

Now I couldn't help but be surprised. "Really? I was kind of starting a line of inquiry on that myself. From what I hear, the guy was a fraud of the phony psychic variety. I also heard on the news this morning that the police think there was some kind of cultlike activity involved."

The mayor looked puzzled. "You started your own inquiry? Who have you been speaking with?"

"A friend of mine over at the *Clarion*," I said.

His Honor's face started to flush. "You spoke to the newspapers!"

Mom raised a hand. "Calm down, Vincent. Jason said he spoke with a friend of his, and at the time he did so, he had no knowledge of your situation. I'm sure no harm was done."

"May I ask, what situation are we discussing?" I asked.

Mayor Addison sifted in his seat. "My daughter, Anna," he said slowly, "was one of Messenger's . . . followers."

I pictured the banner of the *River City Clarion* with the headline MAYOR'S DAUGHTER IMPLICATED IN CULTIST HOMICIDE! No doubt about it, my friend Roland would gladly sell the soul he didn't have to get the byline to a story like that. "Oh, boy," I heard myself mutter aloud.

"Yeah," the mayor agreed sourly. "So you can see my position. I need some independent oversight on this investigation. I can't ask the city attorney's office for an investigator because it'd look like I'm abusing taxpayer money. So I need someone from the outside. Someone I can trust to do the right thing."

"As long as it's understood," Mother said seriously, "that you may not like what our investigation discovers, and that I'll not stand for compromise, nor be a part of any kind of cover-up. Agreed?"

Mayor Addison looked Mom in the eye and then ducked his head once in agreement. "Understood. All I want is a complete and independent report." He stood up and buttoned his suit jacket. "I'll have the paperwork sent over by courier today." A brief smile quirked his lips. "Then I'll give Police Chief Archuleta the news. He'll love that. I trust you'll handle this personally?"

He was looking at Mom when he said it, but his head snapped in my direction when she announced, "No, Jason will be the primary investigator on this case."

"What? Why?"

"Vincent," Mom said as if explaining to a child, "my son is more than qualified. It was Jason who managed to solve the Castle Theater homicides in October. Something the police had failed to accomplish, I might add. Besides, I happen to have a commitment to another client, and my time and attention belong on that case. Rest assured, I'll be available to advise Jason should he feel the need to consult with me."

All through Mom's speech, the mayor subjected me to a

minute examination. Finally he said, "Okay, Vicki. If you say so. I'll be in touch."

Mom walked His Honor to the door. "Good-bye, Vincent. We'll give you our very best." She shut the door and turned to face me. "Well, kiddo, looks like you've got yourself a project."

"Are you sure? I don't think your friend the mayor was convinced I'm the right guy for the job."

"Make no mistake," Mom said, "he's no friend of mine. But I did some work for him years ago, so he has come to trust my judgment. As for you working on this case, consider this your second chance."

"Second chance at what?"

"Second chance to do the right thing. I'm not at all pleased that a man came to our office for help and was turned away."

I started to speak, but Mom held up a warning hand as she said, "I know you couldn't possibly see what was going to happen, but nevertheless, I feel it's our responsibility to see what we can do now. Besides, if I'm not mistaken, I think this whole affair has been bothering you, too. Why else would you be looking into the matter on your own time, eh?"

"Guilty." I sighed. "I admit it. I couldn't shake the feeling that I messed up somehow."

"Well, just don't mess up round two. That's an order."

"Yes'm. So let me get this straight, we're supposed to do our own investigation of an active homicide? Won't that kind of hack off the regular authorities?"

"Big time," Mom said with a smile. "It's well known that Mayor Addison and the chief of police hate each other's guts. I think what Vincent is really looking for is to make sure that the chief doesn't try to squeeze a little political mileage out of all this."

"Politics. Great. My least favorite subject. So you don't think this is really about the mayor's daughter?"

Mom shrugged. "Sure it is. To what degree, who knows? I can't say I'm particularly surprised to find her mixed up in something like this. The girl was a real witch back when I first met her."

"What do you mean?"

"That prior case I worked on for the mayor. It was five or six years ago. Vincent Addison was just a city councilman then, and he hired me to find his runaway teenaged daughter. I tracked her down to a motel room where she and this thirty-something guy had signed in as husband and wife. She was fifteen at the time. It took some convincing to get little Anna to come home."

"Convincing?"

Mom smiled thinly. "Well, I wound up having to thump on the guy and then stuff Anna into the trunk of my car for the ride home."

"How come I never heard about that caper?"

Mom shrugged. "I gave my word."

"Okay. So now what?"

"Now we wait for the documentation from the mayor's office to get here, the most important part of which will be a letter stating that the bearer is entitled to courtesy and cooperation from city offices." Mom shot me a look. "Just the thing for getting out of parking tickets. Then you'll probably have to hook up with someone in Homicide to get access to their casebook. After that, you're on your own, kiddo."

"What, pray tell, will Her Royal Highness be doing in the meantime?"

"Working. I wasn't kidding when I told Mayor Vinnie I had another client. Seems one of River City's more clueless patrons of the arts got taken in by a paint-by-numbers Monet. But I should be around town if you need me."

"Aye, aye, Captain. Well, I wonder which detective I'll get to go out with?" I suddenly got a bad feeling in my gut. "You don't think there's any chance that I'll be stuck with that damn Lori Banks, do you?"

■

# CHAPTER FIVE

I was beginning to feel that I was developing my own psychic powers—and I didn't like them one bit.

A courier had brought over a package from the mayor's office less than an hour after His Honor had left the Midnight Agency. The papers included a portrait-sized photograph of a pretty woman with light brown, shoulder-length hair and large, slightly almond-shaped brown eyes, along with a handwritten note explaining that this was a picture of Anna Addison and including her date of birth and last known address and telephone numbers. I made a guess that the photograph was an old one; it looked like a high school graduation picture. But the main attraction in the package was the letter on official stationery from the mayor's office that stated that the bearer was to be extended every possible courtesy by all city agencies.

Armed with my new passport, I began a bureaucratic odyssey of epic proportions. I made the mistake of first driving to the main downtown police station, looking forward to seeing the old place again. It was a relic of a bygone era, with its Ionic columns and carved stone façade, and was one of the few remaining city buildings that retained any class, in my humble opinion. There, a harried-looking desk sergeant told me that I needed to go to the South River Precinct. That building was an ugly, four-story concrete block that concealed a Minotaur's maze within.

Too bad I hadn't brought a ball of string to trail behind me. I spent the better part of two hours being shuffled from one officer to another, running the gauntlet of authority from the lowly patrolman at the front desk to his sergeant to the lieutenant over to the watch commander and finally up to the office of the captain of detectives for this precinct. All along the way, I held on to my letter from the mayor's office. It was like a magic shield that cast a spell, causing consternation and confusion whenever someone gazed upon it.

When I was finally ushered into the captain's office, though, I saw that my troubles were just beginning. The bad feeling I got certainly didn't come from Captain Raymond Cory, a big, square-jawed, grizzle-haired man in a rumpled open-neck shirt with a loosely hung tie. Unlike everyone else I'd met at the precinct, he radiated all the good cheer of a used car salesman. My bad feeling came from the woman in his office wearing a beige business suit, one that clashed with her stringy beige hair. The look she shot me radiated, too, but it wasn't good cheer.

Captain Cory got up and came around his large, untidy desk toward me. "Hey, come on in. So you're the son of the living legends, huh?" He gave my hand a shake that would have done a grizzly bear proud.

"Well, sit down and let's get the ground rules straight."

I parked myself next to Lori Banks, who sat in her chair, arms folded. "First off," Captain Cory said as he seated himself, "I don't suppose I have to tell you what a political shit storm you've caused. I've been getting phone calls from everyone but the pope. Bottom line is, Chief Archuleta has given the okay for us to let you in on what's going on with this case. But in exchange, you've got to give us all your notes and copies of your reports before anyone else gets them. Got it?"

"Yes, sir."

He nodded. "Good. Now, just what were you expecting to do here?"

"Well, for starters, I'd like copies of all the police reports so far, along with a list of the witnesses and suspects."

Captain Cory nodded again. "Not going to happen," he said pleasantly. "At least not right away. The initial investigation is still ongoing right now, and I won't ask my detectives to stop what they're doing to transcribe their field notes for you. You'll get copies as soon as they're ready."

"Okay," I said carefully. "So what are my chances of tagging along with your detectives in the field?"

"Zip. I can't have my detectives distracted by someone looking over their shoulders while they're trying to work."

"I see. So what you're telling me, sir, is that all I can do is wait for you to release the reports, which, if I'm not mistaken, will probably be about the same time they're sent to the district attorney's office."

The captain smiled. "That's about the size of it. You'll get full disclosure when the reports are finalized. Detective Banks here will act as liaison. Anything you get will go through her, and I'll expect you to provide her with all your reports on this matter, right?"

No doubt about it, I was getting screwed. I did appreciate Captain Cory's reasoning—he wasn't going to take the chance of some outsider messing up a homicide, and I really couldn't blame him—but I wasn't about to let myself get frozen out of this case without a fight, either. I looked over at Banks and said, "So, if I need anything, I should go through the good detective here?"

"Yep," the captain said.

"Very good, sir. In that case, I guess I'll just go and look over the crime scene. I assume by now the Crime Scene Investigations Unit has already come and gone?"

The captain's smile seemed to freeze in place. "Uh, yeah. Probably."

"Okay, then. If Detective Banks will be so kind as to show me the way, I'll just go and take a look around."

The captain and Lori Banks traded looks. "Now?" Banks asked.

"Sure," I said, checking my watch. It was just coming up on five o'clock. The Friday night rush hour traffic was probably going to be a problem, but I was betting I could go take a look at where the murder took place and still have time for a late dinner with Jenny.

Banks looked me up and down. "You might want to think about this for a minute. The murder scene is down by the river. You're not dressed to go slogging around out there."

I smiled. I was wearing what I call my working uniform, a midnight blue suit that looked and wore like silk but was made from some space-age fabric. I could go rolling around in the mud and then throw the suit into the washer and dryer and have it come out looking brand-new. My shoes were waterproof as well. "Don't worry about me, Detective," I told her. "I'll be all right."

Banks looked to her captain in mute supplication, but he just gave her a slight nod of his head. "Okay, kids. I'll let you get to it. Lori? Don't lose him anywhere, okay?"

I said as I stood up, "Not to worry, sir. I promise not to go wandering around unescorted." I made a gracious after-you gesture to Lori Banks, and the look I received in return told me that she would rather have given me a gesture of her own. A rude one.

Banks and I had no more cleared out of the captain's office than she spun around and said to me in a low, venomous tone, "Goddammit, Wilder, I don't know how you got yourself involved, but you are not going to screw this case up. Got it?"

"Sure. Last thing I'd want to do. Now can we get moving? Or do you want to stand around here and chitchat?"

"Wait for me out front," she growled as she turned away and marched up the hall. I made my way down to the first floor, surrendered the visitor's badge, and walked out the glass double doors into the cold early twilight. As I walked to my car I checked the messages on my cell phone, happy to see a call from Jenny. I dialed and got her on the first ring.

"Are we still on for tonight?" she asked. "I've got a babysitter lined up who won't let me cancel."

"Won't let you cancel? Who's that?"

"You call her Mother."

"Queen Victoria is babysitting?"

"Yep, and she said something about how you might be late tonight. What did she mean by that?"

"Ah, yes. I've got a bit of a case. In fact, I'm just about to go out and look for clues and stuff, but I'm thinking I shouldn't be too late. Tell you what, call Marilyn's and ask them to hold a table for us."

"Sounds good. How late do you think you might be?"

"I just want to take a quick look around a certain place and get my bearings. I figure I'll come back tomorrow for a better look in the daytime. Where do I pick you up?"

"Over at your mom's."

I caught sight of Lori Banks behind the wheel of an undercover Ford, driving toward me. For a moment, I wasn't sure if I should get ready to jump out of the way. "Okay, Beauty," I said to Jenny, "gotta go. The Beast has arrived." I closed my phone on Jenny's chuckle.

Lori Banks gave me a look and nodded toward the passenger door. "Just a minute," I called. I went over to my Mustang, opened the trunk, and unlocked my briefcase. I wasn't sure what I'd want with me for my first look at the murder scene, so I started loading up my pockets. All the gear in my briefcase was efficient, state-of-the-art miniature tools. I distributed the camera, voice recorder, flashlight, pocket tool, and monocular among my pockets; they didn't even make a wrinkle. I briefly considered slipping my revolver on, but I decided against it. I didn't want Pit Bull Banks to have any more reason to be suspicious of me.

I closed the trunk and sauntered over to the impatiently waiting Detective Banks. Before I even had my seat belt engaged, she took off.

"Where are we going?" I asked her.

"Crime scene," she said shortly. She chewed some gum noisily while doing her best to treat me as a nonexistent passenger. I noticed that she had donned a shoulder holster and was packing a semiautomatic pistol under her jacket, which did wonders for her bustline. I smiled and looked straight ahead as she joined the traffic on the crowded streets. The only conversation in the car was coming from the police radio.

I let her drive in silence until she made her way to a northbound freeway on-ramp. Fortunately, at this hour, most of the traffic was heading out of town in the opposite direction. I broke the silence and said, "Okay, Banks, spill. What do you know about the late Mr. Messenger?"

She shot me a sour sideways look. "Why should I tell you? You're going to get all the reports."

"Because you're my official liaison. Besides, if we talk it may make our time together seem shorter."

She barked a short laugh. "Well, I don't know much," she said.

I resisted the urge to make the natural response to an opening line like that and said instead, "Yeah, but I'll bet you pumped your friend Detective Navarro after he dragged you out of bed. So come on, spill."

"Well," she said finally, "from what I hear, that Messenger guy was supposed to be some kind of witch or warlock or whatever you call it. When Patrol first got on the scene, they met a bunch of guys running around, looking like they were having some kind of costume party. Only it turns out that they were all members of some kind of cult and all this happened at one of their rituals. Everyone was decked out head to toe in black robes. Including the stiff."

"Who found Messenger first?"

"Don't know. All I heard was that one of his fellow cult members dragged him from the river. Someone had perforated him with a big-ass knife." I got a chill at the thought of that, one that made the scar on my side start to itch.

Banks had driven us off the freeway and onto the South Levee Road to South Gate, one of the older and more affluent areas on the outskirts of the city. The large homes were separated from each other by expanses of lawn, and the streets were named after characters out of mythology. Banks pulled up short just before she reached the front drive of one house that looked like a rose-colored copy of the Texas Alamo, complete with a large wooden double door at the apex of a semicircular driveway. The three cars and a van parked in the driveway were unmistakably River City police vehicles. "Hey, Banks," I said, "looks like you got us here in time for a party."

"Dammit," she muttered, "they're supposed to be gone by now." She twisted in her seat to face me. "Look, Wilder, the house is off-limits. You got that? You're just here for the crime scene."

"What's going on?" I asked as nonchalantly as I could.

43

"None of your business, that's what."

I tried to affect a look of hurt innocence. I figured that sometime during the day Detective Navarro or someone else got a search warrant and the cops were now going through Messenger's house. I briefly considered trying to finagle my way in but realized Lori Banks wasn't just assigned to be my liaison; she was mainly my watchdog, and she wasn't about to let me get away with anything if she could help it. "Okay," I said resignedly. "Which way is it to Messenger's Last Stand?"

Banks pointed straight toward the levee. "Up and over. There's supposed to be a trail that leads to the water. Apparently you'll find an area where they set up a campfire. Should be marked off."

"You're not coming with me?"

"Hell, no. You fall into the water, you're on your own. How long you gonna be?"

"Why? You have a hot date or something?"

"Don't be a smart-ass. I just want to know how long to give you before I send someone in to start dragging the river for your body."

I opened the car door and stepped out as I said, "Your concern is touching, Banks." She opened the door on her side and got out as well. With the sun down, it felt colder than ever. I buttoned up my topcoat. Banks went around to the front of the car, fished out a cigarette, and lit up.

"Hey, Banks, tell me something. How'd you get stuck babysitting me?"

She blew a plume of smoke up into the night air. "You wouldn't believe me if I told you."

"Try me."

"I volunteered."

"You're kidding."

In the near darkness, I could make out the ghost of a smile

on her face. "Nope. When I heard you were getting some kind of special permission to stick your nose in this case, I called the captain and told him I'd act as the liaison."

"Why?"

I heard her sigh. " 'Cause I felt bad. Because I blew off Messenger, thinking he was just a whack job, and I keep thinking that maybe I should've done things differently with him. No one was blaming me, mind you. All the same, I thought I should be doing something. Even if it's just keeping you from fouling things up."

I was hoping it was dark enough that she couldn't see my expression, whatever it was. I shook my head. Just when you think you're starting to get to know someone. "Okay, Banks. I won't be long."

"Better not. Hey, Wilder, you got a gun on you?"

"No."

"Jesus," she muttered. She pushed herself away from the car. "I'd better go with you after all. Strange stuff happens around the river."

"Forget it, Banks. I'll be all right. I'll be back before you know it." Before she could argue any further, I turned and marched up the levee and toward the river, looking to find the place where Elijah Messenger died less than twenty-four hours before.

# CHAPTER SIX

I trudged up the side of the levee, stopping at the top to get my bearings. From my vantage point I seemed to be on the border of two different worlds. Looking behind me, I saw the large houses with a mad array of twinkling Christmas lights, brighter and more numerous than the stars above, and to the north, I saw the spires of River City, like an amber-tinted Oz at this distance. But ahead of me the trees were a dark and chaotic mass, moving with an apparent life of their own in the cold breeze, like an ocean on a stormy midnight.

Sweeping the area with my little Surefire Executive flashlight, I saw a light-colored trail to my left that led down the other side of the levee. I walked along the top, noticing the old, half-buried railroad tracks that crowned the man-made hill. When I reached the trail leading down and into the woods, I looked back and saw that the path seemed to lead directly from the back of the high-walled border of the Old Spanish–style home.

I made my way down carefully, my footsteps crunching along on tiny bits of rock and gravel. With every step I took, the temperature seemed to keep dropping from mere cold to freezing, with a wet overlay that hurt my nose and lungs as I breathed. Playing my light ahead of me, I saw that some helpful police officer had tied a strand of bright yellow crime scene tape between two trees across the path that led toward the river. A narrow blacktop road ran across my path, obviously a stretch of the River City Parkland bicycle path, which runs for miles along the greenbelt of the city. I slipped under the tape and took a few steps inward.

There was a completely different feel to this area, a combination of sound and smell alien to my urban-acclimatized senses—and yet something familiar as well. Growing up in these parts, I spent many a youthful hour down by the river in the summertime, and all of a sudden the scents brought back a flood of long-buried memories. But this was no time to indulge in adolescent reminiscence. I played my light around the thick, tangled branches of the trees, seeing how the shadows moved with a life all their own. I decided I didn't want to linger around here any longer than I had to. Because of the cold, of course, I told myself.

The rustle of the branches in the trees and the crunching sound of my footsteps on the gravel path accompanied me as I walked the narrow and winding trail, which rose and fell as it twisted this way and that, until I came to a clearing bordered with the yellow tape I expected. There was a break in the foliage overhead, and I could see a bright three-quarter moon that trailed a rough silver ribbon across the river beyond.

I ducked under the flimsy barrier and carefully stepped toward the center of the clearing, waving my light ahead. The ground here was hard-packed with flat, smooth stones. Closer toward the river was a dug-out depression, ringed with larger stones surrounding a mass of charred wood in a bed of ashes. In the glare of my light, I saw that someone had painted a red border around the fire pit, a circle that straight lines and right angles disturbed here and there. It took me a moment to trace the pattern: a five-pointed star, with one of the spokes pointed toward the river.

I finished my tour at the river's edge, where I clicked off my light and waited for my eyes to adjust to the darkness. Through the wind in the trees I could hear the faint sound of the river as it coursed along its way, slow-moving liquid ice. With a shiver, I thought of Elijah Messenger winding up here. With cold steel shoved into him.

"Are you a cop?"

All my years of combat training made me spin toward the unexpected voice, which in turn made me lose my footing on the uneven ground. I don't know if I yelled on the way down or only after I crashed painfully on the unyielding stones at the water's edge, but the freezing fire that shot up my submerged right side seemed to shut my lungs down. I scrambled away from the water, getting my feet tangled in the hem of my overcoat, until I flopped flat on the rocks. I was twisting my head around looking for a threat—and my flashlight—when I heard a high-pitched feminine voice say, "Jesus! Are you okay?"

My brain started to get itself into gear and told me that I wasn't under attack. Unless it was from instant pneumonia. I looked up and saw a ghostly face, washed in silver moonlight. Then the apparition revealed its earthly origins by demanding, "Who the hell are you? And what are you doing here?"

I found my footing and cautiously raised myself up, shaky from the adrenaline rush and sudden icy bath. "Jason Wilder, and at the moment, I'm freezing to death. Who are you?"

My ethereal companion took a few steps back into the shifting shadows. "Are you a cop?" she asked tremulously.

"No. Private detective." I sensed that the woman was gathering herself up to make a run for it. "Wait," I said quickly. "Don't go. I just want to talk to you."

"You said you were a detective," she said in an accusing tone.

"Private detective. Not a cop. There's a world of difference. Cops enforce the law. I, on the other hand, have to work for a living."

"What are you doing here?" she demanded. "Are the cops still up at the house?"

"Yeah. At least they were when I started down here. And the reason I'm here is a man named Elijah Messenger."

I heard her catch her breath at the mention of Messenger's name. I took another gamble as I said, "You were here last night, weren't you?"

A pause, then she said sharply, "No. No."

I made my voice as gentle as I could while trying to keep my teeth from chattering. "Now, now. It's not nice to lie to strangers. Especially ones you've just met."

"That's stupid," she said flatly.

"Sorry. Best I can do under the conditions. So who are you, and what are you doing out here?"

"What did you mean when you said you were here because of Elijah?" she asked.

"He came to see me yesterday."

"He did?" she asked breathlessly. "When?"

"Late afternoon. A few hours before . . . well, before he died."

"Oh," she whispered. Her moonlit face turned down, lost in the shadows, and I faintly heard her say, "I was hoping."

"Hoping he was still alive?" I sensed more than saw her nod. I said gently, "I'm sorry." I reached into my pocket and retrieved my keys. One of the more useful items I keep on the ring is a small but powerful emergency flashlight. I turned it on her, aiming low so as not to blind her. The light revealed her to be wrapped head to toe in some silky black material, complete with hood. She jumped a bit when the light came on, and in the reflection I could see she had a pale, pleasantly rounded face with large, almond-shaped eyes.

"Steady," I said, trying to reassure her. "I just didn't want to go stumbling around in the dark again." I switched the light to my other hand, since the one that had gotten wet was becoming a numbed, frozen lump. I took a few steps toward the woman. "What's your name?"

She hesitated before finally saying, "Anna."

"Anna Addison?"

Her eyes flashed. "How did you . . . ?"

"Relax. As a matter of fact, your father hired me."

"My father!" she hissed. "What the hell does my father have to do with this?"

"I kind of got the impression he was concerned about you."

"That's a laugh," she said contemptuously. "You can tell that bastard—"

"Look," I interrupted her, "all I know is that my agency was hired to see that your involvement in all this, whatever that may be, is handled fairly."

"You mean Daddy hired you to cover up, is that it? Keep the little girl out of the big, bad newspapers, because Daddy wouldn't like that, now, would he?"

"I don't care about that," I said wearily, "and I'm certainly not here to cover anything up. Speaking of which, have you spoken to the police yet?"

She pulled her cloak tighter. I could see in the diffused light that she was shivering. "No," she said flatly. "I don't like cops."

"Well, like them or not, you're going to have to talk to them eventually. Better sooner than later. They tend to get annoyed if you put them off. What were you and Messenger doing out here last night, anyway?"

50

She didn't answer; instead, she walked unsteadily over to the water's edge. "You wouldn't understand."

It was eerie, the way she said that; it was the same tone Elijah Messenger used when he told me the same thing. "So you were here last night," I said.

She shivered again, more violently this time. "Yeah."

"What happened?"

She shook her hooded head. "I don't know. All of a sudden, there was noise, and some kind of explosion, then . . . someone said Elijah was in the water. I ran to look. I couldn't see very well, but . . . but when I did, someone said he was . . . gone. Dead. So I ran."

"Where?"

"Back to the house. Later I heard the sirens, and I ran again. I didn't come back until now."

"Did you see how Messenger died?"

"No," she whispered. "I just saw him being dragged out of the water."

Now it was my turn to shiver. "Anna? Look, you're going to have to talk to the police sometime soon. Why don't you come with me? I'll help you."

She started shaking her head, slowly at first, then more and more violently. "No. No way. Not now."

"So what are you going to do? Stay out here all night?"

"No, Robert's back at the house. He told me he'd come and get me when the cops left."

"Robert who?"

She turned to me. In the illumination of my flashlight, her face suddenly looked cunning and calculating. "I'm not sure I want to talk to you anymore," she said. "And you can't make me, can you, now?"

"Look, I'm just trying to help you."

"Help me? Or my father?"

For a brief moment, I was severely tempted to just grab the woman and march her over to Detective Banks—for her own good, mind you—but I figured the mayor probably wouldn't take kindly to me assaulting members of his family. Although I wondered if he'd make an exception in Anna's case. "All right, you win," I conceded.

I turned back to where I recently took my cold-water bath and played my key-ring light around. I spotted my Surefire flashlight lying just under the water at the edge of the bank. I reached into the icy water with my already numbed right hand. I gave it a couple of shakes and turned the switch; the little stainless steel device was completely waterproof. I said to Anna, "Here, take my light. No sense sitting in the dark if you can help it." I got my wallet out and handed her one of my cards. "Take this, too. It's got my phone number on it. Just in case you change your mind."

"You're leaving?" She almost sounded disappointed.

"Yeah. I'm freezing to death, and since I'm not hiding from the cops, I'm going to where it's warm. I strongly suggest you do the same."

She blinded me suddenly by hitting me full in the face with the powerful light. I threw my hand up in self-defense. "I just wanted to see what you looked like," she said simply.

"Satisfied?"

She lowered the light, and in the fading flare of the afterburn I head her say, "Maybe. Just maybe."

I lit my key-ring light and made my way back to the trail. Emerging from the wooded area was like escaping from an enchanted forest into the beckoning glow of the lights of civilization just over the hill. From the crest of the levee, I could look down and see that Lori Banks was still outside her car and was now talking to Detective Navarro, wearing a blue windbreaker with the word POLICE emblazoned in yellow.

Banks spotted me first. "Damn, Wilder, about time you got back here. I was starting to wonder if you had fallen in the river or something."

"You're psychic, Banks," I said sourly.

Navarro looked me up and down. "What happened, Mr. Wilder?"

"Just took a bad step and an impromptu bath."

Lori Banks clapped a hand to her mouth, trying in vain to catch a snorting laugh. "Serves you right, Wilder," she said with evil glee. "I told you, you shouldn't be playing around that river at night."

"What on earth were you looking for?" Navarro wondered aloud.

"I thought I'd just poke around and take some pictures, seeing as how I'm not allowed to do anything else."

"Ah. I see," said Navarro. "Well, Detective Banks, you'd better take charge of our guest before he catches a cold."

I suppose my pride was stung by the smug attitudes of Banks and Navarro. For a moment, I was tempted to be a good citizen and tell them that a homicide witness they were looking for was just over the hill. *Screw them*, I thought. If they weren't going to play fair with me, then they could go and do their own damn police work. Instead, I gave in to an impish impulse and said, "So, did we get any information from Robert tonight?"

Navarro's head snapped in Banks's direction. Banks caught the look and threw her hands up. "Don't look at me. I didn't tell him anything."

Detective Navarro tilted his head to one side as he said, "How did you know about Robert?"

I gave an expansive shrug. "Maybe I'm psychic," I said with a grin. "Come on, Banks, let's go."

I let myself into the car while Navarro just shook his head, waving at Banks to proceed. She got in the driver's side, shut the door, then turned to look at me. Finally she grinned and fired up the engine.

"One's thing's for sure, Wilder."

"What's that?"

"As a psychic, you're all wet."

# CHAPTER SEVEN

Banks and I drove back to the South River Precinct in silence. I could tell she was itching to ask me how I pulled the name Robert out of the air, but she kept her thin lips clamped shut. She settled for a little casual torture by driving back to the police station with the heater off and her window down while I suffered in frozen silence, not about to give her the satisfaction of me asking for a little human consideration. She dropped me off at my Mustang and left me with a "See you later, Wilder."

"Not if I see you first," I said to her departing vehicle. I stowed my gear and aimed my car toward the offices of Midnight, cranking the heater up to full blast. On the way, I checked my messages and found one from Roland Gibson, who advised me to "Bring lots of money and gratitude and meet me at the Boathouse for breakfast around ten. Have I got a story for you!" I thought about calling Roland back, but at this hour he was more likely engaged in chasing a skirt than a story. Besides, I was hungry.

I had just about thawed out when I reached Her Majesty's castle, warmed further by the sight of Jenny Chance's van parked in the driveway. I wasted no time in parking the car and hurrying into the house through the back way. The downstairs kitchen was deserted, and I called up the stairs to the living quarters, "Hello! Home is the conquering hero!"

I heard a girlish giggle in response as I jogged up the stairs. I turned the corner to the hallway and saw little Angelina waiting for me with open arms, wearing pink and white pajamas and a smile three times her size. "Jason!" she squealed. "Fly me!" She ran to my arms and I lifted her up and spun her around while making the now-traditional whooshing noises. "Hey, Tinker Bell," I said as I reeled her in for a hug. "Where's Mom?"

Angelina gave me a squeeze, then sniffed the shoulder of my topcoat and loudly exclaimed, "Ew! You stink!"

I carried her to the doorway of the upstairs den, where I saw Mom and Jenny seated on the couch, Beowulf lounging at Her Majesty's feet. The lady of the house was decked out in her silk kimono, while Jenny was attired in a black velvet dress. She had her shoes off and her feet tucked under her on the couch, looking both comfortable and entirely desirable. Angelina broke the spell by announcing to all present, "Jason stinks!"

"You're not the first girl to tell me something like that," I told Angelina as I gently placed her on her feet. She immediately went over and sat cross-legged next to Beowulf, throwing an arm around the dog's neck, leaning in and giving him a comparison sniff. "And just where have you been?" Mom inquired with a raised eyebrow.

"Working," I replied.

"Ah. How was the experience?"

"Cold. Not to mention wet."

"What happened?" Jenny asked.

"I took a small fall in the river."

Jenny and Mom exchanged looks, Mom adding, "You see

why he needs a keeper?" Her Majesty turned her attention back to me. "Well, tell you what, you go and make yourself presentable, inasmuch as that's possible, then you two can be on your way. Angelina and I have our evening plans, too, you know."

"We're having a slumber party!" Angelina explained. "I'm staying over with Beowulf."

"Really? I thought you had a case you were working on," I asked Mom.

She smiled. "Oh, I've been spinning my webs, make no mistake, but at the moment I'm waiting to hear from a colleague of mine down in Santa Teresa. In the meantime, I'm certain the case won't need my attention for at least a day or so. So move it, kiddo. Don't keep a lady waiting."

I saluted and headed for my old room, where I keep clothes for just such an emergency. I took a minute to scrub myself down, then changed into my spare suit and the white dress shirt I keep handy, in case I need to go testify in court on short notice. Normally I hate wearing neckties with a passion, but I decided to make an exception in tonight's case and wrapped a midnight blue one around my neck. I have quite a collection of ties I never wear. Roland Gibson, knowing my abhorrence of such things, never fails to gift me with the ugliest example he can find every Christmas. I grabbed a raincoat and headed back to the den, where all the ladies present decided I was now fit to be seen in public—as long as it was relatively dark, Mother opined.

"By the way," Mom said as I was helping Jenny into her full-length black leather coat, "I ran some background information on your Mr. Messenger. I sent a file to your computer."

"Anything I need to know right now?" I asked.

Mom glanced at Angelina, who was busy petting Beowulf.

"Not that should be discussed in mixed company. Besides, you're off the clock at the moment, kiddo. You two go and have a good time."

"Thanks, Victoria," Jenny said with a smile. To Angelina, she said, "All right, you. Come over and give Mommy a kiss good night. And you be good for Victoria, you hear?"

"Can I watch *Peter Pan*?" Angelina asked.

"Only if it's okay with Victoria," Jenny assented.

I got a good-bye kiss, too; then Angelina released Jenny and me and returned to Beowulf's side. As Jenny and I went downstairs, I asked her, "Didn't she used to call the dog Beywoof?"

"Oh, yeah." Jenny smiled at the memory. "You can't turn your back on kids for a minute. They'll grow up on you when you're not looking. So what happened to you tonight?"

I felt myself make a face. "Don't ask. I'm working on a top-secret case. So secret, in fact, that I myself am not allowed to know what's going on. I'm pretty sure I'd have to take cyanide or something if I talked about it. But I'm sorry it made me late."

"That's okay," Jenny said agreeably as I opened the back door for her. "I'm not too particular about how you smell. Within reason, of course, and as long as you don't show up reeking of another woman's perfume. I've had that experience, thanks to my soon-to-be-ex-husband."

As we walked to my car, I asked her, "Is everything okay on that front? Have you heard from him recently?"

"No, thank God. Whatever Troy is up to these days, he hasn't tried to get hold of me. Or his daughter, for that matter. But I swear I keep thinking he's going to pop up here someday. I keep worrying that he might try to make a play to get Angelina. Not that he wants her, mind you, but as a way to get back at me."

"Well, at least you can quit worrying about that tonight. If

Troy Chance or anyone else made a move on your daughter, he'd have to go through my mother first. And believe me, it'd be safer to put a live cobra down your pants than to mess with Her Royal Highness."

Jenny beamed a smile. "Thanks. That does make me feel better."

"Good." I wanted to change the subject—not just for her sake. I opened the passenger door of the Green Hornet for her and said, "Okay, since I can see that I'm powerless to resist your interrogation, I guess I'm forced to talk about my case."

I loved her laugh. *Hell, I'd throw myself back into the river,* I thought, *just to have her make that sound again.* After I tucked her in the car, I ran around to the driver's side, and soon we were heading up Hurricane Street on our way to one of my favorite restaurants.

"So," I continued, "seeing as how you're going to twist my arm, all I can tell you is this: I'm stuck working with the police, and they've made it pretty damn clear that they don't want me around. On top of that, I'm supposed to be working with Detective Lori Banks."

"Banks?" Jenny asked sharply. "Isn't she the one who arrested me?"

"Uh-huh."

"And now you have to work with her?"

"Not exactly," I said. "I'm pretty sure her job is to keep me from actually getting involved with the case. I'm just sort of appointed to keep the police honest. Which in this town could be a full-time job by itself."

"So this is all tied up in that murder you were called about last night?"

"Yeah." I was just about to make the turn on Twenty-fourth Avenue when Jenny said, "So you're working on the Elijah Messenger homicide?"

Her casual remark almost made me miss my turn. "What? How did you know that?"

"Elementary, Sherlock," Jenny said confidently. "I heard about the case on the news. You got the call early this morning, and you said you were down by the river tonight. Two and two equal four. That, and the way you nearly wrecked the car when I said his name."

I made the turn onto Jib Street and took the opportunity to slip into the first parking space I saw, feeling lucky to get one on the same block as Marilyn's at this hour. "And you call me Sherlock," I grumbled.

"So is it true?" Jenny asked. "About all that satanic cult stuff? The news reports were a little vague."

"Sorry I said anything," I admitted as I got out of the car. I dutifully opened Jenny's door and escorted her to the restaurant.

"Oh, sure," Jenny said good-naturedly as she slid her arm through mine. "Tease a girl, why don't you, and then hold back on the juicy details."

"Forget it. Like Mom said, I'm off the clock. I promise to give you all the dirt when the case is over. In the meantime, no more shop talk."

"Okay, Sherlock. Lead the way."

I did so, taking Jenny into the foyer of Marilyn's, one of River City's better dining establishments. It's a place that makes you feel like you've stepped back in time. The elegant Deco décor makes the room a fitting shrine to its patron deity, Marilyn Monroe, whose life-sized portrait smiles down from her place over the carved mahogany bar.

Throughout the sumptuous meal (braised lamb with rosemary for her, and for me a steak, medium well, that must have been half the cow) I was happy to just sit across from this lovely woman, with the soft sounds of a jazz trio in the background and the candlelight from the table illuminating her lustrous blue eyes. It's nights like this that make everything else I deal with worth it.

I was just in the process of wondering if dessert would put me into a coma when Jenny asked me, "So, what do you want for Christmas?"

"Me? Oh, the usual, I guess. Peace on earth, goodwill toward men, and a lot of cool toys. How about you?"

Jenny leaned slightly toward me, candlelight dancing in her eyes. She brushed back a strand of her raven-dark hair as she said in a low, sweet tone, "You want to know what I really want?"

I could feel the blood beat in my ears—just before my damn cell phone bleated for attention. I sat there frozen, hoping the annoying sound would just go away. "You'd better get that," Jenny said as she leaned back. "It could be your mom."

I wasn't about to answer the phone at the table, feeling that such behavior is one of the signs of the downfall of Western civilization. With a sigh, I got up, saying, "I'll be right back." I hurried over to the bar section as I checked the number on my receiver, frowning when I didn't recognize it. I answered the phone. "Wilder here."

"Took you long enough," Lori Banks complained.

I felt a sinking sensation in my recently pampered stomach. "What do you want, Banks?" I asked without enthusiasm.

"Thought I'd invite you to a party," she said.

"Party? What the hell are you talking abut?" I turned to see Jenny, her lovely face full of concern, looking over to me. I shook my head, trying to telegraph the idea that Angelina was all right. "Come on, Banks," I said. "I'm in no mood to play games."

"Aw, too bad," Banks said. "And here I was going to ask if

you wanted to come out and see how the real cops do things. We're getting ready to make an arrest in the Messenger case. Since you're the guy who's supposed to be watching our asses, it was decided to invite you along. Not by me, of course."

"You're going to make an arrest?" I checked my watch and saw that it was close to eleven. Looked like Detective Navarro managed to pull it off just before his Golden Day ran out.

"So, look, you coming?" Banks asked. "Or can we go ahead without you?"

I was torn between looking over at Beauty, sitting at the table, and listening to the grating sound of the Beast on the phone. "Who's getting arrested, Banks?" I asked.

I heard Banks's cackle. "Some chick named Anna Addison," she said sarcastically. "You may have heard of her? I think she's related to a certain client of yours. What do you say, Wilder? You want to be in for the kill on this thing?"

I felt my heart sink down right next to my stomach. There are times, such as these, when being a private detective blows. Big time. I looked over to the lovely Jenny as I said, "Yeah, Banks. I'll be there."

I heard Banks's evil laugh again. "So much for your hot date, eh?"

■

# CHAPTER EIGHT

Where and when is all this going down, Banks?"

"Navarro is putting an arrest team together now. We're all going to nine-forty at the train depot in Old Town, but the target is supposed to be at some place called Tantalus."

"Nine-forty" is police radio code for making a rendezvous. "Tantalus?" I asked. "I never heard of it."

"It's some nightclub down in Old River City," Banks said. "Navarro got a tip that Anna Addison is supposed to be there now. You better get a move on if you're gonna make it."

I looked across the dining room to Jenny, who was waiting expectantly. "Yeah, Banks. I'll be there directly." I hung up the phone and headed back to my table.

As soon as I was within earshot, Jenny asked, "Is everything okay with Angelina?"

"As far as I know. That was your friend and mine, Detective Banks. I'm being invited to go and watch our client's daughter get arrested for homicide."

Jenny's lovely blue eyes narrowed sharply. "Oh, really?"

"I'm sorry. Really. But this is something I have to do."

Jenny stared at me with an unfathomable look, then suddenly said, "All right, Sherlock, what are you waiting for? Let's go."

"What do you mean? I can't take you with me."

"What, you were just going to send me off in a cab? Or park me at the bar here? Forget it. Nice as this place is, I'm not going to sit around waiting for you. You can find some out-of-the-way spot for me wherever it is you're going. Preferably one with a vantage point where I can watch you work."

I opened my mouth to protest, but I read the look in her eyes, the one that plainly stated that there was no use in arguing. "Check, please," I said instead.

I was able to pay the bill, retrieve our coats, and have Jenny and me driving toward Ironside Street in less than five minutes. As soon as we were under way, I put in a call to Her Majesty. When Mom answered, I asked for Jenny's sake, "How's Angelina?"

"Sleeping like an angel," Mom said quietly. "Of course, I had to wear her out a bit first. The girl's got stamina."

"Listen," I said, "bad news. I just got the call that the police are going to arrest Anna Addison tonight."

"Wait one," Mom said softly. After a moment, she continued. "Okay, I wanted to get out of Angelina's earshot, just in case. You say Anna Addison's heading for the police hotel, eh?"

"That's the word. Banks called me and asked if I wanted to witness it."

"Where are you now?"

"Driving to meet the police at the old train depot. Supposedly Anna Addison's at a place called Tantalus in Old Town."

"Is Jenny with you?"

I shot a glace at my traveling companion. "Yeah. I didn't have time to drop her off anywhere."

"Can you swing by here and let Jenny and me trade places?"

"That'd be my choice," I agreed, "but the police haven't been what you'd call team players to this point. Chances are they'd love an excuse to start without me."

There was a pause, and then Mom said, "Okay. Keep me posted, and for God's sake, don't let anything happen to Jenny. I'll give His Honor the mayor a call in the meantime. Do you know what kind of evidence they've got on Anna?"

"No."

"Well, find out," Her Majesty commanded.

"Aye, aye. Over and out." I snapped the phone shut and gave the Mustang a bit more gas.

Sometime during my conversation with Mom, Jenny had pulled out her own cell phone. "Okay, thanks," she said, and hung up. To me, she said, "Front Street between First and Second."

"What is?"

"Club Tantalus," she replied. "I called Information for directions."

"Damn," I said softly. "You're both useful and decorative."

"And don't you forget it," she admonished.

I turned my attention to driving. At the bottom of Ironside Street, just under the overhead freeway, was the archway to Old River City. Back in the mid-1800s during the gold rush, the miners brought their hard-won treasure out of the surrounding hills to the river, where paddlewheel boats ferried gold to the mints in San Francisco. If the river was the vein that pumped the gold to market, River City was the leech that attached itself to that vein and bled off what it could. The lure of gold drew in all manner of con men, gamblers, prostitutes, and politicians. The end of the gold shipments caused the town a bit of a recession, until the blessings of Prohibition in the 1920s brought the liquid gold of illegal liquor and a spurt of new life to the city. By the 1970s the place was a total slum, and then some entrepreneurs found a new type of sheep to fleece, namely tourists. Now the place was a booming re-creation of an Old West town, complete with a couple of steam-powered paddlewheel boats at the docks. Jim Bui, a rabid western history aficionado, sometimes wondered aloud what the likes of Wild Bill Hickock and Wyatt Earp would think of the place now. At least they'd still have no difficulty finding a place to drink.

As I angled around Saloon Street, I slowed down, anticipating the jarring vibration caused by driving over the century-old cobblestone streets. Old River City these days is just about evenly divided between the tourist traps and specialty shops that cater to the daytime trade and the restaurants and nightclubs that service the evening crowd. I saw that Christmas had made its mark here as well; many of the Old West façades were now festooned in strands of flickering lights. Crossing into Old River City felt like crossing over to another time and place, especially now as the fog was starting to creep in, muting the streetlights into a soft, translucent glow.

I slowed down when I turned onto Front Street, peering ahead and looking for Club Tantalus. When I was roughly half a block away, I heard it, a rhythmic, thumping noise with a heavy metal overtone. Following the electronic trail, I spotted a black sign with glowing, bloodred lettering: TANTALUS.

"You take me to the nicest places," Jenny said with an impish grin in her voice.

I was busy surveying the cluster of people hanging around outside the club, which was apparently down below street level. The entrance was bathed in strobing red lights that arced up from somewhere below, backlighting the girls and boys who milled about and smoked near the street. "Stop the car," Jenny said suddenly.

I did. "What? What do you see?" I asked.

She opened the door and slipped out all in one smooth motion. "See you inside, Sherlock. Don't keep me waiting too long. I might start looking for a new date." With a devilish smile, she shut the door and spun on her heel, marching over to the doorway to the club.

I called out to her a couple of times—and, I confess, muttered a few things under my breath I'm glad she didn't hear—until an impatient driver behind me started honking his horn. Damn. I'd just have to play this one out. I put the Green Hornet back in gear and drove ahead toward the Old River City Depot, where I had no difficulty spotting the cluster of so-called undercover police vehicles crowded together in the fog-laced darkness.

I parked a bit away from the official cars and walked over to a group of dark-clad men and women. Through the gloom, I could see that most were decked out in black jumpsuits with heavily laden gun belts and armored vests emblazoned with the word POLICE in bright yellow letters. "Am I late for the costume party?" I asked no one in particular.

"Over here, Wilder," I heard the flat, unwelcome tone of Lori Banks call to me. I followed in the direction of her voice and found Detective Banks and Detective Navarro leaning against one of the police cars. Navarro was again dressed in his dark raincoat and was sipping from a jumbo-sized foam coffee cup. Banks was still in the beige suit with her ugly fleece-trimmed denim coat over it. Navarro pushed off the car as I approached and said in a voice that was weary yet not without humor, "Well, now that we're all here." Louder, he said, "All right, people, gather round. Let's get this ball rolling."

Detective Navarro clicked on a flashlight, aiming the beam at the hood of his car as his troops formed a tight semicircle around him. Navarro set his coffee down on the hood and picked up a page-sized color digital photo of the woman I now recognized as Anna Addison, a picture that was apparently a blowup of her driver's license photo. Judging from what I could see, and comparing it in my mind to the photograph her father provided, the picture was taken some years ago, showing a smiling girl with light brown hair.

"This is Anna Lucille Addison," Navarro announced. "She's listed as twenty-two years old, five foot six, one hundred and twenty pounds." I faintly heard one of the officers behind mutter, "Damn. I'd do her."

"She's wanted in connection with a recent homicide," Navarro continued. A different voice behind me said, "Dude, sounds like she'd do you instead." There was some muted laughter. Navarro patiently waited for it to subside before saying, "We got a tip that she's in the nightclub down the street called Tantalus."

"Who called in the tip?" I asked.

In the backwash of Navarro's flashlight, I saw him smile. As if I hadn't said anything, Navarro continued. "Mr. Wilder here is along with us tonight as an observer. Please treat him with all due professional courtesy." *Professional disregard is more like it,* I thought. I could feel the slight shifting of the officers nearest me as they gave me a bit more room, just in case whatever it was I had was catching. Navarro went on, ignoring my interruption. "Now, this picture of Ms. Addison is a few years old, and I'm not sure how much her appearance may have changed. The owner of the club, a Mr. Archimedes, knows her, and I'll expect him to point her out to us if she's here." Navarro looked over to me as he said, "Mr. Wilder? You'll stay back here with Detective Banks until we get the situation under control."

*The hell I will,* I thought. I didn't like the idea of Jenny being in that place, and I'd be damned if I was just going to sit around here waiting for the cavalry to go charging down there without me. I raised my hand. "Detective, I just spoke with

Anna Addison today. If she's down there, I should be able to spot her."

I was rewarded by the sound of Lori Banks noisily spitting out a mouthful of coffee as she said, "Say fucking what!"

Navarro stared at me for a long moment, and then he said, "What do you mean, you spoke with her today?"

"Just what I said. I met her down by the river earlier tonight when Detective Banks took me to the crime scene."

Navarro's voice was heavy as he said, "And you're telling me this now?"

"Hey, I just found out she was your major suspect. Don't blame me. You're the one who's been keeping me in the dark."

"Okay," Navarro said with slow anger in his voice. "New plan. Mr. Wilder will accompany the team."

"One more suggestion," I said quickly. "Rather than go charging into the club with this herd of storm troopers, why don't you let Detective Banks and me head in first? Might go a lot smoother if the two of us just go and get her out."

There was a pause, and then Navarro turned to Banks. "Any objections?"

Even though the night was chill, the look Banks gave me warmed me considerably; it was if she were trying to will me to burst into flames. "No," Banks finally said bitterly.

"Fine." Navarro sighed. "The team will stay back until Banks gives the word. Everyone stay on channel seven. Lori, grab a radio."

"Come on, Banks," I said for everyone's benefit. "Let's go."

Banks opened the door of her car and leaned in, treating me to a view of her beige posterior. I looked away in an effort to save my eyesight, and shortly thereafter she came up with a handheld police radio. Without a glance at me, she started marching across the cobblestone street toward the opposite corner. I hurried to keep up, saying as I finally got abreast of her, "I sense you're not entirely happy with me."

"Damn you, Wilder," she said around clenched teeth. "You could have mentioned you found a witness out by the river tonight. But no, you had to play some goddamn game."

"Game," I repeated. "Oh, you mean like the game Let's Keep Jason in the Dark? If you had played fair with me and at least given me a list of the players involved, I'd have played fair with you."

Lori stepped up to the wide plank sidewalk and stopped, grabbing my arm in the process. She looked up at me and said, "You really would have come clean with us? Really?"

I shrugged and smiled. "Nah. Probably not."

Banks smirked. "At least you're honest. At the moment, anyway. All right, Wilder, do me one favor? Just point this bitch out to me. Then I don't want you to do another damn thing. You got that?"

"Got it."

"Good."

"What have you got on Anna Addison that makes her out to be the murderer?"

Banks looked away, over to where an endless parade of cars vibrated along the cobblestones through the fog. She made a small shrug, then said, "They got a match on the murder weapon. Bloodstained fingerprint."

Ouch. "How did you get a match so fast?" I asked.

"Oh, Addison's prints are on file. She's been picked up before, mostly as a teenaged runaway. She's also got a very interesting trespass arrest on her record."

"What's so interesting about a trespass?"

"She was caught in the Old City Cemetery some years ago," Banks said with a grin. "Looks like your new girlfriend has a thing for satanic rituals."

"Do you have any eyewitnesses that pin the Messenger murder on Anna?"

"Some that put her there at the scene. No one's come forward and said they actually saw her shove the blade into him, but no one else apparently touched the weapon, either."

There it was again, that awful, queasy feeling that I was learning to associate with sharp objects being rudely introduced into human flesh. There was a crackle on Banks's radio, and I heard, "We're in position," followed by Navarro's voice saying, "Ten-four. Make your move, Banks. Call it in if you spot her." Banks raised the radio and replied, "Copy that. Let's go, Wilder."

We walked along the wooden sidewalk past a couple of shops closed for the evening, drawing ever nearer to the loud heavy metal music coming from Tantalus. Black-clad people in twos and threes huddled near the entrance, smoking. The air tasted heavily of clove cigarettes; the strobing red light flickered in time to the music. Standing guard at the door was a large, beefy guy with a shaved head and a mustache and goatee, wearing leather and chains, complete with a metal-spike-studded dog collar. In defiance of the chill night air, his open black leather vest, sans shirt, displayed enough tattoos for an entire circus. He gave Banks and me a smirk as we made our way toward him, thrust out his hand, and shouted over the music, "Five-dollar cover charge. Each."

I smiled as I produced my wallet. "Certainly, my good man," I said over the din of the music. "The wife and I just love your quaint little place, don't we, dear?"

Banks, her mouth hanging open, said nothing as I handed the bouncer the money. We headed down the flashing-red-lit steps, but not before I overheard him say behind me, "Freaks."

Descending into Tantalus, I slowed, hoping to become accustomed to the visual and audible assault. The bottom of the stairs opened out to a low-ceilinged room that seemed to amplify the music into shock waves that pushed their way through my body. To my left, I saw the bar, aglow in a halo of ultraviolet light, and was relieved to see Jenny Chance lounging at the corner. The black-light lamps made her eyes look as if they were lit from within, and her wide smile put me in mind of the Cheshire Cat. Lori Banks pulled my arm, lowering my head to her level as she yelled into my ear, "You see Addison anywhere?"

I shook my head and started scanning the room, crowded with boys, girls, and gender indeterminates, most sporting an assortment of black leather fetish wear, tattoos, and body piercing. Across a dance floor awash in artificial fog, I saw more people, but it was impossible to distinguish features in the hyperactive lighting. I started making my way through the crowd, feeling Banks follow in my wake. The walls of the place were covered in one continuous mosaic of demons, death's heads, and the damned, all madly intertwined. I'd managed to get roughly halfway across the room when I spotted a small group in the far right corner, keeping apart from the other revelers. Angling closer, I saw a woman in a black corset and thigh-high boots who I thought at first was Asian, with long black hair and bangs. As I got closer, I caught a glimpse of the same almond-shaped eyes and high Nordic cheekbones that I had seen illuminated by moonlight earlier.

Anna Addison saw me, too. For a moment, indecision animated her face. She turned to someone behind her and said a few words, then started walking toward me with a look of determination.

Before I could say anything, Detective Banks shoved her way past me, holding out her badge at arm's length, aiming right at Anna Addison. I heard Banks yell above the pounding music, "All right, Addison, you're under arrest!" Anna's eyes popped wide, and she spun around and made a dash back to her corner, screaming words I couldn't make out.

Then Anna, her face locked in a soundless snarl, shot her arm out toward Banks and me, pointing her black-gloved finger like a gun. The next thing I knew, the human mass clustered in the corner behind her seemed to erupt and disgorge a flock of black-clad demons.

Heading right at us.

# CHAPTER NINE

This is why I don't like to wear neckties.

Between the crowd around me and the charging stampede ahead, there was absolutely nowhere to go. The overhead lights flashed into a schizophrenic syncopation, and before I could do more than shift my body to a defensive stance I was hit by a human avalanche. Over the thunderous metal music I heard Detective Banks give vent to a scream of rage. I felt myself getting pummeled to the hard ground. I saw a flash of a grinning, maniacal face appear inches from my own, and I managed to slip a hand free to smash a heel-palm strike into it. Suddenly the human wave washed over me and I was no longer being pounded into the floor. I rocked myself into the kneeling position, trying to get my bearings in the chaotic environment.

I looked up and saw a tightly packed line of people forcing their way up a black metal staircase. It was on the back wall and led to an emergency exit. At the same time, two River City policemen were trying to get down the same stairway to the floor level like a pair of salmon swimming upstream. I stood up too quickly, feeling my head spin, and looked around for Banks. She was on hands and knees in the swirling artificial fog, but before I could reach her, I was grabbed from behind and jerked around—to see the glistening shaved head of the beefy bouncer. The next thing I knew, I was being yanked up on my tiptoes and fighting to breathe as he grabbed a fistful of my necktie and used it as an impromptu noose to hang me with.

*Not me, you idiot!* is what I wanted to say, but all that came out of my throat was an inarticulate gargling sound. Fortunately my body seemed to know what to do, since my brain, badly rattled and now oxygen deprived, was no help at all. My hands clamped themselves to the arm that clutched my necktie, one to the wrist and the other to his tattoo-covered elbow. A quick twist in opposing directions, followed by a half turn of my body, and I had Bouncer Boy bent over double with his arm locked up tight in a classic arm-bar hold. The problem was, my damn necktie had been pulled into a strangling knot, and I still couldn't breathe. I shoved the bouncer away into a pack of gawkers who had ringed themselves around us, knocking over a couple of them, and reached up and dug my fingers under my collar, trying to tear open a breathing space.

I yanked my collar apart, feeling the fabric rip against my neck, and grabbed a couple of grateful breaths, just in time to see the bouncer pick himself up and take aim at me for round two—but then he launched forward, his arms flailing outward as he crashed to the ground, and through the man-made lightning I saw a wildly smiling Jenny Chance step out from the ring of people and take up a martial arts fighting stance, the lovely velvet dress hiked up her lovelier thighs. The bouncer, now on hands and knees, shook his head and pushed himself to his feet. Or he would have if Jenny hadn't spun around and slammed her heel into his head, sending him sprawling across the floor. I looked at Jenny, transformed into a wild Amazon in the joy of battle, and saw her mouth the words "Come on!" as she beckoned me to follow her to the back.

I shook my head, then looked for Banks. The two jump-suited policemen were on either side of the detective, each one now holding an expandable baton and looking around for something to use it on. Abruptly the music stopped and harsh white light exploded from the ceiling. Jenny ran over and wrapped herself around me as the crowd started to buzz like a giant hive of bees. "Are you all right?" she demanded. I drew in a breath to answer but had to stop as a lancing pain stabbed through my right side. My free hand reached for my rib cage; it felt like someone had shot me with an arrow. "Jason!" Jenny exclaimed.

"I'm okay," I heard myself utter. Sometime during the melee, someone must have landed a good solid kick to my midsection. Someone wearing steel-toed boots. I looked around for any sign of Anna Addison in the crowd. With the lights full on, the clubgoers now resembled a circus of zombies caught out after sunrise. I glanced over to the two officers near Detective Banks.

"Hey," I called, "who's watching the back door?"

In perfect unison, the officers looked at each other and said, "Oh, shit!" before running to the stairs, leaving a bloody-nosed and bewildered Lori Banks in their wake. To my left, the crowd parted to allow Detective Navarro through, leading a line of his men. "Banks!" Navarro called. "What happened?"

I kept my eye on the bouncer as he slowly picked himself up, looking around as if to find wherever it was that his brains had wound up. In my peripheral vision I saw Banks shake her head. Navarro spotted me and led his procession over in my direction. "What happened, Wilder? Was Anna Addison here?"

"Yeah," I answered, "but it looks like she got the hell out while some friends of hers created a diversion. Your boys upstairs came charging in, and I figure she must have gotten past them. Her and the rest of her army."

Navarro's dark, sunken eyes flicked to my side. "Who's this?"

Before I could think up a semiplausible lie, Jenny said, "I'm a friend of Jason's, and I saw him get attacked by that thug over there." She pointed an accusing finger at the bouncer, who'd recovered sufficiently to realize he was now the center of unwanted attention. The crowd was starting to get restless. The sound of their grumbling voices began to swell.

From over my right shoulder, I heard a deep, cultured voice say, "Detective Navarro, is it? Could you please explain what you and your men are doing here in my club?"

I turned around to look and had to crane my neck back to see the man's face. He was easily six and a half feet tall and reed thin, with angular features and a crown of jet black hair with impeccable white wings at the temples and at the corners of his goatee. Like just about everybody else in the club he was dressed in black, but in his case it was an expensive-looking tailored suit. His pitch-dark eyes, standing out in contrast to his pale skin, flashed as he said, "I demand an explanation."

Detective Navarro seemed to bunch himself up in his rumpled coat as he answered, "Police business, Mr. Archimedes. I'm looking for Anna Addison."

The man smiled thinly. "For that, you come barging into my club? Really, I'd expect better from the police. Shouldn't you be out looking for whoever killed poor Messenger?"

"I am," Navarro relied flatly. "Did you talk to Anna Addison after I interviewed you today?"

The man named Archimedes gave a slight shake of his head. "No. I haven't seen her since last night. Now, may I resume my business? Feel free to look around all you like, of course." He snapped his fingers. In an instant, Club Tantalus transformed back to the thunderous, flashing-red-lit mayhem that I had descended into, much to the noisy approval of the crowd.

Archimedes made a silent, theatrical bow, a secretive smile on his lips, and turned and melted back through the masses. Over the harsh, grinding sound of the music I heard Navarro say, "Smug bastard." He pointed toward the entrance. The line of officers reversed course and moved out, while Navarro collected a still-dazed Lori Banks. I spared a look back at the large bouncer, only to see him staring at me with an expression that could charitably be described as pure hatred. Jenny put her arm around me, unfortunately landing right on my almost certainly broken rib, and guided me out behind the line of police. As we wended our way through, snide, sarcastic remarks were tossed at us by the local denizens.

Climbing up the stairs and emerging into the cold, foggy night and away from the hammering music felt like an escape from hell, but the flashing red lights from below were replaced by the flashing red lights of the River City patrol cars that now blocked off this end of the street. I could see the officers of the arrest team starting to form a loose circle around Navarro. Handing my car keys to Jenny, I said, "Here. Get ready for a fast getaway."

"What do you think you're doing?" she demanded softly.

"I'm going to try to weasel a little more information out of the local constabulary. I'll meet you back at the car. It's parked over at the old railway depot across the corner there."

Jenny's lovely lips took a downward turn. "Fine," she said shortly. "Just don't start any more riots in the meantime. I won't be here to rescue you."

"My hero," I said with a laugh that made the pain in my side kick in again. I watched Jenny step out into the fog-shrouded street and then tried to angle casually over toward Navarro to eavesdrop, but the echoes of the music emanating from Tantalus made his words difficult to catch.

I stepped in closer, only to hear a startled expletive burst forth from Detective Banks. All eyes looked her way. She was wild-eyed, staring at nothing as she frantically beat the sides of her coat as if trying to put out a fire. "God damn!"

"What?" an officer called out.

"My gun!" Banks cried. "I lost my goddam gun!"

Banks's words stopped me in my tracks. I've never been a policeman, and never will be one, but I was raised by their kind, and even though I occasionally wondered aloud if I wouldn't have been better off had I been raised by wolves, I grew up steeped in all the lore and legend that goes with those who carry the badge. I knew that given a choice between losing their sidearm and their reproductive organs, every cop in the world would choose to hold on to that gun.

Detective Banks had just admitted before her peers that she had committed one of the few completely unpardonable sins in the police world. My instincts told me I should get the hell out of there. I faded back into the night and went to my car.

Jenny had the engine running. I tapped the window on the driver's side, only to have her toss her head toward the passenger seat. I capitulated and tucked myself into it, trying not to groan from the pain in my side.

Jenny reached down and rubbed her left leg, the one she'd used to kick the brains out of Bouncer Boy. "Well, Sherlock," she said, "you certainly know how to show a girl a good time."

"Are you okay?"

"I banged up my foot some, and I ripped the bejeezus out of my dress. Do you know how much this thing cost me?"

"Sorry. I'll buy you a new one. If I still have a job, that is."

I gingerly reached to my belt and got out my cell phone. "Her Majesty isn't going to like this," I said as I punched in Mom's number.

Her Ladyship answered right away. "Well?" she inquired.

"Anna Addison gave the boys in black the slip," I said. "Oh, and if there's a news report of a small riot at Club Tantalus, rest assured that any reports of my demise are slightly exaggerated."

"Really?" Mom said. "Is Jenny all right? Is she still with you?"

I stole a sideways look at the woman next to me. "She's fine. As a matter of fact, Little Miss Brown Belt in Tae Kwon Do managed to rescue your favorite son." In the near darkness, I saw the shadow of Jenny's smile.

"I'm not surprised," Mom said with a certain satisfaction. "I take it Anna's a fugitive from justice now?"

"It would appear so."

"Well, then. We're just going to have to find her first. I spoke to the mayor after you called the first time. He's not happy, to say the very least."

"He's not the only one."

"Did you manage to get any more information on what the police have against Ms. Addison?"

"Yep. And it's not so good."

"I see. Well, you kids had best come home. Sounds like you'll be working tomorrow."

I sighed. "I kind of figured that. Wait a sec, I got another call coming in." I clicked my phone over to receive my new caller and was greeted by an angry, slightly hysterical female.

"Why the hell did you come down there looking for me!" the voice demanded.

It was Anna Addison.

# CHAPTER TEN

For just a moment, I was tempted to hang up the phone, but either reason or lack thereof prevailed. I said to Anna Addison, "I just wanted to talk to you."

"You brought the cops after me!"

"Yeah, well, the police have this crazy idea about you. They think you killed Elijah Messenger."

I heard her suck her breath in. "What? That's insane! I didn't!"

"Don't tell me, Ms. Addison. Tell the police. They're the ones looking for you now." I waited for her response, wondering if she was going to keep talking or just hang up. Finally I heard her say, as if from off in the distance, "I can't go to the police. Not now."

"Why not?"

"I just . . . need to do something first."

I was glad Anna Addison couldn't see the face I was making at the phone. I was shaking my head, trying to imagine what could possibly be more important than an innocent person wanting to clear her name of a homicide charge, when she said, "Help me."

"What?"

"Help me, please," she whispered hoarsely. "I need . . . I

need someone to go to the cops and tell them I'll talk to them later. I promise."

Yeah, right. Like that would go over with Navarro. "Look, Ms. Addison, I want to help you—"

"Then do it!" she shrieked.

"Tell you what," I said as reasonably as I could. "Meet with me, anywhere you like, and we can talk about it, okay?"

"No cops?" she asked suspiciously.

"No cops."

"Anywhere I say?"

"Yes." There was a pause, then she said, "You know the West Gate Bridge?"

"West Gate Bridge? Sure."

"Meet me under it. On the other side from here."

The line went dead. "And just what was that all about?" Jenny asked.

I stared at the phone in my hand as I replied, "That was the whacko daughter of our client."

"And she's accused of murder?"

"It's starting to look that way."

"That doesn't sound good," Jenny opined.

I tried to twist in my seat to see what the police were up to, but all I managed to do was to give myself a jolt of pain in my abused side. "Are the police still out in front of Club Tantalus?" I asked.

Jenny reached up and adjusted the rearview mirror. "Looks like it. I can see a patrol car from here. Why?"

"It's decision time," I said as I held up my phone. "Looks like I just managed to implicate myself. Anna Addison called me from another cell phone, probably her own. Once the police get a search warrant for her phone records, and believe me, they will, they'll see that she made a call on this date and time to a number that comes back to my personal phone. It's only a matter of time until they know I've been in communication with their primary suspect."

"So what decision do you have to make?"

"Whether to meet with Anna Addison by myself or take the cops with me and let them arrest her."

Jenny sat very still in the darkness of my car. Finally she asked, "Do you think she's guilty?"

"Not being psychic myself, I have absolutely no idea."

"Well, then, the choice looks clear to me. You have to meet her."

"I do?"

"Yes," Jenny said decisively. "Besides, you're not a cop. You're a private detective. It's not your job to go around arresting people."

"True, but—"

Jenny cut me off. "And until you think that your client's daughter is a menace to society, I don't see where you need to do the police's job for them, right?"

"Yeah, but—"

"Besides," Jenny interjected, "I seem to remember another woman of your acquaintance who was once wrongly accused by the police. As I recall, you didn't turn her in."

Even in the darkness, I could see Jenny Chance bat her eyes at me. "I had an ulterior motive in that particular case," I admitted. "I wanted to date the suspect."

"And in this case?" Jenny asked quickly.

"I'd have to tell her I'm sorry, but my social calendar is quite full with the tall brunette and the short blonde I date. Infrequently as that may be."

"Good," Jenny said. "So, where are we going? You mentioned a bridge."

"One suitable for jumping off of, if I'm wrong about any of this."

"Not on your life, pal," Jenny said sharply. "This date isn't over yet. So what's the plan?"

"I guess I'm supposed to meet Anna Addison at the West Gate Bridge. I'll find a good place to drop you off, then I'll call you when I'm done."

"Think again," Jenny said as she slipped the Green Hornet into gear and smoothly spun us out of the parking lot. "You're stuck with me. What's the best way to the bridge?"

We hit the cobblestone street, and the vibrations did absolutely nothing good for the pain in my ribs. "Get us out of Old Town," I said. "Then take a right on Sixth Ave and head over to Mast Street. Go west from there and it takes you right to the bridge."

"Aye, aye. And you're not dropping me off anywhere. I'm sticking with you until you decide to call it quits tonight."

I sighed. "Okay, but pull over as soon as you get the chance." Jenny spotted an open alleyway between two of the Old West–style buildings and pulled in. "I'll need the keys," I said.

Jenny shut the engine down and handed me the keys. I managed to get out of the car without groaning and made my way to the trunk, popped it open, and unlocked my briefcase. I glanced around, but no one seemed to be nearby, so I took out my Ruger Speed Six revolver. The gun is a compact stainless steel .357 Magnum that used to belong to my father, and he had a few modifications installed. Unless you're wearing a special magnetic ring, the lock built into the grip of the gun won't allow it to fire. Dad had the ring made with his personal signet: a clock face with the hands at the hour of twelve. I stored the ring in a pocket of my briefcase.

I slipped the ring on and checked that the high-powered .38-caliber cartridges were loaded in it. Knowing that Anna Addison or one of her confederates probably had possession of Lori Banks's service pistol didn't make me feel any better about meeting up with her in a dark, secluded spot, but at least I was ready for real trouble now. I dropped the gun into my topcoat pocket, then picked up my digital voice recorder. I frowned when I remembered that I'd lent my little tactical flashlight to Anna Addison earlier tonight.

I eased myself back into the car and shut the door. Jenny resumed our bumpy progression out of Old River City and said, "Do I get a gun, too?"

"Sorry. I only have the one. Besides, you're strictly on the sidelines in this caper."

Jenny made a haughty sound as we got off the cobblestone road and accelerated on real pavement. "For your information, I've been taught how to operate everything from an old western six-shooter to an AK-47. I'm a damn good shot, too."

"With what? With blanks? This isn't one of your Hollywood movie stunt gigs."

"Hey, we may have fired blanks on the film sets, but I learned it all with live ammo. And the stunts were called gags, not gigs."

"Gigs, gags, whatever. You're not to get out of this car under any circumstance. You're way too important to your daughter. And I'm kind of fond of you myself."

Through the glow of the traffic lights, I saw Jenny radiate a smile. "Sweet talker," she said quietly.

As Jenny drove us toward Mast Street, I got out my phone and called the Queen. As soon as Mom picked up the phone, I said, "I found Anna Addison."

"What took you so long?" Mom shot back.

"Sorry. Just a born slacker, I guess. Anyway, I talked her into meeting with me. Alone."

"Really?" Mom said. "And just what do you intend to do with her then?"

"I'm playing this one by ear. I'm supposed to meet her on the West Gate Bridge. Did you speak to the mayor again?"

"Yes, and I imagine he's burning up the phone lines even as we speak. I advised him to arrange for an attorney for Anna."

"Good move. I think the kid's going to need one real soon."

"Do you want James or Timothy to rendezvous with you?"

At the moment, having either one or both of the most dangerous men I knew would have been a godsend, but I knew there'd be no way for them to get to me in time. "Nah," I said reluctantly. "Besides, at their age, they need all the rest they can get."

"Take care, son. And for God's sake keep Jenny out of harm's way."

"Easier said than done," I grumbled as I clapped the phone shut. Ahead I could already see the gold-painted steel-girder sculpture of the West Gate Bridge that connects River City proper to its poorer cousin, West River, a low-rent, run-down hodgepodge of homes and businesses that were barely keeping themselves above the title of slum. As Jenny and I passed under the metal archway of the bridge's entrance, I once again read the words emblazoned there: WHEREVER THE RIVER FLOWS, THERE ALSO FLOWS ALL GOOD THINGS.

Yeah. Right. Tell that to Messenger, I thought.

Jenny slowed down as we reached the end of the bridge. Traffic was relatively light, and I directed her to pull over where she could park. "This is it?" Jenny asked.

I looked around. The lights from the bridge made the fog glow amber. Ahead I could see the twinkling lights of West River's Main Street, but in the area near the bridge it was all shadows and darkness. "Yeah, this is my stop. Wish me luck."

Jenny grabbed me by my loosely dangling necktie and pulled me close—and kissed me. I was briefly aware of the pain in my neck and side, and then there was absolutely nothing else in the entire world but Jenny and this moment.

The kiss melted, and our faces drew slightly apart. "That's to remind you to come back to me," she said in a voice of pure silk. "There's more where that came from."

I drew in a breath. "Count on it, lady," I said. I threw my door open and stepped outside, feeling ten feet tall and ready to take on anything the night could hold. I took a long look around; a few cars drove past. *Okay,* I thought to myself, *Anna said "under the bridge"; now all I have to do is see if I'm on the right side of the river.* Looking down, I saw a low guardrail that ran parallel to the road. On the other side was a hard-packed dirt trail that led down through the fog to the water's edge, out of sight of the passing traffic.

With a shrug, I stepped over the guardrail and sidestepped cautiously downward. It would be one hell of a time to go sliding down into the black, icy water. As I neared the shoreline, I slipped and halfway slid on the shifting pebbles, just as a blinding light swept out from the darkness under the bridge and speared me in the eyes. I did lose my balance then, flopping hard on my butt and sliding a few feet down. I threw up my hand to ward off the light as I heard Anna Addison say, "Jesus. 'Bout time you got here."

"Would you get that light out of my eyes?" I asked. I was suddenly cast into total darkness. "On second thought," I said, "could you turn that thing back on until I can get over to you? It's a bad time to go swimming."

The light came back on and lit an area near my feet. Keeping my eyes off the light source, I painstakingly stepped up toward Anna, all the while trying to see if there was anyone else nearby. I sat down on the slope next to her, close enough that I could sense she was shivering.

"You're alone?" she asked in a shaky voice. "No cops?"

"No cops," I said truthfully, "but I still think your best bet is to turn yourself in. I just heard that your father is getting you a good lawyer."

"I don't need a fucking lawyer," she said bitterly. "I didn't fucking do anything."

"Okay, okay," I said as soothingly as I could. "So, while we're slowly freezing to death here, why don't you tell me what happened to Messenger last night? You were there, right?"

With a shaky hand, Anna lit a cigarette, and I could now see her face, shrouded in lank black hair, the thick black makeup around her large eyes smeared and runny, like a mask that was melting. She was hunched up inside a black trench coat that was way too big for her. She blew out a smoky breath, and said, "I gotta know one thing first."

"What's that?"

"Do you believe in magic?"

# CHAPTER ELEVEN

There I was, with a young girl of questionable sanity, sitting in the cold, damp darkness on hard concrete while the sounds of traffic overhead echoed strangely around us. I'd had better Friday nights, that was for certain.

As I sat there in the dark with Anna Addison, I reminded myself that the real art of investigation lies in the ability to get people to talk to you, and the last thing you want to do is give them the sense that you don't believe them. I said to Anna, "What I believe in doesn't really matter. I'm just trying to find the best way I can help you. To do that, I need you to tell me how you got involved with Elijah Messenger in the first place."

Anna sucked on her cigarette and shot out a smoky plume before answering. "I guess you could say that Elijah was supposed to be my teacher."

"Teacher of what?"

"Magic. Sorcery," she said in a matter-of-fact voice. "I'm a witch."

"Okay," I said slowly. "Suppose you take me through this from the top."

I heard her rustle inside her oversized trench coat as she shifted her weight. The fog-diffused lights from the bridge overhead came in from either side, letting us see each other in silhouette. Anna said, "Guess I can't blame you. Most mundanes don't believe in the arts."

I translated "mundanes" to mean people who weren't clinically insane, but I kept my opinion to myself and just said, "Go on."

"I've studied the Path for years now. Read the Book of Shadows and learned all I could. Went through my initiations and leaned how to perform the rituals of protection, banishment, stuff like that." She grew quiet, then said, "But I guess you think all this is bullshit, don't you?"

I was glad of the darkness. God knows what kind of toll her words were taking on my poker face. I said, "Please. Tell me more."

Before resuming, Anna took a last hard drag of her smoke and threw the butt away; I watched it bounce on the slanted concrete. "Okay. You asked for it," she said. "A couple of months ago, I was asked if I was ready for more. Ready to learn the Hidden Path."

"What was that?"

"The real thing," she said simply. "Stuff that really works. That's when I met Messenger. The Magister."

"Is that anything like magistrate?"

"It's an old Latin word. It means both 'master' and 'teacher.'" Through the darkness, I felt more than saw her shiver again, and she said in a quiet, shaky voice, "The things he could do."

"Like what?"

"I'd never seen anything like it," she said wonderingly. "Elijah has . . . had . . . power. Real power. When I saw that, I knew I wanted it."

"You say he had power? Like what?"

Anna wrapped herself tightly in her coat and starting rocking back and forth as she sat. "You name it, Elijah could do it. Including the power of materialization. Physical manifestation. It was fucking unbelievable. And he chose me to be his maiden."

"Maiden?"

"Yeah. All true covens have one. It's one of the steps you take before you're ready to be chosen as high priestess."

I kept my voice carefully in neutral as I said, "Okay. So how did you meet Elijah?"

"Through Archimedes. He knew him first."

"Archimedes? The owner of Club Tantalus?"

"Yeah. He was also there last night. When . . . when it all happened."

"Did you see Archimedes tonight?"

"Yeah. For a minute. I went to his office to find out what's been going on. He blew me off. Said he didn't have time to talk to me."

"When was this?"

"Right after I got there. Maybe ten o'clock or so. Why?"

"Just curious," I said. Privately I was wondering why Archimedes lied to the police when he said he hadn't seen Anna tonight. Not that I myself haven't shaded the truth when speaking with the constabulary from time to time. "Who else was there last night?" I asked.

"We were five. We were supposed to do a summoning." She gave a bitter bark of a laugh, then said, "Well, we sure as hell summoned something."

I tried to steer her back on track. "And the five people were?"

"Well, me, for one. Elijah, of course. Robert, Aurora, and Archimedes made five. Oh, Stone was there at Elijah's house, but he never participates."

"Who's Stone?"

"That's Archimedes' boy. He's like a bodyguard or something."

"Was he at the club tonight? Big guy, shaved head with a mustache and goatee, thinks spiked dog collars are fashionable this year?"

"Yeah. That's him."

"Okay, now who are the rest? Archimedes I met tonight, but who are Robert and Aurora?"

Anna went looking inside her trench-coat cocoon and came up with another cigarette. "Want one?" she offered.

"No, thanks."

She shrugged and lit another match, briefly lighting up her pale, painted face. "Robert Hanson is another one of Elijah's students. He's always been nice to me. Aurora is just a total bitch."

"Why?"

"Why? Because she just is," Anna said irritably. "She's also a fucking poser who's been hanging around Elijah for a while, always asking a bunch of damn questions. I think she's a phony. Elijah just mostly ignored her. He once told me privately that she really didn't have what it took. Not like me, anyway."

The freezing cold of the concrete I was sitting on had slowly and inexorably crawled up my backside to the base of my spine, and I was starting to wonder if the creeping cold would eventually start to affect my brain. "What happened at the summoning?" I asked.

Anna's back-and-forth rocking increased in tempo. "Like I said, Elijah called us all together last night. Said the stars were right for a ritual of summoning. I don't have any idea why he wanted that bitch Aurora there, but she made five, and Elijah said we had to have five."

"Why was that?"

"I dunno. I thought it might have to do with the Third Degree of Initiation and the Five Points of Fellowship or something."

I was sorry I asked. "Okay, so what happened then?"

Anna sighed and said, "We all met at Elijah's house, as usual. Elijah told us to prepare, then come to the circle in half an hour."

"That's the place by the river? Where I met you tonight?"

Anna's shadow nodded quickly. "Yeah. So I went to my room and got ready. While I was waiting, I heard something from down the hall. I peeked out my door and saw that bitch Aurora hanging around the door to Elijah's room. I guess it was locked. I don't think she got in. Anyway, after the time was up, we all got together in the courtyard, and Robert led us to the circle. Elijah was waiting for us."

"What happened then?"

"Elijah . . . damn . . . Elijah took the fire from Robert's torch. With his bare hand. And lit the fire in the circle."

"You mean he took Robert's torch and lit the fire?"

Anna shook her head once, quickly. "No. I mean he took fire from Robert's torch. Held it right in his hand like you'd hold a pet or something, then bent down and lit up the fire pit. Just as cool as you'd light up a cig."

"What next?"

"Well, we were all given tools to bring. I was charged with carrying the chalice," she said with some pride. "Aurora had the broom. But it was Archimedes who brought the Athame."

"The what?"

"The Athame," Anna repeated. "It's like a big knife. It's used in rituals."

"Oh. Go on."

Anna threw her cigarette away. "Damn," she said softly. "It

was . . . weird. After Elijah lit the fire, he made an invocation. I was kinda having a hard time staying with it. It was really cold, you know?"

"Where was everybody standing at this point?"

"Well, Elijah was at the head of the circle, closest to the water. We were standing all around in the circle."

"So, if we were going clockwise from Elijah, where was everybody else standing?"

Anna paused to think, then said, "Okay, Aurora was on Elijah's left. Then Archimedes, then Robert and me. I was to Elijah's right. Where I was supposed to be."

"Got it. What happened next?"

"Anyway, Elijah performs the incantation, calling on the Elements of Earth, Air, Fire, and Water. And all of a sudden, it was like the whole goddam fire pit exploded. I felt something singe me and heard Robert screaming something about how he couldn't see, and the next thing I knew there was this god-awful stink and black smoke everywhere, and then I couldn't see. My eyes felt like they were on fire."

"What happened then?"

I heard the catch in Anna's voice before she said, "We were all just kind of stumbling around in the dark, blinded from the explosion, I guess. The fire was almost out, like it just blew itself out all at once. And we were all just like, whoa, what the hell happened? Then Aurora started asking, where was Elijah? It got real quiet all of a sudden then."

Anna seemed to crumple up inside her coat, and she said very quietly, "Then Aurora screamed something about the water. I could hear Robert, and he kept saying stuff like 'What's happening?' Archimedes ran over to the river, then I saw him bend down and start dragging something back. I . . . I went to get a look, and that's when I saw him."

Anna sort of tipped over toward me and started shaking,

wracked in silent sobs. I reached my arm around her and pulled her in close to me, waiting for her inner storm to pass. Holding her in my arms, I became aware of her scent, a strange cross between tobacco smoke and something that reminded me of dusty roses.

After a while, I'm not certain how long, she sniffed and arched her back. "You okay?" I asked as gently as I could.

"Fuck no," she said hoarsely. "I can still see him. Elijah. There was enough moonlight by now, and I guess my eyes had adjusted enough to see. Archimedes had dragged Elijah up to where I could see the Athame. It was sticking out of his chest. Archimedes tried to, I dunno, shake him like he was just asleep or something. Aurora started screaming *He's dead!* over and over. Archimedes said something about going for help. That's when I guess I kind of lost it. I ran back to the house, got my clothes and my car, and just kept going."

"Where did you go?"

"I just drove. I finally managed to get myself to a friend's house. I stayed there until I got it together. Then I went back to Elijah's place, hoping that maybe someone could tell me what the hell happened. But the cops showed up and I ran out the back down to the river. That's when I met you."

"You said you went to a friend's place. Who was that?"

"Not saying," she said defiantly. "I don't want anyone else dragged into this crap."

I waited for what sounded like a large truck to finish rumbling on the bridge overhead before I asked, "So why haven't you spoken to the police? You have any idea how bad that makes you look?"

"I got my reasons," she answered stubbornly.

"Well, your reasons are making you look like you've got something to hide."

"I didn't kill Elijah!" she shouted.

I waited a moment for her to calm down a bit, then said as reasonably as I could, "I'm only saying that what you're doing is making you look bad. The best thing you can do now is let me take you to see someone, and then you can explain your side of the story."

"That someone being a cop, I suppose? Forget that, man. Not right now, anyway."

"What do you mean, not right now?"

"Look, like I said, there's something I've got to do first. Okay? Then I'll talk to the cops."

"What are you planning to do in the meantime? Live under the bridge here?"

She puffed a brief laugh. "I'll be all right. I've got friends waiting to pick me up."

"Your friends from the club? The ones who stomped on my ribs to give you time to get away?"

"Yeah. They're my, well, I guess you'd call them my acolytes."

Great. Little Anna had her own private army. That reminded me of something. "So where's the gun?" I said quickly.

"What gun?"

I was glad the darkness could hide my disappointment. Anna answered my question without the slightest hesitation, so unless she was a good enough liar for the World Poker Tour, she didn't know what had happened to Detective Banks's service pistol. "Just so you know," I said, "I think there's a good chance that one of your acolytes may have made off with a police officer's handgun. If that's true, then I want it back. Soon."

"Okay," she said uncertainly.

I shoved myself off the slanted surface and swayed a bit as my cramped legs tried to reorient themselves while I swallowed a moan that seemed to come straight from my bruised ribs. "You sure I can't take you somewhere? I don't feel right leaving you here."

Through the gloom, I caught the faintest gleam of her smile. "No. I'll be fine."

"How do I get in contact with you?"

"Leave that to me," she said with an irritating smug certainty. "After all, I summoned you in the first place."

"Say what?"

"I did," she said serenely. "Tonight. When I was at the river. I was scared, and I kept thinking of rituals of protection and warding. I guess you could say I was praying for something. Something that would protect me. And then you appeared."

She reached out her hand, touching my chest as if to make sure I was real. Then, in a voice that was tinged with awe, she said, "I summoned you."

# CHAPTER TWELVE

I thought about picking Anna Addison up and dragging her to my car to stuff her in the trunk, like Mom had, but judging by the steep angle of the concrete foundation, we'd probably just go tumbling down into the icy river if I attempted such a stunt. "Look, kid," I said instead, "like I told you before, the reason I'm here is that your dad hired me to look after you. I wasn't summoned, as you say. Now, why don't you just come with me and I'll take you someplace warm?"

"I'm not a goddam kid!" Anna shouted. "You can go tell Daddy that I can look after myself."

Well, legally speaking, she was an adult. Despite the way she was acting. "Okay, then. If you're sure I can't take you someplace safer?"

"Go on," she said, so softly that I almost lost her words in the roar of the traffic overhead. "I'll be fine."

I felt myself make a face at her, glad she couldn't see it, then reached in my pocket for my key-ring flashlight. At the top of the path, I stepped over the low railing, opened the car door, and eased myself into the blessedly warm seat. "I have a message from your mother," Jenny said.

"What's that?"

"This," she said while punching my shoulder with an extended middle knuckle for emphasis.

98

"Ouch! What was that for?"

"Ask her," Jenny replied simply. I called Her Majesty, noting that my phone's battery was getting low.

Mom answered on the first ring. "Did you get my message?"

"Yes. With feeling. What did I do to deserve that?"

"That, kiddo, was for making Jenny and me worry ourselves sick over you. Honestly, a meeting with a suspected murderer under a bridge at night? Speaking of whom, is Anna Addison with you now?"

"No. She's still under the bridge."

"You're leaving her there?"

"She refused to come with me. Besides, I've got a feeling that she won't be down there much longer. I think she has some acolytes lurking nearby."

Jenny said, "If by acolytes you mean three guys in a black Cadillac Eldorado that's seen better days, then you'd be right. I've seen that car cruise back and forth across the bridge about half a dozen times now."

"Aha." I relayed this to Mom, then asked Jenny to take us off the bridge, turn us around, and shut off the lights. Jenny slipped the Mustang into gear and shot forward. As soon as we were over the rise of the levee road, she spun the car in a gut-wrenching, tire-squealing turn that made my ribs want to scream. Before I could utter a protest, she had the car over to the side of the street and facing the bridge, headlights off.

From my phone, I heard my mother ask, "What was that?"

"That," I answered through gritted teeth, "was the last time I let a retired Hollywood stuntwoman drive my car."

Jenny whispered "big baby" under her breath as Her Highness said, "What are you doing now?"

"Waiting to see who picks up Anna Addison. Stand by." Less than two minutes later, I watched as a large passenger sedan crept across the bridge in our direction. Sure enough, it pulled over to the side, allowing a three-car parade to pass it by. Through the smoky fog, I saw a shadow run up from under the bridge and jump into the car. The vehicle wasted no time as it accelerated in our direction. As the car shot past us, I twisted my body to try to get a look at the license plate, only to have my entire torso go on sudden strike. "Dammit!" I said, clutching my side. "I missed getting the license numbers."

"I didn't," Jenny said serenely. "I made a mental note when that car came around for its third pass."

"Three things, my son," I heard Mom say from my phone. "One, come on back to the corral. Sounds like we have a few things to discuss."

"Aye, aye."

"Second," Mom continued, "I'm probably going to have to fire you over tonight's escapades."

"Again?" I asked. "So what's the third thing?"

"Ask Jenny if she's ever considered a career in professional private investigation. The Midnight Agency may have a sudden vacancy."

I clicked off the phone and said to Jenny, "I think I've done as much damage as I possibly could for one night. Let's go back to Mom's."

Jenny fired up the Green Hornet as she said, "So tell me, is your life always like this?"

"Nah. Sometimes it's almost exciting."

"Seriously."

Jenny took us across the West Gate Bridge as I cautiously shifted in my seat, trying to find a position that didn't aggravate my aching side. "Well, as Her Highness puts it, you have to develop a relaxed attitude toward chaos to survive in this business. It's not always crazy like this, though."

"Good. Because for the record, this is not exactly how I wanted to spend my evening with you."

"Can I get a rain check?" I asked hopefully.

"Rain check? More like you owe me big time for this night, boy."

I smiled and tried to relax as Jenny drove us smoothly through the city streets with their fog-softened street and traffic lights. She managed to avoid the more congested main drags and soon had us back in front of the office of the Midnight Agency.

As I expected, Her Majesty was waiting for us in her office, the lit fireplace making a welcome addition to the scene. Jenny went upstairs to check on Angelina, and the moment Mom had me to herself she said, "Okay, kiddo, give it up. All of it."

"May I have a drink first? For medicinal purposes, of course."

"Only if you can prove you deserve one."

"Slave driver," I grumbled as I handed over my pocket voice recorder. "Here. You can listen to my interview with Anna yourself."

Mom smiled as she took the recorder, looking as pleased as a kid getting a Christmas present. "Ah. Excellent. I may avoid firing you tonight after all. Now, you go upstairs and tell Jenny that she should spend the night here. No sense moving Angelina at this hour. Then you go and get some sleep yourself. Something tells me you've got a busy day tomorrow."

"What about my drink?"

She made a dismissive wave toward the carved mahogany liquor cabinet in the corner. "Take one to go. Just don't poison yourself into a hangover."

I saluted, selected a bottle of Bacardi and a pair of glasses, and left the Inner Sanctum through the concealed panel that leads to the kitchen. I stopped off just long enough to put together a pair of Bacardi and Cokes with ice and carefully carried them upstairs, where my first stop was the medicine cabinet in the bathroom off the upper hall for aspirin, with which I treated myself. Then I went looking for Jenny. I found her in the guest suite, with the lights low and soft piano music playing on the stereo. "Hey, lady," I whispered. "Can I interest you in a nightcap?"

Jenny padded over to the doorway on bare feet and gently pulled the door partially closed behind her. "Angelina's sleeping," she said softly.

"Good. By order of Her Royal Highness you two are to stay in the castle tonight. Here's your drink."

Jenny sipped, then said, "And what about you?"

"I'm a prisoner. I'll probably have to sleep in the dungeon."

"Well, at least I won't have to worry about you for one night. How are you feeling?"

I took a long drink, closed my eyes in appreciation, and said, "Better soon."

"So what's next? You still on this case?"

"Haven't the foggiest," I admitted. "I assume Mom will give me my marching orders on the morrow."

Jenny finished her drink and handed me the glass. "Well, in that case, soldier, I'll let you get some sleep." She reached up, grabbed a handful of my battered necktie, and pulled me to her warm, lush lips. Twice in one night. I could get used to wearing ties. The kiss did far more to warm me up than any drink ever did. She then gave me a gentle shove away, saying, "Good night," as she faded back through the doorway, closing it softly after her.

I have no idea how long I stood in front of that door, empty glass in each hand with what must have been an idiot's grin pulling on my cheeks, but I finally regained enough sense to head for my old room. I went to bed with Jenny's kiss lingering on my lips.

The next kiss I got was an altogether different kind.

I woke up with a sputtering grimace, trying desperately to focus on the beastly apparition before me. I pulled my head back in an attempt to get away from the warm, wet assault on my face, only to see one-eyed Beowulf grinning back at me. A giggle came from the doorway, and I heard Angelina say, "Mommy! Beowulf's kissing him!"

I rolled over toward the door, getting a sudden, sharp reminder of the damage to my ribs, and saw Jenny and Angelina peeking in at me. "Are you decent?" Jenny inquired.

"Matter of opinion," I grunted. "Give me a moment. And take the beast with you."

Angelina patted her hands together. "Come on, boy!" she commanded. With a last tongue-lolling look at me, Beowulf turned and trotted to the door. As Jenny let him pass into the hallway, she said, "You mother told me to tell you that you've got less than thirty minutes to prepare for company. She wants you down in the War Room."

"What time is it?"

"Just after 7:30."

"Gah. Doesn't anyone get to sleep around here?"

Jenny grinned. "Consider yourself lucky. Angelina's been chomping at the bit to come and wake you for at least an hour. We're just getting ready to leave now."

"Wait," I implored. "Give me a minute."

Jenny nodded and shut the door. I threw off my covers and drew in a deep breath. The effects of my alcohol-and-aspirin nightcap had long worn off, and I wasn't looking forward to motion of any kind. Fortunately, if you could call it that, I had recently acquired a lot of experience in moving my body while keeping my abdomen locked straight, courtesy of my recent sword-related injury. Knowing I had an audience just outside my door, I stopped myself from groaning. I found my pants and slipped them on, gave myself a moment to compose myself, and opened the door to be greeted with "Fly me!"

I looked down at little Angelina, all smiles and open arms. Under her mother's watchful eye, I performed a deep knee bend, got hold of Angelina, and lifted her straight up, all to the accompaniment of my less than musical moaning. It didn't help that Angelina accidentally gave me a knee in the ribs as I lifted her. When I finally got her to my eye level, she announced, "You're funny."

"Looks aren't everything, Tink," I told her.

Jenny chimed in with, "I think you're going to have to be more careful with your toys, girlfriend. This one's starting to look a little worn out."

I noticed that Jenny had Angelina's overnight bag in her hand. "So," I asked, "just like that, you're leaving me?"

Jenny nodded. "Yep. Victoria told us this morning that you have chores to do and can't come play for a while. Speaking of which, you'd better get a move on. Come on, baby," she said to Angelina. "Give Jason a hug and let him go."

"Nope," Angelina announced while burrowing into my neck. "I'm not letting go."

"Sorry, Tinker Bell," I said, "but I've got some grown-up stuff to do today."

Jenny gently disengaged Angelina, but not before the little one gave me a final squeeze. "Come on, sweetie," Jenny said to her. "You need to help me with house hunting today." To me, Jenny said, "So when will we see you again? Any idea?"

"No. Not right away, anyway. I'll call you when I know something, but if Her Highness said I've got work to do, then I'm thinking it's not going to be anytime soon."

"Call us when you know," Jenny said. Then, with a quick wink to me, she said to Angelina, "Come on, gorgeous. We girls have our work to do, too."

I watched as Jenny and Angelina walked to the stairs, Angelina stopping to throw me a noisy kiss, and descended with Beowulf following behind.

As soon as they were out of sight, I wasted no time in cleaning myself up as best I could. My dark blue suit seemed to have weathered last night's exertions well enough, but my shoes and topcoat had taken an obvious beating. I raided my emergency travel kit for clean socks and underwear and found a heavy dark red pullover to wear. Moving to the upstairs bathroom, I shaved and showered in record time, taking just a few minutes to check out my sore spot in the mirror. A painful probing with my fingers didn't reveal anything broken, and I wondered how soon the dark bruised point on my side would flower into a rainbow of color. I briefly considered going to the doctor but decided that there was nothing that could be done short of taping my ribs, and I had already spent way too much time as the Human Half Mummy from my recent encounter with a sharp object. I decided to tough it out.

After making myself as presentable as possible, I found Mom in the back section of the house: the War Room. It's where she puts all the unsightly necessities of our profession, which must include me since that's where I keep my own desk. The white-painted brick walls also contain the workstations for Jim Bui and Tim O'Toole as well as Felix McQuade, our resident computer whiz kid. Just about every square inch of wall space in the windowless bunker is taken up with the machinery of the Midnight Agency, from the locking, fireproof file cabinets to the copying and fax machines to the widescreen television. In the center of the room is a round discussion table where we'd often meet to strategize over our current cases, that is, when we weren't playing cutthroat poker, of course. I wondered if both Jimmy and Timmy were getting called in to work today because of my recent escapades.

My senses were cheered and my curiosity forgotten when I smelled the coffee that Mom was putting on the table. She was decked out all in black today, from her loose-necked sweater to her tailored jeans to her low-heeled leather boots. I also noted she had four places set out in a circle. Looked like I'd be subjected to both of the Terrible Twins today. I reached for the coffeepot, saying, "Looks like you've saved my life."

Mom smiled as she moved the carafe in my direction. "Help yourself. Did you get a chance to say good-bye to Jenny and Angelina?"

I grabbed a cup and the pot, pouring carefully as I said, "Yeah. Sorry I messed up your night. How was the little one?"

Mom's smile went up in voltage. "Great. We had a wonderful time. She fell asleep while watching her movie."

"Let me guess, you watched *Peter Pan*. That's her current favorite."

"Oh, yes. She seems to be under the impression that you are personally going to take her off to Never Never Land."

"Really? Hmm. I may have said something like that."

Mom tilted her head and gave me a quizzical look. "I seem to recall that *Peter Pan* was also one of your favorite stories. You used to have me read it to you over and over. I'm starting to wonder now if telling you about a boy that wouldn't grow up was such a good thing for you after all."

A thumping came from the armored side door to the War Room. "Ah, company calls," Mom said. "Would you be so kind?"

I set my cup down and headed for the door, wondering why Jimmy and Timmy didn't just let themselves in. I opened the heavy metal door, admitting a chilling breeze and an even more chilling sight: Police Captain Raymond Cory, wearing a rumpled tan trench coat and a baleful look. His eyes flashed when he saw me, and he said with a low growl, "Give me one good reason why I don't arrest you right now!"

# CHAPTER THIRTEEN

Policemen seem to think that just because they have a badge, a gun, and the authority to arrest you, they have the ability to throw the fear of God into you, too. That's probably true for most people, but I was raised by some of the best in the policing business. Besides, after working for Her Royal Highness Victoria, Queen of Detectives, I was somewhat jaded, no matter how well a threat was delivered.

So in response to Captain Cory's question, I simply fought off a yawn and said, "Because I haven't had my first cup of coffee yet?"

From over my shoulder, I heard Mom say, "Leave the bluster outside where it belongs and come on in, gentlemen."

Spearing me with a hostile look, Captain Cory marched in. Only after his bulky body cleared the doorway did I see that it was Detective Nicholas Navarro who had been eclipsed. Navarro came in from the side alley, still wearing the baggy black overcoat I'd seen him in the last time and carrying a bulking manila folder, and looking exhausted. He nodded to me; his dark eyes behind his horn-rimmed glasses seemed to have sunk halfway through his head.

"Come and sit down," Mom said. "I have coffee. Sorry, no doughnuts."

Captain Cory stood there as I closed the door, with his

arms folded and his head lowered like a bull ready to charge. "What's this all about, Vicki? You told me on the phone that you had something good on the Addison case."

Mom smiled as she picked up her own coffee cup and said gently, "Ah. Don't you mean the Messenger case? Or have you already decided that the mayor's daughter is guilty of murder and you don't want to get confused with any more facts?"

"I'm not here to play games," Cory growled. "Just give me what you've got, then I'll try to decide if we want to arrest your son here as well."

"Arrest my son?" Mom said with gentle derision. "Come now, Raymond, for what?"

"Interfering with a police investigation, for starters," Cory said.

I chimed in. "Interfering? Hell, I wasn't allowed to get close enough to your investigation to interfere. All you and your detectives have done so far is keep me out of the loop on everything."

Cory shot me a heated look. "God damn it! You were just supposed to be an observer!"

"I was," I countered, "and I've observed plenty. Plenty of incompetence, that is."

The Queen held up a hand. "Gentleman," she admonished sternly. "This gets us nowhere. Now, if you're all through with your primal chest beating, I have some things to propose."

It was Navarro who responded first. "Please. I would like to see something productive happen this morning."

Cory grumbled something under his breath, then said aloud, "All right, Vicki. What have you got?"

Mom held up a mini CD in a clear plastic case, holding it with her thumb and forefinger as if it were a jewel of great price. "This, gentlemen," she said, "is a recording of an interview Jason conducted with Anna Addison last night."

The four of us had remained standing throughout our brief but acrimonious encounter; separated by the round conference table, Captain Cory and Mom looked like a pair of old-fashioned duelists, with Navarro and me acting as their seconds. At Mom's announcement, Cory's mouth dropped open, giving his broad, flat face the appearance of a stunned frog. "That's evidence!" he blurted out.

"Evidence?" Mom asked pleasantly, "or a privileged communication with a client of my office?" Before Captain Cory could respond, Mom continued, "Now, I suppose we have two ways to go here. One, I could voluntarily provide you with a copy of this recording, in exchange for a small and reasonable request, or two, I could make you get a search warrant or a subpoena for it, which would doubtless take a while to accomplish."

Cory's eyes narrowed dangerously during Mom's speech. You could have heard a pin drop in the silence that followed, until he finally said, "All right, Vicki. What do you want for it?"

"Just this," Mom said. "It appears that you have what you consider adequate probable cause to arrest Anna Addison for the murder of Elijah Messenger. All I want is for you to keep to the original deal. In other words, I want access to your information. I assume that you won't be filing for a formal arrest warrant until Monday morning?"

Cory took a sideways glance at Navarro, who nodded. "Yeah, maybe," Cory grudgingly admitted. "So?"

"So the way I see it," Mom said, "Jason and I still have until Monday morning to make an evaluation on the case you have against Anna Addison."

Navarro cleared his throat, then said, "What if Ms. Addison gets arrested before then? I still have our Special Operations Bureau looking for her."

"If she's arrested prior to Monday, then so be it," Mom said complacently. "At that point I'd expect her to get a really high-powered attorney, who will then probably want to hire the Midnight Agency for the defense work. Either way, you would do well to allow us to work with you. You seem to have done rather poorly so far."

"What the hell do you mean by that?" Cory demanded.

"Simply this," Mom replied. "Where your crew managed to miss catching Anna Addison, my son gets her to speak with him. I'd say that puts my team ahead of yours on points, wouldn't you, Raymond?"

It was amazing to watch Captain Cory try to contain himself. It looked like he kept his head from exploding by sheer willpower alone. When his internal storm seemed to have subsided a bit, he ground out, "Okay, Vicki. You'll get your deal, but I'm going to have one of my men with you every step of the way. And I'm warning you, if I catch you or this son of yours or anyone else in your crew so much as thinking about trying to cover anything up, I'll have your license yanked faster than you can blink. You got that?"

"Really, Raymond," Mom said chidingly. "I don't think your promotion has done much for your emotional well-being. You certainly weren't this uptight when you were walking a beat."

Captain Cory spat out the words "Give 'em what they want" to Navarro and stomped out.

As soon as the heavy door swung shut, Detective Navarro said, "May I please have some of that coffee now?"

Mom was the ever-gracious hostess. "Of course, Detective, and please have a seat."

"Thank you," Navarro said. As Mom poured him a cup, he slowly collapsed into the closest chair, saying, "Please excuse me; I've been up over twenty-four hours now. It's been a long day."

"No need to apologize, Detective," Mom said. "I know—I've been in your shoes more than once."

Navarro took a long sip of coffee. "So. What is it you need from me?"

That was my cue to say, "For starters, what makes you think Anna Addison did the deed? When I spoke with her last night, she not only denied it, but she said she never even got close to Elijah Messenger before he was stabbed."

"She did, did she?" Navarro mused. "Well, according to all of the other witnesses present, for a while no one could see anyone else. Everyone said that someone set off some kind of small explosion followed by a smoke bomb. When the smoke cleared, Messenger was dead. Stabbed."

"Okay," I said. "So what makes you think it was Anna and not someone else there? Or some other party lurking around?"

"The forensics team made a positive match on a finger-print found on the murder weapon. That, and the fact that Ms. Addison has been on the run from the police ever since the murder."

"Oh" was all I could say to that. I noticed Navarro's eyes were focused on the CD. I reached over and slid it across the table to him. Navarro held it up to the light, as if trying to divine the contents. "I don't suppose this has Ms. Addison's confession on it, by any chance?" he asked.

Mom shook her head. "No. She denies murdering Elijah Messenger, and when my son asked her why she didn't speak with the police herself, she said only that she had something to do first. It's all quite mysterious."

"But what about motive?" I asked. "From what I got out of Anna, she was definitely some kind of witchcraft groupie, and Messenger was supposed to be her teacher or something."

Navarro made a wan smile. "Well, we may have a case of a woman scorned, according to some of the other witnesses."

"Oh. She didn't mention anything like that," I said. "Okay, I guess I'd better get out and talk to the rest of those other witnesses myself." Out of the corner of my eye, I saw Mom nod in silent agreement. "Could you provide me with the names and addresses?"

"Sure," Navarro said.

"I'd like your impressions of them too," I said as I got up and retrieved a notepad from my desk.

"I'll leave you two to handle the details," Mom said. "Jason, when you're done here, please see me in my office."

Detective Navarro rose in gentlemanly fashion as Her Majesty made her exit. When we were alone, Navarro sank back into his chair and opened up his folder, revealing a batch of loose printouts and a yellow legal pad. Despite its ordinary appearance, I reminded myself, such a file was known in the detective business as the Murder Book. Navarro sighed and sipped his coffee. "Well," he said, "there's Robert Hanson. From what he said, he's been a follower of Messenger for some time now. I also got the impression that he's tried to cover up Anna Addison's involvement. He was pretty adamant about saying he didn't think she could kill Messenger. He was also at the house when we came in with the search warrant yesterday. He had to be pressured before he admitted to speaking with Ms. Addison shortly before we arrived."

"What did the two of them talk about?"

"According to Mr. Hanson, Anna wanted his help in looking for something in the house, but she wasn't specific about what she was looking for. He did finally admit that he didn't think Ms. Addison was acting entirely rationally. Anyway, he was checked when the police arrived right after the homicide. He had no blood on him."

"Okay," I said as I scribbled. "Who else?"

Navarro made a face. "Brandon Archimedes. He's the one who owns the Tantalus nightclub. He's a smug bastard. Had blood all over him the night of the murder, but he claimed he got that way when he dragged Messenger out of the river. He acted like having someone you know killed right in front of you was no big deal."

"Next?"

"I guess that would be the woman, Aurora. Her real name's Theodora Carlyle. She's supposed to be some kind of expert on the supernatural, and she claimed to be here in California for research. She's actually a resident of Arizona. She was pretty hysterical that night and claimed she was nowhere near Messenger. She didn't come up with any blood on her, either. That brings us to Maurice Phillips."

"Who's that?"

"The bouncer at Tantalus. Goes by the name Stone. He claims that he was at the house the whole time everyone else was down by the river. Says the first he heard there was trouble was when Anna Addison came running back to the house all upset. According to him, she just grabbed her backpack and took off. Next thing he says, Archimedes calls him on his cell phone and tells him to get down to the river. Phillips is on active parole, by the way."

"Really? What for?"

"Narcotics violations. He also has a history of assault and battery. Doesn't care much for cops, either."

I took a few minutes to finish with my notes, getting the addresses and phone numbers from Navarro, then I said, "Okay. I think I got it. I guess the next thing is to call Detective Banks and tell her to meet me this morning."

"That's not possible. Detective Banks has been relieved of duty pending an administrative hearing."

"Say what?"

"Over losing her gun," Navarro explained.

*Damn,* I thought. Then I wondered why I suddenly felt sorry for the abrasive and cantankerous Lori Banks.

"I'll have to see which one of my men can be spared to accompany you," Navarro said. "We're stretched pretty thin right now."

I had an inspiration. "How about seeing if you can get Hector Morales assigned to babysit me? He's a patrolman currently working Vice."

Navarro looked at me with suspicion. "Why him?"

"Because I know him. He's not only one of River City's Finest, he's also a friend of mine."

"Assign a friend of yours to go with you? That might look bad, to say the least."

"Mainly because he *is* a friend," I said, "I'd never do anything that would jeopardize his career."

Navarro seemed to digest this thought for a bit, then said, "It may be because I'm tired, but that almost makes sense. At least it spares me from waking up someone on my team. All right, I'll see what I can do."

"Good. Tell you what, why don't you have Hector, or whoever else you assign, meet me at the Boathouse at ten this morning? Least I can do is buy breakfast for the unlucky guy who gets to follow me around."

Navarro made a wan smile. "Last meal for the condemned? You're starting to get a reputation around the force, you know."

"Me? How so?"

Navarro finished his coffee and carefully set his cup down. "Word has it that the son of Captain Midnight is a jinx, and seeing what happed to Detective Banks, rumors like that tend to get a life of their own."

I shook my head at Navarro's mention of Captain Midnight—my father's nickname when he was a River City detective. "I'm not a lot like my dad," I said. "From what everyone tells me, he was some kind of genius at the detective game. It's just a job for me, and I've got to work at it."

Navarro gathered his papers together and rose from his chair. "Yet you followed in his footsteps."

"Well, seemed like a good idea at the time."

Navarro smiled, albeit tiredly. "In a way, I, too, went into the family business."

"Oh? Your father was a policeman?"

"No, he was a garbageman," Navarro said, "and the more I work this job, the more parallels I see. I spend my time keeping the city clean, which involves me getting my hands dirty occasionally, but it's honorable work. You mind a little free advice?"

"Not at all. I usually accept all the help I can get."

"When dealing in garbage," Navarro said seriously, "the important thing to remember is that at the end of the day, you make sure none of it sticks to you. You see what I mean?"

I did. Navarro was giving me a semipoetic warning to stay clean. "Loud and clear, sir," I said as I walked him to the door.

Navarro suddenly stopped walking and bowed his head, as if he were struggling with an inner argument. Finally he spoke, almost in a whisper. "In a way, I'm glad that someone else is looking into the case. It appears that there are people in my department who would be very pleased to see the mayor's daughter arrested for this murder. I would hope that their enthusiasm wouldn't get in the way of the facts." He nodded a good-bye and left.

I went to the Queen's Inner Sanctum, where I was surprised to see Mayor Addison seated in one of the guest chairs. Even on a Saturday morning, His Honor was dressed in a business suit, looking less happy than the last time I saw him, which I wouldn't have thought possible.

"Sit down, Jason," Mom said. "Mayor Addison has some more information for us."

"Oh?" I asked. "Something that will help with the case?"

"Quite the opposite," Mom said darkly.

■

# CHAPTER FOURTEEN

Mayor Addison wore a look of compressed rage as he sat in the high-backed chair. Her Majesty's expression was one I was accustomed to, the one that silently said She Was Not Amused. I'd been on the receiving end of that particular look of hers enough times to recognize it by now. I was glad it wasn't aimed at me this time.

"What's up?" I asked.

"The mayor just received this," Mom said seriously. "Come around and take a look."

Mom's flat screen and computer keyboard were out on her desk. Leaning on the back of her throne, I watched as she activated the screen. From the hidden speakers, I could hear an oceanlike background noise with a low hum while I squinted to make out details on the screen. The video was badly done, with flickering lights and shadows in conflict with each other—until the image resolved into the figure of a naked woman. A masculine voice, oddly echoing, commanded, "Kneel!" As the woman did so, her face came into view. Anna Addison.

Anna's features faded in and out of focus; the light around her appeared to come from a flickering fire. She swayed slightly side to side. Her expression seemed serene, with a little smile, and her large eyes were mostly closed.

She was looking up and slightly to the right of the camera as the deep, echoing voice intoned, "Doth thou accept thy charge?"

Whatever microphones there were barely picked up Anna's reply of "I do." The male voice droned on, asking, "Doth thou come prepared to receive they gift? Art thou prepared to draw thy blood and entwine it with mine? Art thou prepared to pierce the dark shroud?" To all the questions put to her, Anna mumbled a yes. The male voice then said, "Of the mother, darksome and divine, with blade and blood we consecrate to thee."

The camera hadn't moved at all throughout, but the picture suddenly swam in and out of focus as Anna raised up something that reflected a splash of reddish light into the lens. When the image cleared, you could see Anna was holding an ornate and wicked-looking knife in both hands, point downward. She arched her back as she pulled the knife up, the blade sheathed in a slowly moving, viscous red fluid. Anna closed her eyes and a black-garbed arm came into view from the right, taking the knife out of her unresisting grasp. The gloved hand that now held the blade slowly began to draw wet lines over Anna's breast, five slow strokes that made a rough pentagram, as the voice spoke the words, "I consecrate thee. Blood of my blood, flesh of my flesh. Now and forevermore."

The video ended abruptly, and I realized I'd been holding my breath, which now rushed out all at once, deflating me. "Damn."

"Yes," Mother agreed. It was an awkward moment, to say the very least. I had just seen Anna Addison revealed in what could charitably be called a compromising position, and I was in a room with the girl's father. To Mayor Addison, Mom said, "So, when did you say this disk arrived?"

The mayor looked like he was chewing something bitter. "It showed up at my office late yesterday. Someone dropped it off in the mail slot. It was marked 'confidential' and had my name on it. Once the clerks in the mailroom ascertained that it only contained the disk, it was sent to me. I didn't play it until this morning. Then I brought it to you."

"No note?" Mom inquired. "No message of any kind?"

"Just the message you saw there," the mayor said flatly.

"And you still haven't heard from Anna?" Mom asked.

"No. I've called her cell phone a dozen times since yesterday," the mayor said. "She's not answering."

Mom glanced up at me. "Any chance you recognized the voice on the video?"

"It could have been Elijah Messenger's," I said, "but at this point, I can't be certain. The sound quality was pretty bad."

"Yes," Mom agreed. "Almost as if it was meant to be. The only clear thing on this video is Anna Addison and her questionable actions. Well, Vincent, we'll keep the disk and see what we can learn from it. If anything else shows up at your door, be sure to call Jason right away."

Mayor Addison's frown deepened. "I still wish you were working on this case personally, Victoria."

Mom rose from her throne as she said, "Oh, I'll be available. Try not to worry, Vincent. We'll do everything we can for your daughter."

Mom walked the Mayor out of the office. She returned shortly and closed the door behind her, after which she uttered, "Jackass."

"To whom do you refer?"

Mom jerked her thumb over her shoulder. "Vincent. He doesn't fool me. He's more concerned about what that awful movie starring his wacky daughter can do to his career than about the daughter herself. God knows what a field day his political opponents could have if a thing like that leaked to the press. The odd thing is, the video didn't come with an extortion note." Mom glanced at her Rolex, then said, "Uh-oh. I'm late. So tell me quickly, what's your plan?"

"Me? Well, I'll meet up with Roland first; he said he had some background on Messenger. And I thought I'd call Robin Faye over at the crime lab and see what she can get for me. I figure the mayor's letter ought to be good for that much, at least. Then I guess I'll go round up the usual suspects. Maybe if I ask nicely, someone will be kind enough to make a full confession."

"Sounds like a plan," Mom said as she closed up her desk, concealing all the computer gear. She handed me the CD she had removed from her computer's hard drive and encased in a plain, clear plastic case. "Get Felix to work on that disk. Maybe he can enhance it enough that we can find some clue as to where that thing was filmed. Did you notice how the camera never moved?"

"Yeah. Some sort of fixed-mount autofocus job. Might have been a hidden camera."

"Yes. But you'll notice that the man in the video was not only very careful not to be seen, he also made sure he didn't block the camera's view of Anna. If that was Elijah Messenger, he was in on it."

"Agreed. Now what's this about you being late? Where are you going?"

Mom had gone over to her coat tree and selected a short black leather jacket. The jeweled eye-with-the-clock-at-midnight was attached to her lapel. Donning the jacket, she looked like a cross between a ninja and Amelia Earhart. "I'm off by private plane to Santa Teresa. I might have a lead on the art forgery case I've been working on."

"Santa Teresa? When will you be back?"

"Can't say," she replied. "So, while I'm gone, I need you to wrap up the Anna Addison matter, by Monday morning latest. While you're at it, you might as well find out who's got the original videotapes or disks or whatever and get hold of all the copies as well as the original. I'm certain the mayor would gladly pay us a bonus for that."

"Anything else I should do in the meantime? Like find Jimmy Hoffa or solve the Kennedy assassination?"

Mom smiled. "Don't be silly. I'll take care of those little matters when I have time. Call me with updates or if you have any questions. Now shoo. Get to work. Oh, and don't forget to take care of Beowulf while I'm gone."

I let myself out of Mom's lair before I could frame a proper reply. *Great,* I thought, *solve all the problems before Monday.* No pressure, mind you. Checking my watch, I saw I had little more than an hour before I was due to meet Roland at the Boathouse. My stomach growled in anticipation of a decent meal before my day's trials and errors were set to begin. I sat behind my desk and tried to organize my thoughts. Too many things needed to be done all at once. I needed to break all the tasks down into bite-sized pieces so I wouldn't choke on them.

I started by using the investigator's best friend, the telephone. In short order, I placed calls to three people, none of whom seemed happy to hear from me. By a combination of threats, cajoling, and entreaties, I lined up two more people to attend my breakfast meeting. One of my calls was expected; Hector Morales had already gotten the word from Detective Navarro that his new assignment was to keep an eye on me, and the prospect of me buying his breakfast didn't make the news any more palatable.

Having lined up my impromptu teammates, I booted up my computer and located the file Mom sent me on her preliminary research on Elijah Messenger. I found the file just fine, but when I looked at the screen I thought I'd done something wrong. I called Her Highness right away on her cell phone. Sure enough, she was already on her way to the airport. "What's up, kiddo?" she asked.

"My computer must be acting up. I can't seem to open the file on Messenger you sent me."

"What's on your screen?"

"It says 'Results on Messenger, Elijah,' but there's almost nothing here."

"Yes," Mom agreed darkly. "A great deal of nothing. Which is, all by itself, highly revealing."

"What do you mean?"

"Think about it," Mom said. "No public records? No property? No trace of his existence? That leads us to one conclusion: Your Elijah Messenger is a ghost in more ways than one."

"Ah, interesting."

"That's what I thought, too," Mom agreed. "For what it's worth, I'm betting that Elijah Messenger was not your visitor's real name. You mentioned that your friend Roland managed to dig up some information on him?"

"That's what Rollo said. I'll hear it from him this morning."

"Good. Keep me apprised. And be careful, son."

"Aye, aye," I said, and hung up. I stared at the mostly blank computer screen, feeling I was perilously close to having an actual thought. It was when I recalled what Mom said about there being no property records that the embryonic idea in my head received a live birth. I got my notebook out and checked through my scribbles until I found the note to myself regarding Elijah Messenger's address. I ran the street name and number through the city's property database and saw that the registered owners of the palatial residence went by the names Reginald and Nancy Harrington. A quick crosscheck with the online telephone directory produced a number for an R. and N. Harrington with a different address. I called the number, and an elderly-sounding female voice answered.

"Good morning," I said. "My name is Jason Wilder, and I was looking for the Harringtons who own a house on Persephone Street. Am I speaking with that Nancy Harrington?"

"Yes," the woman answered cautiously. "What's this about? Are you from the newspapers?"

I decided to try the truth. "No, ma'am. I'm an investigator working with the police on the murder of Elijah Messenger."

I felt myself wince, waiting for the effect my words would have. I heard a sudden exclamation from Nancy Harrington, then she said, "Oh. Oh, my. I mean, I read the paper and saw . . . but I really couldn't believe it about Elijah."

"Did you know Mr. Messenger well?" I asked gently.

"Yes. Yes, I did. I was one of the inner circle."

"I see. I was wondering if I could have your permission to go over to the house on Persephone and have a look at it. To help in our investigation."

"Well, certainly. I mean, if you think it's necessary."

"It may help us a great deal. Do you mind if I ask you a few questions?"

After a hesitation, she said, "Very well. How can I help you?"

"Did Mr. Messenger rent the house from you?"

"Rent? Oh, no. I was happy to let him stay there. After all he did for us, it was the least Reggie and I could do."

"Reggie? You mean your husband?"

"Of course."

"When was the last time you spoke with Mr. Messenger?"

"Oh, wait. Let me see. It was less than a week ago." I heard her sigh. "I'm still having a hard time believing that Elijah has crossed over. It seems so sudden."

"Crossed over" seemed a somewhat baroque way of saying "got killed," but I wasn't about to argue semantics. "Mrs. Harrington, can you tell me what you discussed with Mr. Messenger?"

"Well, he asked to borrow some money. For his research, you know. Oh, dear, I wonder what's to become of that now."

"What kind of research was that?"

"Well, his work, of course. To be honest, I wasn't quite sure I followed what Elijah said entirely, but Reggie and I always supported him."

"And you loaned him some money? May I ask how much?"

"It was twenty thousand dollars," she said simply. "Plus the usual thousand we gave him every month."

I kept myself from whistling in surprise. Twenty-one grand was a fair piece of change. "And you gave him the money?" I asked.

"Oh, yes. He told me that it would all come back to me with interest. Reggie agreed to it as well."

"I see."

"He was actually asking for more," Mrs. Harrington continued, "but I believe the other members of the circle were able to help him out."

"Mrs. Harrington, what circle is that exactly?"

"Well, that's what Elijah called us. The inner circle. Those of us who helped him with his work."

"I see. And what did Mr. Messenger do to help you?"

"He brought me messages from Reggie."

"Your husband?"

"Yes. Elijah kept us in contact."

I had a sudden sick feeling. "So, Mrs. Harrington, are you saying that your husband Reggie has, uh, 'crossed over' himself?"

"Yes. Didn't I mention that? Elijah was our link. I just don't know what Reggie and I are going to do now without him."

"And Elijah Messenger told you that Reggie said it was okay for you to give him the money?"

"Yes," she said simply. "Reggie always makes the decisions where money is concerned."

I resisted the urge to bang the phone on something and tried to keep my voice even as I said, "Mrs. Harrington, could I trouble you for a list of the other members of your circle? I think I'd like to speak with them as well. It may be important."

"Well, I suppose I could. Although I really ought to call them first, to see if it's all right with them."

"Certainly. While you're at it, would you ask them how much money they lent to Elijah Messenger?"

"I could ask," she said tentatively, "but it's really none of my business."

"Just tell them that it may help us with the investigation."

"Oh. Of course. I'll do what I can, but I hope you understand that this isn't easy for me."

"I understand."

"No," I heard her say sadly. "I don't think you do. But I will do what I can."

"Thank you."

"I just wish I knew what Reggie would want me to do."

I said good-bye and hung up my phone. My hand was cramped from gripping the receiver. So, Elijah Messenger made his money bilking the gullible by using their grief and love for their dear departed. I found myself hoping that if there was such a thing as an afterlife, somewhere, somehow, Reginald Harrington was kicking Elijah Messenger's ass.

# CHAPTER FIFTEEN

As I sat at my desk and gathered my notes together, I reflected on the fact that I was probably over my head and sinking fast. So I figured I might as well take some of the gang down with me.

I called Timmy O'Toole first. "Are you in a jam already?" was how he answered the phone.

"If I'm calling you, I must be absolutely desperate. Listen, I need some of that Irish charm you keep pretending you have. I want you to look up this rich widow I just spoke with and make sure she comes through with a list of all the people she knows who gave money to Elijah Messenger. I especially need to know how much and when. Tell her you work for the nice young man she spoke with on the phone this morning."

"Rich widow, eh?" Timmy asked with evident interest. "You're right, Junior. Sounds like my kind of job. What's the angle?"

"Not sure, but it's starting to look like the recently deceased Mr. Messenger was hitting up people he knew for money. There may be a blackmail angle involved, and most definitely fraud." I gave Uncle Timmy Nancy Harrington's name, number, and address, then hung up and made my next call.

Jim Bui was as enthusiastic as a man digging his own grave.

"Please tell me you don't need to be bailed out of jail this early. I was hoping to get a round of golf in."

"Sorry, Uncle Jimmy. At least you won't be risking pneumonia with the job I have in mind. I'm leaving a video on a digital disk on my desk. I need you and Felix to analyze it."

"Video? Video of what?"

"At first glance, it comes off like a bad old horror flick. Only it's starring the mayor's daughter. Did I mention she's naked?"

"Naked? Really? Where did you get your hands on this?"

"Someone anonymously delivered a copy to the mayor's office. It came with everything but a blackmail note."

Jimmy laughed, softly and darkly. "Okay, I'll call the geek and get over there. What the hell, I've had worse assignments."

I hung up. I was probably going to be late for my breakfast meeting with the Epic Hero Society, but at least I felt I'd matched up the best people with the jobs I couldn't do. Next to Mom, Uncle Jimmy was the most computer literate, and I was betting that if there was anything to be learned from the video disk, he and our resident computer hacker, Felix McQuade, would be the guys to get it. Uncle Timmy, on the other hand, could barely operate a mechanical pencil, but that man could talk to anybody about anything, and I was certain he'd be charming Messenger's inner circle out of any secrets they might be keeping.

Before I left the Midnight office, I made certain that my revolver was ready and snugly packed in my hip holster. I don't make a habit of carrying my gun around; I manage to accomplish most of the work I do without being armed with a deadly weapon. Somewhere out there, though, someone was walking around with Detective Lori Banks's service pistol, and it was a pretty good bet that said someone was associated with Anna Addison.

After wrapping myself up in my worse-for-the-wear over-coat, I marched outside into a bright, windy, and cold-as-hell morning. I eased myself into the Green Hornet, relearning how to go from standing to sitting with the least amount of torso movement so as not to give my bruised ribs any more reasons to complain, and was soon cruising down the streets of River City. Saturday mornings are usually light traffic days, but now we were into the Christmas holiday madness, with wild-eyed shoppers cruising in their cars like sharks out for blood. As far as I'm concerned, the red and green Christmas decorations festooning the city are just so many DANGER signs.

I finally made it to the old dock area and found a parking spot below the wooden planks of the boardwalk. I got my briefcase and climbed the steps to the topside restaurant-and-shop area that overlooks the fashionable side of river, with its high-priced collection of sailboats and motor yachts. A short walk down the planks took me to the long tin-roofed shack that was the Boathouse Restaurant. From the outside, the place looks like an old homage to *Cannery Row*. Stepping in-side, you see the tables appointed with white tablecloths and crystal and the floor-to-ceiling windows that completely fill the riverside wall. The restaurant is a good reminder that you can't judge people or places by their external appearance. I scanned the dining area and saw that my gang had managed to grab one of the tables by the window wall.

I made my way around the other tables, keeping my eyes on my friends, who appeared to be in the midst of a very ani-mated discussion. Roland spotted me first. "There he is," he said, raising an accusing finger toward me.

"Good morning, troops," I said as I seated myself. "You're probably wondering why I've gathered all of you to-gether today."

Robin, Hector, and Roland greeted me with matching looks of suspicion, and I held up my hand in a warding gesture. "Food first," I said, "and lots of coffee. Then we talk business. So order up."

There was a grumbling acceptance of my demands, and then the four of us settled down to the business of breakfast. If there's one thing I've learned in the detective trade, it's that you never know when you're going to have time to indulge in your next meal, and I resolved to take advantage of this opportunity. The four of us made the usual small talk you'd expect among friends who've been together for as long as we have. When we'd finished with our repast, Roland charged into the discussion. He held up a rolled-up newspaper, asking me, "Have you seen this edition yet?"

"No. Haven't had time."

"Well, then, here you go." He reached across the table and smacked me on the head with the paper. I yanked it out of his hand, unrolled it, and saw the headline on the Metro section that read, MAN SLAIN DURING SUSPECTED CULT RITUAL. I scanned the story and read that the River City police were questioning possible suspects in connection with the murder of Elijah Messenger, who was described as a "self-styled spiritualist" and was stabbed to death on the west bank of the Americano River on Thursday night. I was happy to note the lack of names associated with the article; apparently the police were keeping Anna Addison's involvement under wraps for now. I had barely managed to finish reading when Roland asked, "And do you see what's wrong with that story?"

"Uh, no. What?"

"The byline, idiot! This story was credited to that sneaky, unprincipled snoop Kathryn Fossie!"

"As opposed to that sneaky, unprincipled snoop Roland Gibson?" Robin put in gently.

"Damn straight," Roland replied. "What's the point of pretending to be Jason's friend if he won't come up with a worthwhile story once in a while?"

I took a look around the restaurant to make certain that our fellow diners weren't paying attention to us, then drew my friends closer over the table and launched into a recitation of the whole sordid story. When I concluded, Roland whistled. "Damn. This is great! I take back most of what I said about you, boy."

"Hold on, Rollo. You can't put any of this into print yet."

"Oh, yeah? Says who? The people have a right to know, you know."

"Says Her Royal Highness," I said. "If you break this story now, my next assignment from her will be to get a shovel and find a private place to hide your body."

Roland grinned and held up his hands. "Say no more. I'm way too young and pretty to depart this earth just yet. But I get the scoop first, right?"

"Yep. Just as soon as I can figure out who did what to whom. Now, you said you had some dirt on Messenger? From what I can see, the guy didn't leave a paper trail."

Roland's cherubic face took on a smug look. "Oh, ye of little faith. Prepare to be astounded by the power of the press."

"Not to mention the power of the mouth," Hector grumbled.

"Pay attention, class," Roland continued undeterred. "I did a national scan of the newspaper archives. Seems Elijah Messenger first pops up in Arizona some years ago. He was purported to be some kind of mystical shaman or something. He wrote a book some years ago, called *The Illuminated Traveler*, in which he describes his supposedly mystical experiences. It was published by a small press back in the seventies. Looks to me like he was just another con artist bilking the local yokels out of their cash with the old Gypsy scam. You know, 'cross my palm with silver and I'll tell your future' kind of thing. Only in this case, about three years ago, he apparently got hold of some local heiress and got her to sign over her inheritance to him. Which was handy since she shortly thereafter died of cancer."

"Oh, no," Robin breathed.

"Oh, yes," Roland said. "Turns out that old Elijah Messenger was giving her some kind of mystical 'treatments,' and she refused to go to a real doctor. After the girl died, her family threatened to sue the pants off Messenger, and he hightailed it out of Dodge. Then he turns up right here in River City, but the only references I could find on him locally were notices advertising his appearance at psychic fairs and stuff like that."

"Psychic fairs?" Hector asked.

Roland grinned. "I knew you were going to say that. Psychic fairs, my uneducated friend, are where the sheep get fleeced. They're where a bunch of phonies peddle their magical, mystical wares to the morons who are gullible enough to pay for them. Messenger's specialty was talking to dead people. For a price, he was supposed to be able to put you in touch with the dear departed. I figure he must have charged a lot of money. Long distance, you know."

"You don't think it's possible that Messenger had a genuine gift?" Robin asked gently.

Roland snorted. "Gift? Hell, no. There ain't no such thing. Look, you guys ever hear of the Amazing Randi?"

"Amazing Randi?" Hector asked. "Oh, yeah. Isn't she that stripper down at the old Alhambra Club?"

"No," Roland said quickly, then stopped. "Wait. Did you say stripper?"

"Stay on target, Rollo," I advised.

Roland grinned sheepishly and said, "The Amazing Randi

is a former stage magician. He has a standing offer of one million dollars cash to anybody who can prove that telepathy or clairvoyance or any psychic ability is real. So far, no one has collected. So there."

"Fine," I said. "Messenger was a fraud. That still doesn't get me any closer to who may have killed him, or why. Which brings me to you, princess."

Robin's liquid golden eyes were veiled in suspicion. "Yes?" she asked carefully.

"Did you bring me the autopsy report?"

"I brought it with me," Robin replied evenly, "but I don't see that I can legally give it to you."

I reached down to my briefcase, opened it, and retrieved a copy of the mayor's letter. I handed it to Robin. "Here. This should help."

Roland snatched the letter right out of my hand. His eyes danced as he scanned the paper. When he finished, he grinned and said, "By my order and for the good of the State, the bearer has done what has been done."

I shook my head. "What?"

"You know, *The Three Musketeers*? What I was trying to say is that this looks like the mayor himself just handed you a carte blanche. Hey! Can I get a copy?"

"Hell, no," I said as I grabbed the paper back and handed it to Robin.

She looked it over, then shrugged. "Well, as long as you're willing to support me if I lose my job over this, I guess I can play along." She reached under the table and produced a thick stack of paper bound with a spring clip. "I printed a copy of the coroner's preliminary report. Since you said you were in a hurry, all the photos are printed in black and white. If you want color pictures, you'll have to wait until I get back to the office."

I took another glance around the room to make sure we weren't attracting unwanted attention and then started flipping through the report. I found the photographs toward the back. The first one I saw was of an ornate knife. It was photographed alongside a ruler, and I could see that the symmetrical blade measured six and a half inches. The handle looked black, but the guard between it and the blade appeared to be of silver and was shaped like a pair of snakes, coiled up and facing each other; the pommel at the end was a silver ball. I was glad for the sake of my recent breakfast that the picture was black and white; there was an obvious dark stain covering most of the blade.

The next picture stopped me cold. It was a photo of a man lying on a stainless steel table. A handwritten sign at the end of the table near the man's head read MESSENGER, E, with the date and time the photo was shot. I looked up to Robin and said, "Princess, we have a problem."

Robin tilted her head. "What do you mean?"

I turned the report around so she could see. "This doesn't look like the man I knew as Elijah Messenger. Not by a long shot."

■

# CHAPTER SIXTEEN

I expected my announcement to be a shock, to say the least, but while Hector and Roland gave me a pair of wide-eyed looks, Robin displayed a subtle smile on her café-au-lait features that put the Mona Lisa to shame. "Do tell," she said mysteriously.

I looked at the photograph again. "For starters, the man I met who called himself Elijah Messenger had white hair, and lots of it. Full beard and eyebrows to match. This guy has dark hair and no beard."

Robin nodded. "Uh-huh. Anything else?"

I searched my memory. I'd been trained to study faces by their individual componants. "I can't vouch for his eye color. He wore dark glasses. I think his nose is the same. I think."

"But you're sure about the beard?"

"Sure I'm sure," I said, a little irritably.

"Interesting," she purred.

"Okay, I give up," I admitted. "You know something. Care to share?"

"The man in the picture did come in to the coroner's office with a white beard," Robin said, "but it came off during examination."

"Came off?"

"Yes. It was held on with an adhesive. After we saw that,

we ran some tests on the hair on his head. It had been colored recently, but after it had been bleached white sometime in the past. The color hadn't quite set yet. Now, are you certain that when you saw this man his beard was real?"

I shook my head. "Yeah. Pretty sure, anyway. I got a good look at him. I think I would have noticed something like that."

Roland leaned forward. "He was in disguise?"

"And would you testify in a court of law that the man in these pictures is the same Elijah Messenger?" Robin asked.

"Yes," I answered, hoping I sounded more convincing than I felt. "So it appears that between the time I saw Messenger on Thursday and the time he was killed a few hours later that night, he took the time and trouble to give himself a makeover. What other little surprises did the recently departed have to offer?"

Robin said, "Whatever he looked like when you saw him, it looks like he went to some trouble to revert back to his normal appearance. His other body hair, the stuff that doesn't normally get seen, was dark as well. His eyes are brown, by the way."

"Okay. What else?"

"From here it really gets weird," Robin said. "He was brought in dressed in some kind of black robe, which matched the rest of the clothes he wore underneath. But while he was wearing brown leather sandals on his feet, he had a pair of athletic shoes tied to his belt and a pair of socks in his pocket."

I saw Roland scribbling furiously in a small notebook, grinning from ear to ear. "Don't stop now," he pleaded.

Robin continued. "All he had in his trouser pockets, besides his socks, was a pen-sized flashlight, a small pocketknife, and a couple of business cards. One of the cards was yours, Jason, and the other one was Detective Banks's. That was all he

136

was carrying on him, no wallet or keys or anything like that. The robe itself had a bunch of small pockets sewn inside, including on the inside of the sleeves, but there was nothing in them. The examination of his hands was really intriguing."

"How so?" I asked.

"A deceased subject's hands are routinely bagged in plastic. This is done in case the murder victim was able to get hold of something revealing. For instance, there are cases where a victim has scratched his or her assailant and traces of the perpetrator's DNA are recovered from under the fingernails."

"Thanks, teacher," I said. "I think I kind of knew that already."

Robin smiled. "Sorry. Didn't mean to lecture. Anyway, this guy's hands had a lot of chemical traces present."

"Chemicals? Like what?" I asked.

"Iron oxide mostly. Also some traces of magnesium and other elements and compounds. The one thing they all had in common was the fact that they can be used for making explosives and pyrotechnics. Iron oxide, for instance, is used in the manufacture of thermite."

Hector made a face. "Explosives? What the hell is up with that?"

I remembered what Navarro's witnesses had said and what Anna Addison had told me about the bright flashes and dark smoke that came out of the fire right before Messenger was killed. Before I could say anything, Roland beat me to the punch. "Magic act."

"A what?" Hector asked.

"Magic act," Roland repeated. "The flashy stuff a stage magician does to distract the audience from what he's really doing. Only in this case, it sounds like someone else's hand was faster than Messenger's eye."

I picked up the postmortem photo of Elijah Messenger

again. The man in the picture looked younger, maybe thirty-something. I flipped through a couple more pictures until I got a close-up of a clean but gaping wound just under Messenger's sternum. Turning the photo around, I asked Robin, "What can you tell me about this?"

"Ah. Single entry wound by a sharp, double-bladed knife. The knife in question was still in place when the deceased arrived. Do you see the abrasions on either side of the entry point?"

I turned the picture back toward me and squinted at it. "Yeah. What made those?"

"The guard of the knife," Robin explained. "Even though there was only one strike of the blade, it was done with tremendous force, right up to the hilt. Then apparently the knife was worked around inside the wound, long enough to sever the descending aorta."

"Bleah," I said as I put the picture down.

"Sorry if I'm spoiling your breakfast. But you did ask. Anyway, in this case, the deceased lost a great deal of blood. Unconsciousness would have come very quickly, with death following soon after."

"Lot of blood, eh?" Hector asked. "So the perp would have gotten blood on him? Or her?"

"Almost certainly," Robin said. "Mr. Messenger lost quite a bit of it, and with a wound like that, done up close and personal, blood would be bound to get on the perpetrator."

I checked back through my notes. "According to Detective Navarro, the only person left on the scene who had blood on him was Brandon Archimedes, who claimed it was because he was the one who pulled Messenger from the river. The rest turned up clean."

"Could you tell if the guy who stabbed Messenger was left or right handed?" Hector asked.

"No," Robin replied. "There was too much internal damage. Someone really worked that blade around in there."

I felt myself swallow dryly and reached for my water glass, feeling more than a little nauseous as I imagined the path of the knife through Messenger's innards. "So it must have been a really strong dude who did it?" I heard Hector ask.

"Not necessarily," Robin said evenly. "Someone who was very determined could have managed this as well. Say, a seriously motivated woman, for instance."

I finished my sip of water. "Thanks. So much for a workable theory that little Anna Addison couldn't have done it." I found myself looking at my water glass, noticing the fingerprints on the crystal, revealed in the bright sunlight that streamed through the window. "I understand that a fingerprint was recovered from the knife?"

"Oh, yeah," Robin said. "The forensics team managed to lift a good partial print from the blood on the hilt. Once that matched Anna Addison's right forefinger."

"Okay, case solved," Hector announced. "Can we all go home now?"

"Not yet," I said to him. "Your day is just beginning. What did the good Detective Navarro tell you?"

Hector's dark eyes narrowed. "He said that I had to follow you around. He also said to watch you like a hawk."

I got my wallet out and retrieved the company credit card. "Well, then, it looks like Hector and I need to strategize a bit. We have a lot of people to see and things to do."

"Where are we going?" Roland asked with relish.

" 'We' refers to Hector and me," I said. "You, on the other hand, are not invited. Period."

Robin stood up, reaching out and taking Roland by his collar. "Come on, Rudolph. You're not allowed into their reindeer games today." Robin then fixed me with a golden-eyed stare. "You two be careful, okay? Whoever did this to poor Mr. Messenger is a very violent person."

"We'll be fine," I said as confidently as I could. Hector's unstifled moan didn't help, though. I watched as Robin all but dragged Roland away from our table, to the amusement of the other diners. They made quite a sight—tall, black, and beautiful Robin dragging out pale, cherubic Roland, who called back to Hector and me, "Just bring me a story! Call it my Christmas present!"

I shook my head, then found myself staring at Hector. The boy had shown up for breakfast dressed in jeans, work boots, and a gray, hooded pullover sweatsuit top underneath his black Oakland Raiders jacket with white sleeves. "Geez, boy. You expect me to take you out looking like that?" I asked.

He rubbed a hand over his dark chin stubble, which obviously hadn't seen a razor in over twenty-four hours. "Hey, I got woke up after working late last night," he grumbled. "What'd you expect?"

"Well, I suppose if we were going out and speaking with crack whores and junkies, you'd be the height of sartorial elegance, but as it turns out, we're going to be dealing with at least one murderer, hopefully. They have standards, you know."

Hector grinned. "You forget, bro, you're the one gonna be doing the talking. I'm just along for the ride. Which reminds me. Where the hell are we going?"

I opened my notebook as the young and pretty waitress efficiently scooped up the bill along with the credit card. I checked my watch and saw that it was after eleven already. As I ran down my list of names and addresses, I reminded myself that an investigation is frequently driven by the reality of geography. "Let's see," I said aloud. "I want to get back over to Messenger's house and the murder scene sometime before

140

dark to get a good look around. Conveniently, Robert Hanson lives there as well and will hopefully be home. Now, Archimedes' place is the closest. He's got an apartment over in Four Voyagers Plaza. His boy Stone, or Maurice, if you will, lives in a crappy neighborhood down south. The woman who goes by the name of Aurora lives in a midtown motel. So, looks to me that we hit Archimedes, then swing by where Aurora lives, go and hook up with Stone, and finish off over at Messenger's place by the river. All before dark."

Hector shook his head. "Whatever you say, dawg. So what's the plan?"

"Usual routine for a private investigator. Talk to people, look at stuff. Then try to weasel a confession out of someone in between gunfights, hand-to-hand combat, and car chases."

Hector rolled his eyes. "You got me out of bed for this?"

The waitress returned my card, and I made sure I left her a good tip in cash. I got up and took a moment to look out across the river toward the city. With the sun sparkling off the water and the bright blue sky showcasing the city's towers and spires, you could almost forget all the dark and dirty parts that wormed their way through the bowels of the urban landscape. I picked up my notebook from the table. "Let's ride."

As we walked a winding path between the tables, Hector said from behind me, "That's another thing. I ain't your goddam Tonto or Kato or whatever the hell Captain Midnight's sidekick is supposed to be. Got that?"

I stepped outside into refrigerated daylight, hastily putting on my sunglasses to shield my eyes from the glare. "For your information," I said, "it was my dad who was called Captain Midnight. I haven't gotten a cool nickname yet."

"Oh, you got a nickname, bro. Lots of them, in fact. Around my department, I've heard you called 'that crafty SOB PI.' And once I overheard Detective Banks call you a—"

"Yeah, I can imagine," I said, cutting him off. We walked the planks of the dock, heading for my car. After a bit, Hector asked, "So, who was Captain Midnight's sidekick, anyway?"

"Beats me. Wait a minute." I pulled out my key ring, holding up the small brass disk that was attached. It was an official Captain Midnight Medal of Membership, a present from my mother to my father back in the day when they both worked as River City detectives. On one side was a clock face with the hands pointing at twelve. On the other side, a three-bladed propeller divided the circle into thirds, and a face appeared in each section. One was a man in a flying helmet and goggles, Captain Midnight himself. The other two were a male and a female—the one with the most hair looked a lot like Ludwig van Beethoven. I handed my keys to Hector. "Here. See if you can make out the names."

Hector held the keys and disk up to the sun, squinting. "Nah. Can't make anything out. It's too messed up."

"Well, it was made back in the 1940s." I stopped in front of my Mustang and held my hand out to Hector. He just slapped my palm with his free hand as he hip-shoved me out of the way. "Slide over, little boy. Let a real man drive."

I briefly considered putting a wristlock on Hector to get my car keys back, but as he was my regular sparring and shooting partner, he knew almost as many combat tricks as I did, and I didn't have the time to go rolling around on the docks with him. "Fine," I said. "You can drive. That's what Kato did for the Green Hornet anyway."

Grinning, Hector opened the door and slid in behind the wheel, unlocking the passenger's side for me. We were on our way to meet with the last people to see Elijah Messenger alive.

■

# CHAPTER SEVENTEEN

The place known as Four Voyagers Plaza is near the heart of River City. Also known among us locals as the Quad, it's a set of four tall round towers, encased in blue glass, first connected by an artfully designed square park complete with an artificially pumped creek that winds its way around and under arched bridges. The first floors house a collection of upscale shops. If you had enough money, you could live at the Quad and never have to leave its borders. Just about anything you'd possibly want was within a short walk or a long elevator ride.

Hector and I made good time getting over there. Not surprising, since he drove my car with reckless abandon. We found a spot in the maze of the underground parking garage and rode a glass-walled elevator to the twenty-third floor, getting a clear view of River City bathed in bright sunshine. We walked along a curving hallway until we found the door to the apartment we were looking for. After the third time I rang the bell, the intercom speaker came on. "Yes?" said a cautious voice.

"Good morning, Mr. Archimedes," I said. "My name is Jason Wilder. I'm here with Officer Morales of the police department."

The voice from the speaker didn't respond right away. Finally, we heard, "Just a minute." It was more like five minutes before the door opened to reveal Brandon Archimedes, clad in a rich-looking red velvet dressing gown. He stepped aside and waved us in with a flourish. "Come into my humble abode, gentlemen."

I had already taken off my sunglasses, but my eyes were nowhere near ready for the gloom of Archimedes' apartment. I could see sunlight making an attempt to squeeze in under drawn curtains across the way, but other than that, the only light in the room came from a red-shaded lamp on a low table. "Sorry I wasn't ready to receive company," Archimedes said smoothly. "I'm not usually up at the crack of noon. Please, be seated."

Hector and I made our way over to a couch near the center of the room and slid side by side onto the black leather of its covering. Brandon Archimedes took a seat on a matching chair set at a right angle to the couch. In the bloodred light, Archimedes' hair and beard seemed just as perfectly arranged as the last time I saw him. I handed him one of my business cards. "Thank you for allowing us to barge in on you. As I'm sure you've guessed, we're here in regard to the Messenger matter."

Archimedes gave me a brief, thin smile and then looked at my card. "Jason Clark Wilder," he read, "Midnight Investigation Agency? I thought you said you were from the police?"

"That'd be me," Hector said, producing his badge.

"Officer Morales and I are working together on this matter," I explained.

Archimedes crossed his long legs and leaned back in his chair. "I see. Well, I suppose you know that I've already given my statement to the police. So why should I have to speak with you now?"

"Homicide investigations generally involve a number of phases, sir, and this may not be the last time you're interviewed in this matter," I said. "It's a pretty complex process."

"And I suppose you'd like me to go ahead and confess to everything now?" Archimedes asked.

"If it's not too much trouble."

Archimedes smiled, the way a sleek cat would smile when confronted by a pair of fat, stupid mice. "Well, sorry to disappoint you, gentlemen, but I didn't do the deed. However, as I am already awake for the day, go ahead and ask your little questions."

I opened my notebook, and as I did so, I took a quick scan around the room. I felt a tingling sensation course through me. Brandon Archimedes' decorating taste ran to a combination of books and sharp-pointed objects; swords and knives of various designs hung on the walls. The place looked like a cross between a medieval cutlery shop and a library.

"Is there something wrong?"

I shook my head at Archimedes' question. "No. I just noticed your collection."

"Ah. The books or the edged weapons?" he asked with interest.

"The blades. You have quite a lot of them."

"I collect them," he said shortly. "So what questions do you have for me, Mr. Wilder?"

"How did you come to be acquainted with Elijah Messenger?" I asked.

"Oh, let's see, I met him about a year ago. I'd heard about him from people who share the same interests I do; they said I should check him out."

"Check him out?"

"Yes. I have an interest in the occult. I'd heard that Elijah

Messenger had a certain, shall we say, insight into such matters. So I made it a point to make his acquaintance. I wasn't disappointed."

"How's that?"

"Elijah Messenger claimed to have powers and abilities far beyond those of mortal man, to borrow a phrase, and in a way, I suppose he did."

"Powers? Like what?"

Brandon Archimedes smiled. "The power to captivate an audience. Whatever else he was, Elijah Messenger was a first-class magician. Not with any kind of real magic, mind you, but of the stage magician kind. The man always put on a good show."

"So you didn't think he had any kind of real psychic power?"

"Oh, come now," Archimedes said derisively. "If the man had the kind of ability he claimed he had, he'd be a millionaire. But if he wanted to pretend to be a wizard or whatever, who was I to burst his bubble? Besides, I always enjoyed his performances. In fact, I frequently sent people his way."

"What kind of people?" I asked.

"The kind looking for the type of thrill that Elijah could provide. In a way, you could say that Elijah and I were in the same business. The entertainment business. I have people who come to my club because they want to feel wicked and evil. People went to Elijah Messenger because they wanted to believe that such things as psychic power and magic were real. You could say that we both dealt in the art of illusion."

"Did you introduce Anna Addison to Elijah Messenger?"

Archimedes made a rude noise. "Anna Addison? That crazy little bitch? Well, yes. I suppose I did."

"Why do you say that Anna Addison is crazy?" I asked.

Archimedes rolled his dark eyes. "You mean other than the

fact that she and her little playmates go around pretending they're vampires?"

"Vampires?"

"Vampires," Archimedes confirmed. "As in, they drink each other's blood. She's supposed to be the queen of the brood or something like that. Pretty childish, really."

"What can you tell me about her friends?"

"Not much. She always has a retinue with her, but they're a pretty pathetic bunch. There was one I recall, a tall and dark young man who was her chief consort, I think they called him. He went by the name of Raven."

"Raven? Do you know what his real name is?"

"No, but he was always in Anna's shadow, kind of like a pet dog. At least until she started seeing Elijah."

"And you're the one who introduced her to Elijah Messenger?"

"Sure. More as a joke than anything else. She and her little friends were always hanging around my club. I didn't mind, really. They lent a charming Gothic ingredient to the atmosphere. Then Anna started bugging me. I think she was attempting to impress me at first, schoolgirl crush sort of thing, but I found her rather tiresome and immature. So, in order to be rid of her, I told her that if she wanted to learn the ways of real magic, I'd introduce her to an actual wizard. Elijah seemed more than happy to take her off my hands."

"Did they develop a, uh, relationship, shall we say?"

Archimedes stroked his groomed black-and-white beard. "Oh, I think we could say that. Elijah seemed to have an eye for the young ladies. He probably told her there was a quid pro quo to their relationship. You know, the price of learning the power, so to speak. Makes one wonder what he really did teach her."

"So what happened the night Elijah died?"

"Hmm. Let's see. I got a call the night before from Elijah. He said that he was having an event over at his place. He called it a summoning, and he invited me. I told him I'm usually busy at the club on Thursday nights, but he said not to worry, that it would be over by nine o'clock. So I agreed to attend. As I said, he always put on a great show. He did this fire-walking routine once where—"

I cut him off. "Okay, so you showed up at Messenger's house. Who else was there?"

"Well, there was Bob Hanson. He's sort of Elijah's helper. Anna Addison was there. Oh, and that woman who goes by the name Aurora, she was there, too."

"Didn't you have a helper of your own there?"

"Oh, you mean Stone. Yes, I brought him with me."

"Why?"

Archimedes shrugged. "I'm used to having him around. He's useful. In fact, he was very useful that night. He helped me drag Elijah's body out of the river."

"Okay. What do you know about Robert Hanson and Aurora?"

"Hanson is . . . pardon me, *was* Elijah's right-hand man. I guess you could call him an acolyte. He seemed dumb enough to fall for Elijah's silly ruses. Now Aurora, on the other hand, was impressive. She has a rather profound knowledge of occult matters. She told me that she was preparing to write her own book on the subject. I assume that was her interest in Elijah. As intelligent as she seemed to be, it makes me wonder why she wasted her time on him."

"So what happened at the ritual?"

"We all gathered at Elijah's house. Hanson was waiting for us with our robes. When we were dressed for the occasion, Hanson led us out to the garden. I thought that was where we'd see the show, but then Elijah seemed to come out of nowhere and told us we'd be going to the river. Elijah handed me the Athame, that's a type of sword, and gave Anna the chalice and Aurora the broom. Hanson lit a torch and led the way. When we got near the water, I saw that someone had prepared a pentagram on the ground. Elijah started a fire in the center and then began to do an invocation."

"What was everyone else doing at this point?"

Archimedes looked up, eyes unfocused, as he said, "Aurora was to my right, and Hanson to my left. Looking back, it seemed like Aurora was fidgeting with something under her robe, as if she had an itch or something. Hanson just stood there with his head bowed, like a good little sycophant. I really didn't pay any attention to Anna; I was waiting to see what Elijah was going to do. That's when the fire blew up."

"What happened then?"

"I fell back on my ass," Archimedes said with candor. "Couldn't see a damn thing. My ears were ringing from the explosion, but I could hear Anna screaming and Hanson braying to someone about how he was blind. I got tangled up in that damn robe and had a hell of a time getting to my feet. I finally got up and just stood there for a while, waiting to get my senses back. The fire was almost out. Then I heard Aurora scream something about Elijah being in the water. I went over to the riverbank, and that's when I saw him."

"Elijah Messenger was in the water?"

"Oh, yes. There was just enough light from the moon to see the handle of the blade sticking out of his chest. I went in and got him. I managed to grab a leg and pull him partway up, but I slipped and fell into the water. I swear, I think my heart almost stopped, it was so damn cold. I heard Anna scream again, and Hanson kept asking, 'What's going on?' over and over. I got my cell phone out and called Stone. I guess I was a little stunned, because I didn't think to call the police. Aurora had to remind me to do that. By that time, Stone arrived and helped get Elijah up out of the water."

"How did Elijah look at the time?"

"He looked dead," Archimedes said sarcastically.

"Okay, did you notice anything strange or different about his appearance besides that?" I asked.

"I couldn't see him very well. He was wearing the same robe as the rest of us. But I could see enough of his face to know that it was him."

"And he wore a beard?"

Archimedes' hand stole up to his own facial hair. "Yes. He's had one as long as I've known him."

"I see. Tell me, have you spoken with anyone who was present about this incident since that night?"

"Well, Anna tried to see me the other night, but I didn't have time to see her. So no, other than Stone and the police, I've spoken with no one."

"Did Elijah Messenger attempt to borrow any money from you recently?"

"He did. Last Tuesday, he called me and wanted to borrow ten thousand dollars for a week. I told him I didn't have it. He pressed me for whatever I could spare, and I finally agreed to let him have five thousand. Now I wonder if I'll ever get that back again."

"Did he say what he wanted the money for?"

Archimedes shook his head. "No. He just insisted that he only needed it for a week."

Hector surprised me when he spoke up. "Don't mind me saying so, but you seem pretty calm for a guy who's a homicide suspect."

Archimedes' eyes widened in mild surprise. "Suspect? I hate to disappoint you, but I'm innocent."

150

"You were holding the knife or sword or whatever before Messenger was killed."

Archimedes laughed softly. "I was holding the blade that Elijah gave me. I was still holding it when the fire blew up. That blade went flying off somewhere. It wasn't the blade that wound up inside Elijah Messenger."

I quickly thumbed through the photographs that Robin gave me until I came to the close-up of the murder weapon. I held the picture out to Archimedes, who took it and studied it. "Do you recognize this knife?" I asked.

"Oh, yes," he replied with a vulture's smile. "That's the same knife I gave to Anna Addison just two weeks ago."

# CHAPTER EIGHTEEN

I was glad it was dark inside Archimedes' apartment. Hopefully it concealed the disappointment I felt at the news that the murder weapon belonged to Anna Addison, the woman I was supposed to be trying to clear of this homicide. Brandon Archimedes handed the photograph of the knife to me, then leaned back in his chair and tented his fingers. "Well, gentlemen," he said, "is there anything else you'd like to know?"

"Yes," I said. "Why would you give a knife like that to Anna Addison?"

"She asked me for it," Archimedes said simply. "She saw it once when she was over here during a party, so I gave it to her." He smiled. "It wasn't an important one to me, and I never imagined it would wind up where it did. So what did you mean when you said I was a suspect?"

"Someone killed Elijah Messenger, and you were one of the few on the guest list, not to mention the fact that you were apparently the only person who got Elijah Messenger's blood on him. Why wouldn't you be a suspect?"

Archimedes shrugged. "The detectives I spoke with that night seemed to think so as well. I thought I'd die of pneumonia before they let me go. Then after a while they focused on Anna Addison. After all, she was the only one who fled the murder scene, as you call it. Truthfully, though, I thought that Messenger committed suicide."

"Suicide? You think he went to all the trouble of setting up an elaborate ritual and inviting guests just to kill himself?" I asked.

"Why not?" Archimedes countered. "He was a showman. And no one heard him cry out."

Hector and I traded looks, and I said, "Well, thank you for your time, Mr. Archimedes. We may be calling upon you again."

As Archimedes rose slowly, he said, "I take it you'll be speaking to the others? Like Stone?"

I gathered my file and notebook and stood as well. "Yes. Speaking of whom, what did you and Stone discuss after Elijah Messenger died?"

"Just how strange the whole thing was," Archimedes said. "Nothing specific. Although Stone was concerned at being in the vicinity of a violent death. He's a little paranoid about the police. Come to think of it, you'd better have me arrange your meeting with him. He'll show up where I tell him to."

"All right," I said. I wasn't wild about the idea of handing Archimedes and Stone a chance to compare notes and get their stories straight, but they would have had time to do that regardless. "After you get in touch with Stone, give me a call. My numbers are on my business card."

As Archimedes opened the door for us, I said to him, "Tell me, if you had to choose the best suspect for Elijah Messenger's killer, who would that be?"

"Anna Addison," he said without hesitation. "She's crazy enough."

"And I shouldn't think you did it? Why not?"

Archimedes held his right hand up. "Because you have my solemn word as a nonpracticing pagan." As he closed the door behind Hector and me, he added with a low, mocking laugh, "I swear to God."

Hector and I walked down the hall toward the elevators in silence. It wasn't until we were descending toward the garage floors that he said, "What a freak."

"Yeah," I agreed. " 'He plays real hard at being a dark and sinister man.' "

"What?"

I shook my head. "A quote from an old story. Never mind."

"But you gotta say this, the dude has some damn fine toys."

"You mean the sword collection?"

"No, bro. Didn't you see that big-ass home entertainment system in the corner? With the wide-screen TV?"

"Nope. Didn't catch my eye. I must have been distracted by all the cutlery. Well, let's go and see who else we can talk to, shall we?"

Despite some misgivings, I decided to let Hector play chauffeur again. As we left the underground lot and emerged into the bright daylight, I directed him to the address I had for the woman known as Aurora. I jotted down a few notes on the way—not an easy task, since Hector was driving as if we were in an auto rally—and soon we were pulling into the parking lot of a low-rent midtown motel just off the central freeway. The motel was called the Rio Vista, which means something like "view of the river," but unless the rooms were equipped with a fifty-foot periscope, there was no truth to the name.

I was disappointed but not surprised when our knocking at Aurora's motel room door went unanswered. It was after 1:30 in the afternoon. The best time to find people at their residences is either early or late, and this certainly wasn't the kind of neighborhood anyone would hang around in by choice.

"Well, now what, bro?" Hector asked.

I scanned the neighborhood from the creaky worn wooden balcony. It was definitely not the kind of place where you could wait unobserved by the local inhabitants. "I guess we leave a card and try to talk to the manager," I said, wedging said card behind the brass number on the door.

Hector smiled beneath his dark mustache. "Better let me do the talking this time. Come on, I'll show you how it's done."

I followed Hector downstairs to the manager's office, a dingy place reeking of old, cheap tobacco smoke, where a grandmotherly woman—if your grandmother was a Hell's Angel, right down to her oil-stained Harley-Davidson sweatshirt—greeted us. The pleasant greeting evaporated after Hector flashed his badge, but she allowed us to check her books. Theodora Carlyle's rent was paid up through the next Wednesday. Hector seemed pleased with himself for getting the information so quickly, but I knew we were missing a bet here. I sent Hector out to bring the car around. He gave me a quizzical look, but he went without complaint.

When I was alone with the manager, I said, "Thank you for your time and trouble," as I handed her my business card.

She looked at me with open suspicion as she took the card, then her expression thawed slightly as she felt the twenty-dollar bill I had folded beneath it. "No trouble," she said shortly, stuffing the money into her jeans. She took another look at my card, saying, "You're not a cop?"

"Me? No. I work for a living."

She snorted something I took for laughter. "So," I went on, "if you see Ms. Carlyle come in, you'll give me a call?"

"She in any trouble?" the manager asked sharply.

"No," I said with as much sincerity as I could muster, "but I think she may be able to help me. I already left my card on her door."

"We'll see," the manager said neutrally. I took the hint and had started to leave when the woman said, almost under her breath, "She said something about maybe leaving early, like by Monday. Just so you know." I smiled my thanks, feeling that I had at least rented a pair of eyes to alert me when Aurora came back.

I left the office with a jaunty step and swung into the passenger seat of my car, telling Hector, "Let's roll, Kato."

He punched me in the arm before we left the parking lot.

Hector angled the Mustang toward Hurricane Street as he said, "So, where to now?"

"Well, Faithful Companion, we seem to be down to two tasks: talk to Robert Hanson and check the house and crime scene. That should keep us busy until we get a call on either Stone or Aurora. So take the freeway south, then cut over west to Olympus Grove. It's the long way around but probably faster than driving through town with the holiday shopping crowd."

Before I finished speaking, Hector gunned the engine and blasted his way to the on-ramp, where we damn near got airborne as he rocketed up and onto the overhead freeway. In an instant, we were flying in the fast lane with complete disregard for the speed limit.

"I take it back," I said when I was no longer in danger of biting through my tongue. "I ought to let you drive me all the time. I'd get my work done twice as fast."

"Privilege of the badge," Hector said.

"Good. Get me one for Christmas. Speaking of which, what are you getting your wife?"

Hector shrugged. "Becky wants a baby."

A picture of Rebecca Morales flashed into my mind— blond, pretty, petite. "Well, you know," I said offhandedly, "if you need any help in that department . . ." I let my voice trail off.

"Nah, no good. She's already had a real man. So when are you going to quit fooling around and grow up and get married?"

"What is it with you married guys?" I countered. "You always want us wild and free types to join you in captivity." Of the four of us in the Epic Hero Society, Hector was the only one so far to get hitched. Roland either had too many girlfriends at once or none, and Robin always insisted that she would wait for her One True Love.

The discussion of marriage brought my thoughts around to Jenny and her daughter Angelina. I'd been surprised to find that the little one never seemed to subtract from my feelings for Jenny; rather, my feelings for the two of them seemed to multiply into dimensions I'd never before experienced.

I shook myself out of my reverie and brought my mind back to the job. "Is it me?" I asked aloud, "or does it seem that every new piece of information we get just makes Anna Addison look worse?"

"Hey, I'll put five dollars on that creepy dude Archimedes," Hector said. "He looks like the type to stab someone."

"Yeah? Well, if he did, he's being awfully cool about it. At this point, I'm thinking that if Anna did do the murder, we might be able to help with some sort of insanity defense. I mean, what's up with the vampire stuff? Bleah."

Hector and I traded more barbs and banter for the short duration of our high-velocity trip, until we pulled into the circular driveway in front of the pocket-sized mansion that was the Harrington residence. As we got out of the car, Hector let out an appreciative whistle. "Damn," he muttered. "We're with the High Rollers now."

I took a moment to admire the view in the winter daylight. A beat-up grayish Chevy pickup truck with an aluminum camper shell parked along the right side of the driveway stood out in jarring contrast to the Spanish Mission façade of the house; it had a Missouri license plate, I noticed.

Hector and I went over to the large, rounded double doors in what reminded me of a castle's archway and rang the bell. Enough time went by that I was on the verge of giving up and leaving a card when I heard a masculine voice call from the intercom, "Who is it?"

I nodded to Hector, who took the hint and said, "Police."

"Police? Oh. All right, just a minute."

Shortly thereafter, the left-side door creaked open and a lean, lined face masked by a pair of dark glasses and an iron gray beard leaned around the portal. "Are those newspaper guys gone?" the man asked in a hoarse whisper.

"Uh, I guess so," I said.

He hurriedly waved us in. "Get in. They'll come back. Vultures always do."

Hector and I slipped into the foyer, and the man hastily pushed the portal shut behind us. "Goddam jackals been at me for the last two days," he muttered. After locking the door, he turned toward Hector and me and extended his hand. "Hi. I'm Bob. What can I do for you boys?"

I had to quickly revise the mental picture I'd developed of Robert Hanson. Anna Addison described him as a student of Elijah Messenger's, and Brandon Archimedes called him an acolyte, so I'd imagined someone young. The man I was looking at seemed to be in his midfifties, long and lean, dressed in a red plaid shirt with worn jeans and white tennis shoes. His gray hair was pulled back in a rough ponytail.

"For starters, Mr. Hanson," I said, "we'd like to speak with you about the night Elijah Messenger died."

Hanson bent his head and put his hands in his pockets. "Yeah. I know," he said sadly. "I expect you boys are a little upset with me. I just didn't want to believe it at first. I didn't really mean to hold anything back."

"Believe what, sir?" I asked.

"About Anna," Hanson said. "And what she did to Elijah."

Hector and I traded quick looks, and I'm certain we were both thinking the same thing:

Everything I did just made it worse for Anna Addison.

# CHAPTER NINETEEN

I tried to suppress a sigh and asked Robert Hanson, "What can you tell us about Anna Addison that you didn't tell the police the first time?"

Hanson shook his head and said, "I didn't hold anything back that night. It's just that I didn't see how a girl could do such a thing. I mean, I know she was a mixed-up kid and all, but still . . ."

"Can we sit down somewhere and talk about it?"

"What? Oh, sure. Sorry." Hanson turned around and led us into the recesses of the house. I saw that the foyer opened up into a large room with a two-story plate glass wall that looked out over a central garden area. The room itself was all white marble floors and richly appointed furnishings. Everywhere you looked were white marble statues that looked like they came from ancient Greece or Rome. I caught Hector giving the place a once-over and rolling his eyes, as if to say, *Rich people have funny taste!*

Hanson indicated a white leather couch with a round glass-topped coffee table set in front of it. Hector and I sat down, and he pulled up a chair facing us. I opened my notebook and took out my pen as I said, "If you don't mind, I'd like to get a little background first. How did you come to be associated with Elijah Messenger?"

"Me? Well, I guess that started a couple of years ago. You could say I was on a kind of quest."

"Quest?"

Hanson folded his arms and turned his head away slightly. "Yeah. All my life, I'd been hearing about strange things in the world. Stuff like how the government's been covering up what they know about UFOs, and stories about ESP and hauntings. When I retired, I decided it was time to go and have a look. I wanted to see things for myself."

"Okay," I said. "And this led you to Elijah Messenger?"

"Yeah. I read his book, *The Illuminated Traveler*. It explained a lot of things about how telepathy and clairvoyance work. Anyway, I did a little research and found out that Mr. Messenger lived here in California. So I up and packed my truck and came out here."

"When was that?"

"Oh, let's see, I've been here near on a year now. I got to talking to Mr. Messenger after one of his fire-walking events."

"Fire-walking?"

Hanson shook his head again, and said with a tinge of awe in his voice, "Yeah. That's the first time I met him. He taught us that things like pain can be controlled by the mind. Well, I admit I was a bit skeptical at first, but when I tried it myself, I saw it was real." Hanson looked at me through his dark glasses. "I walked barefoot across hot coals. All because Mr. Messenger showed me how to use the power of my mind."

I felt Hector shift uneasily beside me, and I was hoping that my expression was one of open acceptance. "So what happened after that?" I asked.

"Well, I started asking Mr. Messenger all about his book, and wondered if he was taking on any more students. I told him I couldn't afford to pay him much, seeing as I was on a fixed income from my retirement. I used to be a machinist back in Missouri. Anyway, I asked Mr. Messenger if there was anything I could do for him, and I sort of became his assistant."

"What did you do as his assistant?"

"Oh, lots of things. He didn't drive, you know, so I took him to most of his appointments. Mrs. Harrington, the lady who owns the house here, lent us one of her husband's cars. I also kept his appointment book for him, and I handled his correspondence."

"And you've been living here?"

"Yeah. Mr. Messenger let me have a room on the first floor."

"What can you tell me about the others who were here the night Mr. Messenger died?"

Before he spoke, Hanson took off his glasses and rubbed his watery blue eyes. "Sorry," he said quietly. "I'm still not used to the whole thing. Can't quite believe it all happened."

"It's okay, sir. Take your time."

Hanson sucked in a breath, held it, then exhaled. "Okay. Sorry about that. What was the question? Oh, right, the others." Hanson replaced his glasses and said, "Well, there's Anna, of course. She started coming around here a couple of months ago. I thought at first she was trying to be one of Mr. Messenger's students, kind of like me. But she was, uh, well, she was also kind of pursuing him, if you know what I mean."

"Pursuing him?"

Hanson shifted uncomfortably. "Yeah. You know, like trying to get close to him."

"Are you saying that they had a sexual relationship?"

"I guess I am. She spent the night here more than a few times. In his room. Not that it was any of my business, but the last week or so, I overheard a lot of arguments."

"What were they arguing about?"

"Can't really say. My hearing isn't all that good. It sounded

162

angry, though. At least on her part. Mr. Messenger never raised his voice the whole time I knew him. That's also about the same time the threats started showing up."

"Threats? What kind of threats?"

Hanson shook his head. "Stuff started showing up in the mail. First thing was a pair of Tarot cards. One was the card for the Magician, and the other was the Death card."

"Any clue as to where they came from?"

"No. They weren't really mailed, just put in a plain envelope and dropped in the mailbox. No note or anything. But the next thing that showed up really had an effect on Mr. Messenger."

"What was that?"

"It was just a small gold cross on a gold chain. Showed up like the cards did. I showed it to Mr. Messenger, and when he held it in his hand, he turned as white as a sheet. I thought he must have picked up a psychometric trace on it."

"A what?"

"Psychometric," Hanson repeated. "That's the ability to pick up psychic traces from inanimate objects. Whatever it was he felt, it really shook him up."

"I see." My cell phone started vibrating. I chose to ignore the call for now; I didn't want to interrupt Hanson's flow of words. "Did Anna Addison say or do anything else that would make you think she was having problems with Mr. Messenger?" I asked.

"Oh, yeah. For one, there was that ex-boyfriend of hers."

"Oh? Who was that?"

Hanson shrugged. "I'm not real sure about his name, but he started showing up here right after Anna started hanging around. One time, I answered the door and he barged in, demanding to know where Anna was. She must have heard the ruckus, because she came down with Mr. Messenger and told the boy to get lost. Anyway, at one point during the yelling, Anna called him Raven, but later I heard her say something like, 'Leave now, Harold.' Anyway, I think he was kinda hanging around the place, because not too long after that I found some large footprints out in the back garden."

"What did this guy look like?" I asked.

"Big fella," Hanson said. "Face like a full moon. He wore all black when I saw him, a black trench coat, I think it was. And he had long black hair."

"Did Anna Addison have any other problems as far as Mr. Messenger was concerned?"

"Not that I could put my finger on," Hanson replied, "but she did seem real jealous of anyone else getting Mr. Messenger's attention. Anyone female, that is."

"Would that include Aurora?"

"Oh, yeah. Anna had a real problem with her. I overheard Anna say one time, 'That bitch better watch her step,' or something like that. Her words, not mine."

"What was your impression of Aurora?"

"Oh, she's a real nice lady. Real smart, too. Knows all kinds of stuff. She told me she's writing a book, too, just like Mr. Messenger did."

"What was her relationship to Mr. Messenger?"

"She said she was here to do research. For her book, like I said. Anyway, Anna didn't take too kindly to the time Mr. Messenger spent with her."

"Was there anything else to their relationship?"

"Not that I could see."

"What about Brandon Archimedes?"

Hanson's face twisted in a bitter frown. "Now him, I didn't like. Him or that Stone guy."

"Why is that?"

"Mr. Archimedes always seemed to be up to something.

He's the kind of guy who thinks he's smarter than you and makes no bones about it, and I didn't like the way he acted around Mr. Messenger, like Mr. Messenger was some kind of employee or something. Plus that friend of his, Stone, is just plain rude."

"What can you tell me about last Thursday?"

"Well, it had been a pretty busy week. I took Mr. Messenger to a lot of appointments with his clients, and we ran a lot of errands, especially to a bunch of banks, come to think of it. But Thursday was different. First thing he did, he told me to go down to the river and prepare a circle."

"A circle?"

"Yeah. He told me to paint a pentagram close to the water and set up a fire pit in the center. I figured he was preparing for one of his spiritual exercises. Anyway, I did as I was told. Later, in the afternoon, he had me drive him to the police station."

"Did he say why?"

Hanson shook his head. "No. I figured he might have been helping the police out. There've been a lot of cases where psychics have helped the police solve murders and find missing people."

"What happened after that?"

"Well, after the police station, he told me to go to an address on Galleon Street. I'd never taken him there before. He wasn't inside long."

"Was that address in the 1300 block? A brick Victorian?"

"Yeah. Beautiful old house."

Hanson had described the office of Midnight Investigations. "What happened next?"

"Mr. Messenger told me to take him home, and when we got here, he told me to lay out four robes and the Athame, the chalice, and the broom. Then he told me to stay in my room for a while so he could meditate and prepare. I was alone for a few hours, then Mr. Messenger came and got me. By that time, all the others were there at the house."

"The others being Anna, Aurora, and Archimedes?"

"And Stone," Hanson added. "Anyway, Mr. Messenger had us gather in the back garden. He told us to put on our robes and follow him to the river. He also said we all had to be perfectly silent. Then Mr. Messenger had me take a torch and lead us to the riverside."

"Now, that Athame you mentioned, that's like a big knife, right?"

"Right." Hanson nodded. "Mr. Messenger used it in a lot of his rituals. He called things like that 'focusing elements.' He always said that tools like the Athame or the chalice were helpful in achieving psychic tuning. Like using a magnifying glass to see things more clearly."

"I understand that Brandon Archimedes was told to take the Athame?"

"Right. Anna got the chalice and Aurora the broom. We formed a little procession and we all went to the river."

"Had you ever had a, uh, ritual there before?"

"Nope. First time. Whenever we had an event at the house here, it was always either right here in this room or out in the garden."

"Okay. So what happened next?"

Hanson looked down and said slowly, "Well, we all got to the river, all right. Mr. Messenger pointed us to our positions. Then he took the flame out of the torch and lit the fire in the center of the circle."

I tuned a page in my notebook and laid it on the table. Taking my pen, I began to draw. "Let's see now, let's say this line is the water, okay? If I make the pentagram like this, then Mr. Messenger was at the top? Closest to the water?"

Hanson leaned close to the table and raised his glasses, squinting. "Okay," he said.

"So, if Mr. Messenger is at the twelve o'clock position, then as I understand it, Aurora is at two o'clock, then Archimedes at four o'clock, then you at eight o'clock, and Anna at ten o'clock. Is that right?"

"Yeah." Hanson nodded.

"What happened then?"

Hanson leaned back on the couch, replacing his glasses. "Then all hell broke loose," he said firmly. "There was a loud bang and a bright flash. For a second there, I thought someone was shooting a gun. I must have turned my head too quick because my glasses went flying off somewhere, and I dropped the torch and ran. I didn't get too far before I tripped on something and fell down. I couldn't see a damn thing, except a bright spot where the fire was, but I could hear Anna Addison screaming like a banshee. There were more popping sounds, and I still wasn't too sure that someone wasn't shooting a gun. Then it got kind of quiet. I sort of stumbled back to the fire, and I could hear Aurora and Archimedes asking each other what the hell just happened. It wasn't more than a minute or so later that I heard Aurora scream something about what's that in the water, and Archimedes called out Messenger's name. I still couldn't see a damn thing. There was a splashing sound. Then I heard Archimedes say something about how Mr. Messenger had been stabbed."

Hanson took off his glasses and looked at me with watery, unfocused eyes as he said, "That's when Anna took off running like the devil was behind her."

# CHAPTER TWENTY

Everything Robert Hanson told me was consistent with the story I got from Brandon Archimedes. Everything I'd heard so far was also consistently bad for Anna Addison. "What happened after Mr. Messenger's death?" I asked.

Hanson bowed his head a bit. "Well, the police and fire department guys showed up. I still couldn't see what was going on—I couldn't find my glasses—but while the police were talking to Mr. Archimedes, I heard him complain about how he was probably going to catch pneumonia. He was the one who went into the water and got Mr. Messenger out. The police took us all back to the house here and asked us for a statement. I told them everything I could remember."

"Then the police came back the next night, right? With a search warrant?"

"Yeah. Anna showed up first, though."

"What did you two talk about?"

"She seemed real upset," Hanson said. "I asked her why she ran off the night before, but all she said was that she got scared. Guess I can't blame her for that. Then she kept saying how she needed to find something in the house. Something that belonged to her."

"Did she say what that was?"

"No. I told her to go ahead and look around. Then she

asked me if I had the combination to the lock on Mr. Messenger's door. I told her no. Then she tried to talk me into breaking the door down, and while we were arguing about that, the police showed up. We heard them knock real loud and say something like, 'Police officers, search warrant, open the door,' about three times. Anna grabbed my arm before I could get up and begged me not to tell them she was here. Then she up and ran out the back. I let the officers in."

"But you did tell them about Anna being here, didn't you?"

"Yeah. I did. Just not at first. But I decided I didn't want to lie to the cops."

"Did the police find anything in the house that night?"

Hanson rubbed his bearded chin. "Yeah, I guess so, but they didn't tell me about it."

Hector cleared his throat and said, "They should have left you a receipt for anything they took from the search warrant. Where is it?"

Hanson shrugged. "One of the detectives gave me a handwritten paper, taped up, and told me to give it to the owner of the house. I mailed it to Mrs. Harrington this morning."

"Did you read what was on the list?" I asked.

"No, sir," Hanson said, shaking his head. "Not my business."

I wondered what the police found during their search. Whatever it was, Detective Navarro hadn't seen fit to advise me. Hopefully that meant he didn't find anything of significance. "I have just a couple more questions, Mr. Hanson," I said. "If you don't mind."

"Not at all. And call me Bob."

"Okay, Bob. Did you always drive Mr. Messenger to his appointments?"

"Mostly," Hanson answered. "Although in the last couple

of weeks, Mr. Archimedes sent Stone over here to get Mr. Messenger."

"Where did he go on those occasions?"

"Don't know. Mr. Messenger wouldn't say. Oh, and he went out a couple of times with Anna Addison. I guess she drove those times."

"Okay. I'd like you to look at a couple of pictures for me," I said as I offered Hanson one of the black-and-white coroner's photos. "Have you seen this before?"

Hanson slipped his dark glasses up on his forehead and peered closely at the photo of the knife recovered from Elijah Messenger's body. "Yep." He handed the photo back. "That belongs to Anna Addison."

"You're certain about that?"

"Sure. See the way the guard on the knife there looks like a pair of snakes? That's hers, all right. I saw it once when she brought it over to show Mr. Messenger. They talked about having a consecration ritual for it."

"Consecration ritual?"

"Yeah. To infuse the knife with the owner's own power. Kind of like charging a battery, according to Mr. Messenger."

"Did you see them perform this ritual?"

"No. That would have been a private matter."

"So this isn't the blade that Archimedes had the night you were all down by the river?"

"No," Hanson said definitely. "The Athame's bigger and has a bone handle."

"Okay. Do you recognize the person in this picture?"

Hanson squinted at the postmortem photo of Elijah Messenger with darkened hair and no beard. "No. Who is this?"

"According to the coroner, that is supposed to be Elijah Messenger."

Hanson shook his head once, sharply. "No. That's not him."

"Look again," I urged. "Are you certain?"

Hanson took a long look. "Well . . . I guess . . . it could be him . . . but where's his beard? What happened to his hair?"

"Think carefully," I said. "The last time you saw Elijah Messenger, what did he look like?"

"When he came and got me for the ritual, he was wearing his hood, but I saw his beard. I know I did."

I took the picture from Hanson's hand. "Thank you, sir. That's all the questions I have for now."

"Oh. Okay," Hanson said, as if waking up from a dream.

"Officer Morales and I want to look around a bit. We'll try not to disturb anything."

Hanson stood up from the couch a little stiffly. "Okay. Call me if you need me," he said almost absently. "I'll be down here in the kitchen."

"Where's Mr. Messenger's room?" I asked.

"Up the right set of stairs and down the hall to the double doors at the corner. It's locked, though."

"Okay, sir, thanks."

When Hanson was out of earshot, Hector said quietly, "That's one strange old boy. So now what?"

"So now," I said softly, "we go and take a look at Messenger's room. Come on."

Hector and I marched up a curving set of stairs and down a marble-floored hall to the room at the end. "Are you sure this is legal?" Hector asked.

"Relax. I got permission from the owner this morning," I said as I got my phone out and checked my missed call. I hit the redial button, and Mom answered right away. " 'Bout time, kiddo," she said. "What's up?"

"Hello, Mother dear. I'll put it this way: If we were working for the police or the prosecutor's office, I'd say we're doing great. Everything I turn up makes Anna Addison look worse."

"Have you told the mayor anything yet?"

"No way."

"Good. The game's not over yet, kiddo. So what are you doing now?"

"Hector and I are going to check out Messenger's living quarters, then I thought I'd head over and get a look at the crime scene while it's light out. After that, I've still got two more witnesses to chat with. Oh, and I've got Jimmy, Timmy, and Felix working on a couple of things for me."

"Here's one more piece of news for you," Mom said. "The mayor called a little while ago. I told him to check Anna's credit card account since he's a cosigner, and he found out she made a cash withdrawal of over seven thousand dollars last Tuesday. Right up to her card's limit."

"Really? That's starting to fit a pattern. Seems Messenger was hitting up everyone he knew for money shortly before he died."

"Uh-huh," Mom agreed. "I also notice that was a little something that Anna didn't bother to mention to you the other night."

"Must have slipped her mind. So how are things in sunny Santa Teresa? Coming home soon?"

Mom laughed. "Not right away. I'm busy fishing for art crooks. I've got some bait set out. Hopefully I'll catch something."

"Well, good luck. I'm just about to do a little domestic burglary here. I'll give you an update later."

"Good enough," Her Majesty proclaimed. "Tell Hector I said hello. And be careful, love."

"Aye, aye. Over and out." I snapped my phone shut and saw that Hector was examining a massive combination lock bolted to the white-painted double doors of the master bedroom.

"We gonna shoot the lock off?" Hector asked. "If so, I'm going to need a bigger gun."

I took a good look at the lock myself. I routinely carry some small tools designed to open both pin-and-tumbler as well as warded key-type locks, but the combination models are a little beyond my capabilities. I smiled as I looked to the marble floor and found my answer. "No, Hector old boy," I said. "We're getting in the same way your buddies did when they came in with their search warrant."

Hector shook his head. "I don't get it."

I pointed to one of the four screws that attached the hasp of the lock to the door. "See here? This was a really amateur attempt to secure the door for the times nobody's home. Whoever did this just bolted the hinges and lock on the outside. All we have to do is unscrew the hasp, and voilà! Open sesame." I keep a small utility tool on my key ring that snaps open to reveal a knife blade, along with the three types of screwdrivers and a bottle opener. As the screws had been recently loosened, it took only a couple of minutes to get the door open. A gentle push, and I ushered Hector in. "Women and children first," I said.

I'd been curious about the Inner Sanctum of Elijah Messenger, and as Hector and I entered the darkened room, I switched on the light.

"What a frickin' pigsty," Hector muttered.

I couldn't have said it better myself. The large master bedroom looked like it had been converted into an indoor campsite, complete with mostly empty fast-food containers tossed haphazardly around. The king-sized bed was covered with a mass of blankets and obviously hadn't been changed in way too long, while the tops of the dressers and nightstands were piled to capacity with trash. I made my way carefully through a minefield of empty beer bottles and soft drink cans to the far wall, where I pulled the heavy white curtains open, flooding the room with daylight. The extra illumination didn't do the view a bit of good.

"I've been in crack houses that looked better than this," Hector said. "Smelled better, too."

"Well, let's take a look around. Try not to mess anything up," I cautioned.

Hector smiled and headed for the walk-in closet while I took the bathroom. The round tub arrangement, spacious enough for four, needed a steam cleaning. Under a wide mirror wreathed in gold vines and leaves was a marble double-basin sink, buried in debris. Some of the items were intriguing.

I found a mass of straight white hair, along with scissors and a shaver and an emptied box of a commercial hair dye for men. The colored stains left in the sink matched the description on the box. I also found a package from a place called Pirates of Penzance Theatrical that once contained a Deluxe Wizard's Beard along with a bottle of adhesive. This pretty much explained Messenger's change of appearance the night he died. Sometime after he came to see me, he must have come home, cut his hair and shaved, then dyed the hair on his head and applied a false beard, covering up the results with the hood of his robe.

"Hey, I found the porno collection," Hector called.

"Anything unusual?" I asked.

"Nah. Just the run of the mill girls-who-like-girls-and-dress-like-cheerleaders stuff. I think I found the one with your ex-girlfriend in it."

"Keep looking, funny boy." I returned to my own task, but the more I looked at the collection of containers and bottles, the more puzzling it seemed to be—until I came across an empty tin of gunpowder and the remains of hollowed-out road flares. It appeared that Messenger made up his own special effects for his rituals. The stuff in the containers looked like it could produce a loud bang and a bright flash.

I stepped out to the main bedroom as Hector was emerging from the walk-in closet. "Anything else?" I inquired.

"Nah. Bunch of clothes on the floor. Everything this guy owned was black. Looks like he had at least some good intentions, anyway."

"Oh?"

Hector picked up a paper carton from the bed. "Look here. A whole pack of jumbo garbage bags. Maybe he was going to clean up soon?"

The package was open but apparently full of dark green plastic bags. "I didn't find any used ones around here," I said.

"Me either. I almost had to fight my way out of the closet."

"I take it no money showed up?"

"Not a dime."

"Okay, let's give the rest of it a good going-over."

Hector and I left no mossy stone unturned. By the time we were done, the place didn't seem all that much the worse for wear. We didn't turn up any money or contraband, nor did we find any other personal items belonging to Messenger. The only other item of interest was among the clothes on the bed: a black vest that turned out to have pockets sewn on the inside. We took the liberty of washing our hands in the bathroom and then drying them off on each other's pant legs in true juvenile fashion, after which we made our way back to the door. As I was replacing the screws on the hinges, Hector asked, "So now what? Can we call it a day yet?"

"You can call it what you want, but we've still got work to do."

"Slave driver. No wonder no one likes you."

I finished with the lock and checked my watch as I replaced my little utility tool on my key ring. It was close to 3:30. "Come on, Hector, old boy. Let's go visit a crime scene."

# CHAPTER TWENTY-ONE

We met Hanson in the front room. "Thank you again for your time, sir," I said. "May I call you if I have any further questions?"

"Sure. I guess I'll be sticking around for a while, anyway. At least until the police tell me I can leave. Mrs. Harrington was nice enough to tell me I could stay as long as I needed to."

"That's good. So you'll be heading back to Missouri?"

"Nah. Nothing for me back in La Plata. I thought I'd head out for Nevada."

"Nevada?"

Hanson smiled, a bit wistfully. "Yeah. That's where the government's been hiding a lot of their UFO stuff, down around Groom Lake and what they call Area 51. I thought I'd go and take a look-see for myself."

"That's nice," I said automatically. "Uh, before we go, you mentioned that you did Mr. Messenger's correspondence for him. Would you have a list of his, uh, clients?"

"Sure."

"Could I have a copy?"

"Wait here." Hanson went out of the room, returning shortly with a neatly typed legal-sized page. "Here's all the addresses and phone numbers I kept for Mr. Messenger. You can have them. I won't be needing them anymore," he said sadly.

"Thank you, sir. One last thing. Could you show us the route you took to the river the other night?"

Hanson nodded. "This way." Hector and I followed Hanson toward the back of the house, walking past a large kitchen that held a big round table. On the table sat a stack of loose paper and an old-fashioned electric typewriter. "This is where I did my work," Hanson explained offhandedly as we walked past. We went into the dining room and out through a large sliding glass door into a garden, complete with life-sized statues that looked like they belonged in an ancient Roman villa. We followed Hanson down a flagstone path to what looked like a table made of carved stone set on a slightly raised round concrete pad with the symbols of the zodiac carved around the edge. On one side of the table was a five-foot-tall, slightly rusty-looking black metal pole with a fluted cup on top. "This here is the altar. It's where Mr. Messenger usually held his outdoor gatherings," Hanson explained.

The walls that contained the garden were made of the same dusty rose-colored stone as the house, but in here the walls were nearly covered with a dark green, leafy vine that seemed to run everywhere. Past the altar I could see a wooden door in the wall. "Does that lead outside?" I asked.

"Yep. Straight out there is the path to the river."

"Okay. Thanks again, Mr. Hanson. Please call me if you can think of anything else."

"Are you boys heading down to the river?" Hanson asked.

"Yes, sir."

"Do me a favor? If you happen to find my glasses, would you bring them back to me? I can't get around very well at night wearing these prescription sunglasses."

"Sure thing," I said. We shook hands, and Hector and I left

by way of the back door. Once outside the protection of the walls, I could feel the cold wind shoot straight through my clothes.

"Where to now?" Hector asked.

"Over the levee and through the woods," I said.

As Hector and I marched along the path toward the river, I could feel the ache in my side start up again. Cresting the top of the levee, I looked down at the mass of trees, now swaying in the breeze, and spotted the scraps of yellow crime scene tape that marked the path to the water. Seen in daylight, the place appeared a lot less foreboding than it did in the dark. Hector silently followed me down the path and into the trees. Once we were screened by the foliage, with the trees rustling in the wind, the feeling of being completely cut off from civilization sank in again.

We came to the clearing, and the angle of the late afternoon sun bounced off the water, breaking into a million liquid flashes, making me dig out my shades. "So this is it?" Hector said.

"Yeah. Welcome to Messenger's Last Stand."

Hector and I approached the red painted pentagram that bordered the fire pit. I could see a lot of things I had missed when I came here in the dark. The ground was hard-packed clay with smooth, half-buried river stones making up a chaotic mosaic. I walked toward the river, giving the pentagram a wide berth, until I came to the spot where Messenger had stood. On either side, the dense groves of trees swayed as if to music. "Come over here," I said to Hector. "Tell me if I'm making any kind of sense out of this."

Hector came and stood next to me. "Okay," I said. "Now, from what we know, it looked like Messenger was getting ready to make a run for it. He'd gotten a bunch of money together and changed his appearance. I'm guessing that all this ritual stuff was some kind of magic disappearing act. So, if Messenger is ready to run, where is he going from here?"

Hector looked around. "Maybe he had a boat nearby?"

"Not likely. For one thing, I don't know anyone crazy enough to try to navigate the river at night with anything short of a motorboat with lights, and that's not exactly conducive to a stealthy exit. Now, the way I see it, once he's got his audience dazzled with a flashy explosion, he could just walk past them and head back to the house. Only he's got to make a really wide arc to get around everyone, no matter which way he goes."

"Not to mention what if someone else decides to head back to the house," Hector said. "Isn't that where Anna ran off to?"

"Yeah, and Stone was supposedly waiting back there as well. Okay, so the house is out as far as a getaway. That leaves going either left or right along the river's edge."

"Where was his body found?"

"In the water, a few steps to the left of us, from what I gather." Now I saw dark splotches among the flat grayish stones near the shore. "Right about there," I said, pointing to the ominous stains.

Hector grunted his agreement. "So who was the closet person to him at that point?" he asked.

I looked at the circle and saw a small broom, more like a stick with a bundle of long twigs tied at one end. "That's where Aurora stood," I said.

"Ah. And we still haven't talked with her yet."

"Right." I walked over to Aurora's spot on the circle, avoiding the bloodstained rocks, and kept going. "So Archimedes must have stood here," I mused aloud.

"The creepy guy with all the swords and stuff? I'd say he

was close enough to do the job. If Aurora was blinded the way Hanson said he was."

"But then Archimedes would be blinded, too," I added. "On the other hand, he was supposed to be holding a bladed weapon himself, and he was the only one who was seen with blood on him."

"Yeah," Hector nodded. "Then again, Anna took off. She could have been covered in blood, only no one saw her."

"Thanks for reminding me," I said sarcastically. I looked around the ground. "Okay, so where is this Athame thingy? Archimedes said he dropped it somewhere when the explosions went off."

It took Hector and me more than fifteen minutes of pawing through the bushes, but we finally spotted it—a long, shiny blade with a whitish handle. "Aha," I breathed. "Now, I wonder why this ended up here?"

"Maybe because that Archimedes guy got scared shitless by the campfire going boom, just like he said?"

"Or maybe there's a more sinister reason."

"I don't know," Hector said dubiously. "That knife looks pretty clean to me."

I straightened up from my examination, suppressing a groan as my wounded rib reminded me to leave it alone, and called Robin Faye on my cell phone. "Hello, princess."

"Well, hello to you. Now that we've exchanged pleasantries, what do you want?"

"Only to hear the dulcet tones of your voice. Oh, and to ask you if there's any chance that Elijah Messenger was stabbed with more than one knife."

"As to that, all I can say is how sweet and heck no."

"You're sure?"

"I didn't do the examination myself," Robin replied, "but

the conclusions are inescapable. Mr. Messenger was killed by one very powerful knife blow from the weapon that was found still in place in his body."

"And that weapon had the bloody fingerprint of Anna Addison?"

"Yes, dear. It did."

"You're positive?"

"I'm sorry, Jason, but the facts speak for themselves."

"Okay." I sighed. "Thanks, princess." I shut my phone off with a snap. "Crap. There goes another good theory."

Hector nodded his head in sympathy, and we walked around to Hanson's position in the circle. There was a rusty black hollow iron pole lying at an angle with one end near where the fire was. A couple of feet away lay the cuplike end that was the torch part. Together, they'd be a match of the torch that was still standing next to the stone altar back at the house. I picked up the torch end of the thing and saw that there was a wick connected to a fuel reservoir inside. Picking up the pole, I slipped the torch on the end. "Okay, so Hanson is standing here," I said. "The fireworks go off, and he drops the torch and loses his glasses." I let the pole go, and it bounced and clanged on the stones in the ground. Looking around the immediate area, I said aloud, "So where are his glasses?"

"Right here," Hector said from behind me as he bent down, retrieving a pair of black horn-rimmed spectacles.

"Ah, let me see," I said. I took the glasses from Hector and switched them with my own sunglasses. I opened my eyes, then instantly closed them again as I snatched off Hanson's pair. The brief glimpse I got through the lenses made my head hurt. "The dude is blind," I said as I replaced my sunglasses. Looking down, I saw that the black metal torch had come apart again; the head of the thing was separated from the pole, similar to the way we found it.

I slipped Hanson's glasses into my overcoat pocket and walked the rest of the circle to Anna's position. "Which brings us to Anna Addison's spot," I said. "Like Aurora on the other side, Anna's the closest to Messenger. We know that it was her knife that killed him. So why in the hell would she stab the guy, apparently hard enough to shove him back into the river, and then hang around until everyone else saw that he was dead? It doesn't make sense."

Hector was silent as he stared out over the river. Finally he said, "Maybe she thought he'd float away?"

I ran the sequence through in my mind, remembering that Messenger's body did wind up a couple of feet downstream. "Hector?" I said.

"Yeah?"

"I hate you. Remind me to never, ever work with you again."

"It kinda makes sense though, huh?"

"Yeah. Too much sense. Anna doesn't run until after Messenger is found dead."

"Well, bro, if it helps any, I still think that Archimedes guy is a good suspect."

"How do you figure that?"

"Well, it was dark, right? And everyone is wearing black robes? Maybe he sneaks around behind that Aurora woman, stabs Messenger while the fireworks are happening, and then says that he gets blood all over himself when he drags the body out of the water? Sounds good, right?"

I shook my head. "Sounds more like a stretch. Especially if he was blinded by the flashes from the explosions like everybody else."

"So maybe he wasn't blinded. So maybe he was the one who threw the explosive stuff into the fire?"

"Except for the fact that Messenger's hands had chemical traces on them, and the fact that we just found a bunch of explosive-type chemicals in his bathroom. So I'm afraid your theory goes boom, too."

"Hey, I'm trying here," Hector said defensively.

"Yeah." I sighed. "Unfortunately, your first theory is the best. At least Anna's dad can afford a good defense lawyer. Looks like she's going to need one."

"So now what?"

I looked over to the water. The sun was on its descending course and falling slowly onto a bed of low black clouds. "Let's get back to the car. I need to get my camera and take some shots of this place while there's still daylight left. Besides, we can drop off Mr. Hanson's glasses to him on the way."

We hadn't quite finished our hike back to my car when my cell phone vibrated. "Wilder here," I answered.

"This is Shirley over at the Rio Vista Motor Lodge. You the guy looking for the chick in 212?" a gravelly female voice asked.

"That's me."

"Well, I just noticed her car's in the lot. You want to see her, you'd best get it in gear."

"I will, thanks."

"Who's that?" Hector asked.

"That, my friend, is an example of how being nice to people pays off. Well, being nice and slipping people money. Sounds like our girl Aurora just came home. Let's go and make her acquaintance, shall we?"

As we picked up our pace heading down the trail toward

the house, Hector said, "I'll bet you twenty bucks this Aurora just puts another nail in Anna's coffin."

The way this case was shaping up, there was no way I'd take that bet.

## CHAPTER TWENTY-TWO

I tossed my keys to Hector as we semijogged back to Messenger's house. While Hector fired the Green Hornet up for takeoff, I rang the front doorbell, and when Hanson appeared I quickly handed him his eyeglasses and took off with a wave as he thanked me. I jumped into the passenger seat of my car, getting a shot of pain in my side in the process, and then Hector launched us down the circular driveway and out into the streets.

After hooking up my seat belt, I opened up my notebook to put some finishing touches on my scribbles. While I was checking my notes, I discovered something we'd missed. "Hey, Hector? Did you see a chalice anywhere around while we were down by the river?"

"Chalice?" he asked. "You mean, like a communion chalice?"

"I guess. According to what I've been told so far, before the so-called ritual, Aurora was given a broom, Archimedes a knife, Hanson had the torch, and Anna Addison was supposed to have been given a chalice. We found all the other things down there, so where's the chalice?"

Hector shrugged, not taking his attention off the road. "Beats me. Maybe it got tossed into the river?"

"Maybe," I said uncertainly. "On the other hand, I found Anna right there at the murder scene the night after it happened. I wonder if she went back there to get the chalice? And if so, why?"

Hector shrugged again. "You're the big-shot detective. You tell me."

I got my cell phone out and called the Midnight office. Uncle Jimmy answered right away. "How's it going on your end?" I asked.

"I was wondering how long you were going to let us sit around waiting for you," he answered. "According to our resident computer geek, Felix, 'looking at movies of smoking-hot naked chicks' isn't a bad way to spend an afternoon. Timmy, on the other hand, just got in a short while ago. He said that he barely escaped an elderly lynch mob."

Uncle Timmy himself then got on the line. "Jesus Christ, Junior. What the hell did you get me into?"

"What happened, Uncle Tim? Did you get in touch with Messenger's former clients?"

"Did I? By the time Mrs. Harrington was done, she had damn near the whole knitting circle at her house, and when these old broads found out that they'd all given Messenger a bunch of money, they were ready to do him in themselves. Looks like Messenger told them all a different story about why he needed to quote-borrow-unquote money. We figured out that all together, he got away with close to a hundred thousand dollars."

I whistled. "Damn."

"You can say that again, Junior. Now I've got all these old babes looking at me and asking what I'm going to do to get their money back. Some of them trusted him with their life savings."

"Oh, crap."

"No kidding. I want to dig the bastard up and kill him my-self. Any clue where the money wound up?"

"No," I said reluctantly. "He sure didn't have it on him when he got killed, and Hector and I just tossed his room, not that the police would have missed that much cash when they did the warrant search the other night."

"Well," Uncle Timmy said, "this is your case, Junior, but I'm telling you, we need to find that money. I don't take kindly to little old ladies getting scammed."

"When are you coming in?" Jimmy asked.

"Hector and I have one more interview to do, then we'll head for home. Did Felix have any luck figuring out where that video was shot?"

"No, but at least I got him to stop drooling. He wants to know if the girl is single."

"Right." I sighed. "I'll be in as quick as I can." I shut my phone. "I'm running out of time."

In response, Hector goosed the car. I stole a look at the speedometer and saw that he had us cruising near ninety on the freeway. I settled into my seat and tried to clear my mind for the interview with the mysterious Aurora.

By the time Hector and I pulled into the parking lot of the Rio Vista Motor Lodge, the sun had almost set, and the amber streetlights cast a wan glow around the area. As we got out of my car, I spotted an older, dark green Jeep Cherokee 4×4 with Arizona plates. "Must belong to our subject," I said, pointing to the vehicle.

As Hector and I reached the top of the motel stairs, I saw that my business card was gone from Aurora's door. I crept up as quietly as the creaking wooden balcony would allow and listened for a moment or two, hearing what I believed to be a television set. I knocked and said, "Ms. Aurora? It's Jason Wilder. I left a card on your door earlier?"

The TV sound faded quickly, and the door opened a couple of inches and stopped at the length of the security chain. I was greeted by a bright green eye and a voice that asked suspiciously, "What do you want?"

"I'm here with Officer Morales to talk to you about the Messenger matter," I said. Hector obligingly held up his badge. The woman said quickly, "Just a minute," and closed the door. When it opened wide, a tall, generously proportioned woman with a mass of wavy reddish hair greeted us. "Come on in," she said with a voice tinged with a southern accent. "Sorry for the mess, but I wasn't expecting company."

She needn't have apologized. The bed was unmade, true, but aside from that, nothing seemed out of place. Besides the cheap furnishings, the only items in sight were a large, battered brown Samsonite suitcase standing by the foot of the bed next to a black nylon shoulder bag. On the single table was an expensive-looking laptop computer with the top down. The room had that cigarettes-and-Lysol aroma that most low-rent motels seem to acquire, while the lone lamp on a nightstand provided marginal light. Aurora, whom I judged to be somewhere in her middle twenties, was dressed in comfortable-looking jeans with a baggy brown sweater. She gave a helpless little flap of her arms and said, "Make yourselves comfortable, if you can."

Hector leaned against the door. I motioned to Aurora to take the one chair and sat myself down on the edge of the bed, moving the suitcase over to make room. "Sorry to barge in on you like this," I said, "but in homicide cases, it's important to talk to people while the events are still fresh in their memory. Are you planning on going somewhere?" I asked, indicating the suitcase.

"Home," she said without hesitation. "Just as soon as I can. I was hoping the detective would call soon to say it's okay to leave."

"Why so suddenly?"

"No reason to stay," she shot back. "Besides, would you stay in a place like this if you didn't have to?"

"Um, probably not."

"Didn't think so," she drawled with a crooked little grin. "I'm starting to wonder now if I'll ever be able to go to sleep without hearing sirens a dozen times a night." More seriously, she said, "With Messenger dead, there's no reason to stick around."

I opened my notebook. Pen poised, I asked, "Your real name is Theodora Carlyle, but you go by Aurora, is that right?"

"Aurora is my spiritual name," she said, a bit defensively.

"I see. Would you tell me about your relationship with Elijah Messenger?"

"I already told one detective," she said shortly.

"I know," I said gently, "but please bear with me."

She sighed. "All right. Go ahead."

"Thank you. Now, about Elijah Messenger?" I prompted.

Aurora looked up briefly, as if searching the top of her head for the answer. "Well," she began, "I was in the process of studying with Messenger. I was doing research."

"What kind of research?"

"For a book about psychic phenomena."

"Oh. Like the book that Messenger wrote? What was that called?"

"*The Illuminated Traveler*," Aurora said flatly.

"Right. I remember now. And how did you come to meet Mr. Messenger?"

"Oh, I'd heard about him a while ago," she said. "When I learned he was here in California, I came out to meet him."

"And he was helping you with your research."

"Yes. That's right."

"Is that why you were invited to the ritual Thursday night?"

"I guess. Messenger just called me up and told me to come out to his house. He didn't tell me why."

"So what happened after you got to Messenger's house?"

"Well," she began slowly, absently twisting a ringlet of her dark red hair as she spoke, "I first saw Bob Hanson there. He told me that Messenger was getting ready to perform an Elemental Ritual. That's one invoking the Spirits of Earth, Air, Fire, and Water. Anyway, after I got there Brandon Archimedes showed up, and we were told to dress for the ritual. Messenger had robes there for us to put on. Anna Addison was already around the house somewhere. After we all get called to the garden, Bob Hanson passes out the tools, then Messenger leads us to the river."

"When you say tools, you mean the broom, chalice, Athame, and torch, right?"

She looked at me sharply. "Yes. I see you've done your homework. Anyway, Messenger leads us to the circle. He does an invocation, lights up the fire in the middle, and then something must have gone wrong, 'cause next thing I know, there's flames and all kinds of noise. Scared the hell out of me, I can tell you that."

"Could you see what the others were doing right then?"

"I couldn't see my hand in front of my face," she countered. "I was blinded. I could hear Anna and Bob scream, and a bunch of loud pops coming from the fire, then I heard a splash. And that was about it. I just sort of crouched there, holding on to that damn broom for dear life. After a bit, I looked around to see where everyone was. I could just see Archimedes to my left, but I couldn't see Messenger. Then I remembered that I heard a splash, so I looked out over the water. There was just enough moonlight that I could see there was something floating out there. I realized it was Messenger."

"You saw him in the water?"

She nodded, and I said, "What happened then?"

"I guess I did some screaming myself. Archimedes went down and got into the water and dragged Messenger out. I could see he was stabbed. That's when Anna took off like a shot, leaving Bob behind. Bob had lost his glasses somewhere and was stumbling around. I went to go help him, and Archimedes called his friend Stone on his cell phone. Then we called the police. But Messenger was dead before we got him out of the water."

"I see. Let me ask you this: Did Messenger try to borrow any money from you recently?"

Aurora looked surprised. "Yeah, he did. When he called me up Thursday, he asked if I could make a loan to him. I told him that I was sorry, but I didn't have any extra money. He was a little rude after that."

"But he still invited you to come out for the ritual?"

"He'd asked me that first."

"Right before Messenger was stabbed, could you see what the others were doing?"

Aurora paused, then said, "Yeah. We were all at our stations in the circle, right where Messenger told us to stand. I was between Messenger and Archimedes, and Bob and Anna were across the fire from me."

"Did you see anyone make a move toward Messenger?"

She shook her head. "No."

"Are you sure? For instance, you're certain Archimedes didn't go around behind your back at any time?"

"Pretty sure. Although . . ."

"Yes?"

She bit her lip, then said, "When Archimedes started to go to where Messenger was floating, he stopped all of a sudden, and I think he threw something off into the bushes. Then he went and got Messenger out of the water."

"Did you see what it was he threw?"

"No."

"Did Messenger ever talk to you about someone threatening him?"

Her eyes narrowed. "What do you mean? Like what?"

"Like sending him Tarot cards with death symbols on them."

"No. Never."

"Okay." I let my pen slip from my hand and bent over to retrieve it, so I could get a good look at the identification tag on the suitcase. I've been trained practically from birth to pay attention to details, and I'd been straining my eyes to get a surreptitious look at the information written on the luggage tag since I sat down.

What I saw surprised me. As I straightened up, I made an obvious move to check my watch. "Whoops. I just remembered something. Would you excuse me for a moment? I need to make a call."

Aurora shrugged, and I got up and went for the door. Hector's dark eyes shot me a questioning look, but he kept quiet as I stepped outside and walked a few doors down out of earshot. I got my phone out and clicked on Roland Gibson's number. "It's your favorite PI," I said when he answered.

"You're only my favorite if you're calling to give me a hot story," he replied. "Other than that, you suck. What have you got for me?"

"A question. What was the name of the girl that Elijah Messenger knew in Arizona? The one who died."

"I don't know offhand. I left my notes back at the office. Wait. It was something unusual."

"Was it Theodora? Theodora Carlyle?"

"Yeah! That was it. Why?"

I looked back toward Aurora's room. "Because for the last fifteen minutes, I've been talking to a ghost."

# CHAPTER TWENTY-THREE

I went back to Aurora's room and knocked. Hector let me in, and I saw that Aurora was sitting still as a statue with her arms crossed. "I have just one more question," I said to her. "Why the masquerade?"

The way her eyes widened as she gave herself a slight hug told me I'd hit the mark. "What do you mean?" she asked in a half whisper.

I sat back down on the edge of the bed, so as not to appear intimidating. "Your name is not Theodora Carlyle," I said gently. "I know for a fact that the real Theodora is deceased."

Aurora's face twisted and her mouth moved, but no words came forth. "Who was she?" I asked her quietly. "The girl who died?"

Aurora shot out of the chair, her face twisting with emotion and drained of blood. *"Bastard,"* she whispered fiercely.

I started to say, "I'm sorry," but Aurora shouted, "Not you. Messenger!" She then turned her back on Hector and me, hugging herself.

Hector was leaning against the door with his arms crossed and his head down, slowly shaking it side to side. I sighed and ran my mind back to that morning, when Roland Gibson told me that Elijah Messenger had influenced a girl in Arizona to sign over her inheritance to him—because Messenger had convinced her that only he could cure her cancer. The tag on the suitcase read M. BARSTOW with an Arizona address. "Aurora" was concealing her name in more ways than one.

Aurora seemed to regain some control of herself. She turned back to me, shaking her head as she said with a sigh, "Teddy. Her name was Teddy."

"Teddy Carlyle?"

"Yes."

"So you are . . . ?"

She didn't answer at first, slowly collapsing back into the chair. Not meeting my eyes, she said quietly, "I'm in trouble, aren't I?"

I kept my mouth firmly shut to keep from answering. Lying to the police, especially during a homicide investigation, certainly would classify as trouble, for starters, but I didn't want to scare the woman into clamming up, or worse, asking for a lawyer. So instead I said, "Well, let's see what we can do to get you out of trouble, okay? To do that, we're going to need you to tell us the truth. Deal?"

Aurora, or whatever her name was, nodded dumbly, letting her red ringlets cover her face. "Okay," I said gently. "Let's start with who you are."

"Melanie Barstow."

"And who is Teddy Carlyle?"

Melanie's head came up and her green eyes, shining with tears, fixed on me as she whispered fiercely, "Teddy was my friend, closer than a sister. Do you know what that's like?"

"Yes."

"Do you? Do you really?" As if unable to contain herself, Melanie jumped up from her chair and stalked to the back wall. Hugging herself again, she said with her back to us, "Teddy and I grew up together. We were going to save the world."

"Care to explain that?"

Melanie's shoulders heaved once, then she turned to face us but kept her eyes on the floor. "Save the world," she repeated. "When we went to college, we both went into the social studies program. Only Teddy got sick and had to drop out and go back home. I stayed in school, hoping the doctors could figure out what was wrong with her. Well, they found out, all right."

"She had cancer?"

Melanie nodded once, still looking down. I noticed that the southern accent had evaporated. "Yeah. I wanted to take time off from my studies, but Teddy wouldn't hear of it. She told me that one of us had to keep going. And . . . and to be truthful, I had a hard time seeing Teddy waste away like she was doing. I guess I didn't have what it took to stay with her."

Melanie Barstow's words seemed to be hanging by a slender, fragile thread, a thread that could break at any moment. "What happened then?" I urged as gently as I could.

"I went back to school in Florida. Teddy and I kept in touch by e-mail. That's when I first heard about Messenger. Teddy wrote and told me all about this wonderful man she met, and how he was teaching her all about healing herself through a spiritual path, or some such crap. I started getting worried. I don't think Teddy was really in her right mind then. She was taking a lot of pain medications, you know? Anyway, I called her mom and asked what was up with this Messenger guy. Teddy's mom really didn't know, but it seemed clear to her that Teddy was acting more hopeful since Messenger started coming around. So we both kind of figured there was no harm in it. No harm." She gave a dark, contemptuous laugh.

"We didn't know at the time that Messenger was working on Teddy, getting her all confused," Melanie continued. "And with the drugs she was on, that wasn't hard to do. Next thing I hear, Teddy quits going to the doctor, all because she believes she's going to be cured. I tried to call her up, but Teddy didn't want to talk to me anymore. The last time I spoke to her, she told me that I didn't understand what was going on, and that soon I'd see. She told me she was going to make a believer out of me when she got her miracle."

Melanie walked slowly back to the single chair and sat down again. "By the time I could get home," she said in a near whisper, "Teddy was back in the hospital and in a coma. She never woke out of it."

The small, shabby room grew quiet, and the spell of Melanie's words seemed to dissipate as the traffic noise of the outside world leaked in. "What did you do then?" I asked.

Melanie shrugged. "After we buried Teddy, more of the story came out. You know what psychic surgery is?"

"No."

Melanie's lips twisted in a grimace. "I didn't either, but I found out. It's an old trick practiced by so-called medicine men in the Philippines. It's supposed to be a miracle cure, but all that really happens is that the medicine man just does some sleight-of-hand with ground meat, making it look like he's magically pulling the cancer right out of a person's body."

"And people fall for this?" Hector asked from behind me.

Teddy looked up. "Oh, yeah. Remember Jim Jones? The guy who had his own cult in Guyana? The one where he convinced all his followers to kill themselves? He used to practice psychic surgery. And Andy Kaufman, the comedian—when he was dying, he flew to the Philippines looking for a miracle cure, but all he found was the usual unscrupulous con man willing to take desperate people's money. Just like Messenger."

"What did you do then?"

"After the funeral, I pieced together what really happened to Teddy. Then her mom and I found out that she signed over her inheritance to Messenger. We went to the police, but they said they couldn't do anything about it, since Teddy was over twenty-one. Teddy's mom filed a wrongful death lawsuit against Messenger, but after he got served, he just relinquished his claim on Teddy's money and disappeared. After that, well, Teddy's mom didn't want to deal with it anymore, so the bastard got away with it. But not as far as I was concerned. I was going to make Messenger pay for what he did."

"And how were you going to do that?"

Melanie looked me in the eye as she said warily, "Oh, I know what you're thinking—and you're right. I wanted to kill him myself. I planned lots of ways to do it, too, but Teddy wouldn't have wanted it that way. So I was going to fix it so that he wouldn't hurt anyone else ever again. I was going to track him down and get the goods on him and expose him to the world as the con artist that he really is. Or was."

"So you went looking for him?"

Melanie shook her head. "Not right away. I spent some time teaching myself all about how people like Messenger did their tricks. I did a lot of study on con artists and learned how they operated. Messenger's not a unique case, not by a long damn shot, and this kind of stuff's been going on forever. Houdini spent the last years of his life exposing fake mediums and spiritualists. Some people think that his death was actually a murder, because he put a lot of scammers out of business."

"So you and Messenger didn't actually meet until you came out here to California?"

"No. I was all set to tell him exactly what I thought of him when he was supposed to show up in court back home, but he skipped out on his appearance. So, like I said, I studied up on him and his kind. I found his book in a used-book store, but that didn't tell me anything new. The book was supposed to be all about Elijah Messenger and his journeys around the world looking for spiritual enlightenment, but the damn thing is nothing but a bunch of made-up crap for suckers. It reads more like a cheap adventure novel. When I found out he was in River City, I came here to try and get close to him. I was going to get the goods on him and expose him for the fraud he is. Was," she corrected herself.

"So that's why you called yourself Aurora?"

"Sure," Melanie said with a shrug. "I was going to do a con to catch a con. I even had some business cards made up. 'Aurora, Psychic Researcher.' Turned out I needn't have bothered. Elijah Messenger apparently fell for my line. He was more than happy to talk to me. That's when I got my first surprise."

"What do you mean?"

Melanie shook her head again, her red curls swaying with the motion. "He was a smooth talker, all right, but the guy didn't know jack about witchcraft or pagan practices or anything he professed to be an expert on. Hell, I'd quote his own book to him and he'd just give me a blank look. But he still managed to fool people."

"People like Anna Addison?"

Melanie made a bitter face. "Messenger's groupie? She's one twisted sister. That little freak was like his personal pit bull. She's the only one who gave me any grief. She threatened to cut me up once, saying I was trying to move in on her territory."

"She said that?" I asked.

"Her words," Melanie confirmed.

I tried to hide my disappointment as I asked, "What about

the rest of the people who were there for the ritual the night Messenger was killed?"

"Ritual?" Melanie said contemptuously. "Now, there's an example of what I was talking about. Messenger didn't know his rituals from a hole in the ground. The timing was all wrong, for one."

"All wrong for what?"

"For anything," Melanie said with a tone of frustration. "For instance, if Messenger was supposed to be doing a ritual according to pagan tradition, it should have either been on October thirty-first for the feast of Samhain, or on December twenty-second for Yule. Hell, it wasn't even a full moon yet."

"Okay," I said, "so Messenger was a little, uh, nontraditional, shall we say. Did Brandon Archimedes ever say anything to you about that?"

"No. That Archimedes guy looked like he was just coming around for kicks. I don't think he took anything Messenger did seriously."

"What about Bob Hanson?"

"Another groupie," Melanie replied. "At least he's a nice enough old fart. He seems like he's the true believer type. Trouble is, he seems to believe in just about everything, from UFOs to the Loch Ness Monster, and he'll take up your whole day talking about any whacko subject you want. I think he's damn near memorized Messenger's book."

"So if you didn't kill Elijah Messenger, who did?"

My question stopped Melanie like a bucket of ice water to the face. Her eyes narrowed as she said slowly, "I don't know."

"What do you know about threatening messages?"

She seemed to sink in her chair a little as she said, "Oh. Those. Those were from me."

"You sent Messenger the Tarot cards and the gold cross? Why?"

"I was getting frustrated," she said. "I was hoping to, I don't know, shake Messenger up a little. Make him make a mistake. I guess I wasn't really thinking. The cross I sent him belonged to Teddy. I gave it to her years ago. I knew it was something Messenger would recognize."

"So, getting back to the night Messenger died, what did you see happen?"

"Not much," Melanie said. "I was really only paying attention to Messenger, wondering what the hell he was up to. When the campfire blew up, I'm afraid I just ducked down until the noise was over. When it got quiet, I thought I'd heard a splashing sound, so I looked at the water. I saw Messenger there. I think I kind of lost it for a moment. I went to the edge of the river, but Messenger was too far out to reach. I remember how cold the river was when my hands touched the water. Next thing I knew, Brandon Archimedes slogged right in and started dragging Messenger back to the shore."

"Did you see anyone else get close to Messenger that night?"

"No. Anna and I were the closest, but I didn't see anyone else get near him."

"Could Archimedes have gotten to Messenger by going around behind you?"

"Maybe," Melanie said slowly. "Maybe. I don't know. Anyway, when we saw that Messenger was dead, Archimedes called his friend on his cell phone. Then we called the cops. I had to go and help Mr. Hanson. He'd lost his glasses, and by that time Anna had taken off."

"Why did you lie to the police and give them a false name?"

Melanie looked down to the floor again, her wavy red hair

falling into a concealing curtain. "Just panic, I guess. It was all like some bad dream. I mean, here I wanted Messenger dead, and all of a sudden, there he was. My wish come true. Only now I was afraid the police would find out how I'd been kind of stalking him and leaving those threatening notes, and I thought they might blame me. So I blurted out Teddy's name and address when the officer asked me for my name that night. Truth is, I wasn't sure what I was going to do to Messenger when I came out to California, so I used Teddy's name when I rented this room."

"Didn't anyone at the crime scene ask to see your ID?" Hector asked.

Melanie gave a wan smile. "Yeah, but I just acted all flustered and told the cop I couldn't remember where my purse was. I wasn't really acting all that much." She bowed her head as she said, "I'm in big trouble, aren't I?"

I resisted the urge to look back at Hector for confirmation as I said, "Well, giving false information to a police officer is bad, especially in a case like this, but I think Detective Navarro might at least understand what drove you to it."

"Actually," Melanie said slowly, "I think it's worse than that."

"What do you mean?"

She looked up and stared me right in the eye as she asked, "What's the punishment for withholding evidence in a murder case?"

# CHAPTER TWENTY-FOUR

I was glad that the light was dim in the shabby little motel room. I was pretty sure that my expression was less than welcoming. "What kind of evidence have you been withholding?" I asked casually.

She didn't answer at once. Then she said, "I've been secretly tape-recording all my conversations with Messenger. Including what happened last Thursday night."

"Wait. Do you mean to say that you've got a tape recording of the murder?"

"Yes."

"What the hell were you thinking?"

"I'm sorry!" she almost shouted. Then, calmer, she said, "Look, I didn't know how much trouble I'd get into for tape-recording people without their knowledge. I mean, I knew it was illegal, but I thought that if I could get something incriminating on Messenger, it'd be okay. I didn't know what was going to happen that night."

"Do you have the tape here?"

She swallowed once before saying, "Yeah. I've been trying to figure out what to do with it. I thought I might be able to just, you know, anonymously drop it off at the police station. On my way out of town."

I sat down again, collecting my notebook and pen. I took

a deep, calming breath, then said, "Okay. You know you're going to have to tell Detective Navarro all of this, right?" She nodded, and I continued, "Good. Now, where is the tape?"

Melanie got up and went to her suitcase. She unzipped it and rummaged around inside, coming up with a microcassette that she handed to me. I saw that she had written the date of the murder on the label. "What's on it?"

"I started taping when we were back at the house. I stopped the tape while we all walked to the river, then started it again when Messenger started speaking."

"Ah. Good. So you got a recording of the whole event."

"Not really," she said almost shyly. "I must have accidentally pulled the microphone plug out after the fire pit started exploding. The tape shuts off right about that point."

*Damn,* I thought. That was inconvenient, to say the least. Or maybe a little too convenient. "So you've listened to this?" I asked.

"Over and over," Melanie said, "but I still couldn't figure out what happened to Messenger."

"Okay. Now, is there anything else you haven't told anyone? Anything else you've been holding back?"

"No. I swear."

I looked over at the open suitcase and saw a paperback book with a black cover and the words *The Illuminated Traveler* in bold red letters. "That's Messenger's book?"

Melanie picked it up and handed it to me, a grimace of distaste on her pale features. "Here. You can take it. I never want to see it again."

I flipped the book open and saw that it was old, with cracks in the spine and pages turned brown and dog-eared. According to the first page, the author was Elijah Messenger, and it was published in 1974 by Golden Goblin Press as "the true tales of a modern-day challenger of the unknown worlds."

"All right," I said. "Are you ready to talk to Detective Navarro?"

Melanie's green eyes widened. "Now?"

"Trust me. It's the best time."

She searched my face for a moment, then nodded. I went to the phone on the desk, found Navarro's card in my wallet, and dialed his number. He didn't take long to answer. "Navarro here."

"Hi, Detective. This is Jason Wilder. I'm over at the Rio Vista Motor Lodge in room 212. There's a lady here you'll want to speak with again."

"Who?"

"You know her as Theodora Carlyle, who was going by the name Aurora, only she's actually Melanie Barstow."

There was a pause on the line, then Navarro said, "Mr. Wilder, have you been drinking?"

"No, sir. I'll let the lady explain it all to you. Hector Morales and I have found what may be evidence. I'll let Hector hold on to it for you."

"Evidence? What evidence? What are you talking about?"

"As I said, I'll let the lady explain. Call me after you've spoken with her and we'll compare notes." Before Detective Navarro could get another word in, I covered up the receiver and said to Melanie, "Okay, just tell everything to the nice detective, and I'm betting you should be able to keep yourself out of trouble, okay? And if you think of anything else, call me. You've got my card." Under normal circumstances, I'd have stuck around to make certain Melanie Barstow gave the good detective the same story she gave me. But I had to hurry to make my own copy of the tape she made.

I handed the phone to Melanie and nodded to Hector. As he and I slipped out the door, I heard Melanie take in a deep breath, like someone about to dive into cold water, and say to Detective Navarro, "Hello, sir? I think I owe you an apology—and an explanation."

The cold night air was an almost welcome change from the claustrophobic closeness of the motel room. As Hector and I marched down the creaking stairs, he said to me, "Okay, so I guess we can scratch her off your suspect list."

"What makes you say that?"

"Well, for one, she came clean with you, didn't she?"

"Yeah. She also has the best reason to kill Elijah Messenger I've heard yet."

As we walked through the parking lot to my Mustang, Hector said, "Oh, yeah? Tell me this, wise guy. If she actually did the killing, then why would she hand over that tape recording to you? Which, by the way, you told Navarro that I was going to keep for him."

"Oh, you'll get the tape. Just as soon as I can make a decent copy. As for letting Aurora/Theodora/Melanie off the hook, you'll note that she said that the tape of the murder stops just a little short. Like maybe at the point where she's stabbing Messenger? Now give me my car keys back."

Hector, albeit reluctantly, tossed me my keys. As I opened the doors, he said, "You're reaching. She didn't get any blood on her that night, remember?"

"Uh-huh. And do you remember the part where she said how cold the water was at the river?"

"Yeah. So?"

"So what if she was washing blood off her hands?"

Hector didn't say another word as I started up the car and pulled out on to the street, aiming for the Midnight office.

When we turned onto Galleon Street, he said, "Okay. Maybe I'll buy your wild-ass theory. So why is she confessing so much now?"

"Sometimes people will admit to small sins when they're caught, thinking that they can still cover up the larger sins. One of the things I've learned in the detective business: When you've found out one lie, be ready to find some more. Also, there's another angle I just thought of."

"What's that, bro?"

"Everyone's been saying that Anna's been looking for something. Something she says belongs to her. I've been assuming that she's been looking for that movie that was already sent to her daddy the mayor. What if she's been looking for something else?"

"Like what?"

"Like what if someone stole her knife, the one that was used to kill Messenger?"

"You're reaching," Hector said. "How do you explain the fingerprint on the knife? You know, the one left in blood?"

"Did I mention that I never want to work with you again?" I responded.

We made pretty good time driving to Midnight Investigations. I parked in the alley next to the stately old Victorian and led Hector in through the side door directly to the War Room, where I was warmly greeted by my fellow investigators.

"What the hell took you so long, Junior?" Tim O'Toole called out from behind his disaster of a desk. "You get lost again?"

"Leaving us to slave away here," Jim Bui added. I was stopped short from making what I'm certain would have been a witty rejoinder by the sight on the screen taking up most of the back wall. Anna Addison, larger than life and completely naked, stared out at nothing with upraised arms, frozen in time.

"You call that working?" Hector asked of no one in particular.

"I'm getting paid," came a voice from the darkest corner. Felix McQuade, long, lean, and dressed in his customary all-black attire, which matched his long black hair, flashed a jack-o'-lantern grin beneath his round purple-tinted glasses. He had his feet up on his desk, which, as usual, looked like someone had blown up a computer and let the parts fall where they might. "Who's the dude?" Felix asked.

I made the introductions. "Felix McQuade, this is my friend Hector."

Felix uncoiled from his corner and came up to shake hands. "Welcome to the asylum, dude."

"Felix is our resident geek," I explained.

"Yeah, I'm slowly bringing the old geezers into the 1970s," Felix added.

"Here," I said as I handed Felix the microcassette I got from Melanie Barstow. "I need a good copy. And be damn careful with that."

Felix held the tape up to the light, peering at it from above his glasses. "Speaking of 1970s technology. So what are you looking for?"

"I want to see if parts of that tape have been intentionally erased. Can do?"

"We'll see," Felix said casually as he strolled to the inner door. We keep a lot of our older equipment in the basement, including stuff to copy tapes and photographs. I set my notebook and attaché case on the round conference table and took off my topcoat and suit jacket. "Okay, what have we got so far?"

"So far," Tim O'Toole said, "I've had to work here under god-awful conditions. How am I expected to get my job done if I'm forced to see naked girls? It's been hell, I tell you."

"I'm surprised you remember what one looks like," Uncle Jimmy said. He was at the phone on the round table, dialing a number. I heard him say, "The pigeons are assembled," as he put the phone on speaker. "Can you hear me now?" he asked.

"Perfectly," came Her Majesty Victoria's voice from the phone. "Hello, boys."

"Hey," Timmy said. "This is just like *Charlie's Angels.*"

"Yeah," I agreed. "Except instead of hot babes, I'm here with a bunch of ugly men. How are things in Santa Teresa, Mom?"

"Just fine, love. I'm in the process of wrapping things up here and should be home soon."

"So you found your artistic thief?"

"Caught 'em and cleaned 'em," Mom responded happily. "This guy had a pretty good little scam going. He had a genuine work of art in his possession. What he'd do was bring out the original for inspection, and then after the sale make a switch with a really good copy. Only this time the trick was on him; I switched the original with the copy he sold my client. With any luck, I'll be out of here before he figures it out. How are things on the Anna Addison case?"

"The case is going great," I said. "The case against her, that is."

"I see," Mom replied. "So what new developments have there been?"

I looked over to Uncle Timmy, who cleared his throat and said, "Well, I've spent my day with Elijah Messenger's sucker brigade. Looks like he hit up every person he knew for money, and he wound up with close to a hundred thousand dollars."

"You can probably add another seven thousand from Anna Addison's credit card," I said. "Oh, and that reminds me. Wait a second." I flipped through my notes and found the typewritten list of clients that Bob Hanson gave me. I walked over to Uncle Timmy and handed him the list. "How does this compare with what you got?"

Tim ran a hand through his wiry gray hair as he looked at my list and compared it with a paper on his desk. "Crap! There's a bunch of names here that I didn't get, but all of the old gals I talked to today are here. Where did you get this, Junior?"

"From Elijah Messenger's assistant. So, I take it there could be even more missing money involved?"

Uncle Timmy rolled his eyes. "Looks like I got a few more people to talk to."

"You know," Hector said, "there could be another explanation for the seven grand that Anna Addison got her hands on."

"What's that?" I asked.

"Maybe she knew she'd need that money to make a run for it. Like right after she killed someone?"

I regarded Hector bleakly as I said, "That's it. You're fired."

"Pay no attention, Hector dear," Her Majesty stated grandly. "It's certainly a point worth consideration. And what of you, James?"

Uncle Jimmy folded his arms and said, "Felix and I reviewed the video starring Anna Addison. I think Felix said it best when he called it 'fairly crappy porn.' "

Like everyone else in the room, I was staring at Anna's image on the wall. With her long black hair in bangs and her exotic eyes, she looked like an Aztec priestess in the middle of a sacrifice. "Can I get a better view of the knife she's holding?" I asked.

"Sure," Jimmy said. He picked up a remote and Anna's image shifted frame by frame until the knife was in the picture, held in both her hands. I found my photograph of the knife from the coroner's file and took it with me as I went over to the screen. The hilt of the knife, with its twin-snake-shaped guard, was a perfect match.

"Looks like Anna's holding the same knife that was used to kill Messenger," I reported.

"Any clue as to where or when the movie was made?" Mom asked.

"No," Jimmy replied. "Not yet. Felix was able to enhance the background somewhat, but it's still pretty dark."

"And the sound track sucks," Felix said as he returned to the War Room. He tossed me the microcassette. "Here. I made a copy on digital tape."

I handed the original cassette to Hector, who carefully placed it in an inside jacket pocket. "What do you mean, the sound track sucks?" I asked. "I could hear everything that was said the first time I saw the movie."

Felix shook his head. "Not the dialogue, the sound track. You know, the music?"

"Music? What music?"

"That's what I mean," Felix said. "You can barely hear it."

"Show me," I said.

Felix went back to his desk, saying, "I had to isolate the music from the dialogue. It's almost like background noise. There." Suddenly there was a loud hissing sound that almost covered up the faint rhythmic beat of drums. I closed my eyes and could barely make out a kind of syncopated shouting.

Then I realized I'd heard something like this very recently.

"Club Tantalus," I said.

"What was that, Jason?" Mom's voice asked.

"Club Tantalus," I repeated. "The music. I heard music like

this when I was at the nightclub that Brandon Archimedes owns."

"The club down in Old Town?" Mom asked.

Jim Bui's hand slapped down on the round table like a pistol shot. "That's it!" he shouted. "Old Town!"

The sudden outburst from the normally cool and collected Jim Bui took everyone by surprise. "What the hell are you talking about?"

Uncle Jimmy's face took on a cast of wicked cunning. "I know where this little movie of yours was shot," he said darkly. Jimmy slowly walked toward Anna's frozen image as he said, "Someone took this girl down to the Under City."

# CHAPTER TWENTY-FIVE

What the hell is the Under City?" I asked the room.

Uncle Jimmy opened his mouth, but Mom's voice from the speakerphone beat him to the draw. "It's one of the more polite terms for the tunnels and catacombs that run under the streets of Old River City. The underground is an absolute maze in some parts."

"You're kidding," I said. "Who would build such a thing?"

"It wasn't exactly planned that way, partner," Uncle Jimmy said in his best cowboy drawl. "Back in the late 1860s, River City was damn near wiped out in a flood. After that little event, the main city and the docks were built up right on top of the original foundations. Most of what used to be rooms on the first floor became basements, but a lot of these areas were just sealed off. Later, all those abandoned parts came in handy. Anytime people needed a private place to conduct a little illegal business, all they had to do was set up shop underground. At one time or another, there were brothels, opium dens, and even speakeasys all just a few feet below the main streets."

Hector said, "Huh. You'd think the cops back then would have figured that out."

Tim O'Toole barked a laugh. "God, you kids are naive."

Mom cut in. "What Timothy is trying to say is that historically the River City police always knew what was going on, but in most cases they were paid to look the other way."

Jimmy grinned. "Hell, in some cases, they ran the businesses."

"What's pertinent to us," Her Majesty continued, "is the fact that someone may have used one of the abandoned tunnels or cellars to make that bizarre movie with the mayor's daughter, and that someone then took the trouble to send a copy to the mayor. Jason, you say you've spoken to the owner of Club Tantalus?"

"Oh, yeah. Brandon Archimedes. A dark and sinister man if there ever was one."

"Really?" Mom's voice was tinged with amusement; she got my Peter Pan reference. "Well, then, gentlemen, I believe a visit to Club Tantalus is in order."

"For two reasons," I added. "One of the witnesses in the Messenger matter works for Archimedes, a parolee named Maurice Phillips, also known as Stone. Archimedes said he'd have him contact me today, but so far, he's been a no-show. There's a good chance he'll be working at the club tonight."

"Hell of a way to spend Saturday night," Uncle Timmy groused quietly.

Felix McQuade, who had been unusually quiet throughout, suddenly burst in with, "Can I go, too? Huh? Can I? You guys are gonna need me."

"Need you?" Timmy snorted. "What for? Bait for the giant rats?"

"Aw, come on. Underground tunnels and stuff? This is gonna rock! Wait. Did you say rats?"

"Uh-huh," Timmy confirmed. "Big ones. Size of goddam pit bulls."

"Forget that," Felix muttered as he shook his head and returned to his desk.

Mom's voice said, "We're going to need to check the city property records to see what part of Old Town Mr. Archimedes owns. That'll give us a clue as to where to start looking."

Uncle Jimmy hurried to his desk and slid into his chair. "I'm on it," he said as his fingers flew across his computer keyboard.

I was just about to bring Mom up to speed on my interview with Melanie Barstow when the phone on my desk rang. "Midnight Investigations, Jason Wilder speaking," I answered.

"Well," Detective Navarro said, "do you have any other little surprises for me today?"

I cupped the phone in my hand to keep the good detective from overhearing any of our plans. "Why, hello, Detective Navarro," I said for the benefit of the room. "How did your talk with Ms. Barstow go?"

"It was informative," he said neutrally. "How did you get her to cough up who she really was?"

"Um, could we just say I'm a good investigator and leave it at that?"

He laughed. "I'll have to give you the benefit of the doubt on this one. Is Officer Morales still with you?"

"Yes, sir."

"And he has custody of the tape recording Ms. Barstow made?"

"He does."

"Have you listened to it?"

"No, sir. I haven't played it," I said truthfully. I didn't bother Detective Navarro with the fact that I'd had Felix make a copy of the recording.

"Okay. Good. Put Officer Morales on the phone."

"Sure. Oh, before I go, Hector and I were over at the crime scene today. I think there's something missing from it."

"Something missing? Like what?"

"Supposedly Anna Addison was given some kind of chalice to hold during the ritual. I didn't see it there."

"Oh." Navarro sounded relieved. "No mystery there. We have it. When I found out that Ms. Addison held that object, I had the crime lab people take it for fingerprinting. The prints matched on both the chalice and the murder weapon."

"Oh. I see."

"There was something else, too," Navarro said. "There was residue inside the chalice. I got a report from the lab that said there were traces of Rohypnol found inside the cup."

"Say what now?"

"Rohypnol," Navarro repeated. "Otherwise known as the date-rape drug. It causes people to lose both their inhibitions and their memory. Evil stuff. It keeps showing up around town in clubs and bars."

I found myself looking up at the wild-eyed image of Anna Addison. "Really," I said. "That's interesting. You say that you find this stuff in local clubs?"

"Don't you watch the news?" Navarro asked, almost irritably.

"I guess not, sir. Here's Hector." I waved Hector over and handed him the receiver. He rolled his eyes at me with a forlorn look. From that point on, Hector's part of the conversation consisted of saying "yes, sir" repeatedly. Finally he hung up the phone. "Navarro says I need to get myself over to South River headquarters and book this tape into the property vault pronto. So what's the plan, guys?"

Jim Bui checked his watch. "It's a little after six now. I

guess the question is, when's the best time to go skulking around this nightclub?"

"I guess sometime around ten tonight," I said. "We may need the music from the club to help us home in on wherever it was they shot this video."

Timmy nodded. "Makes sense."

I tossed Hector my car keys, then sent my company credit card sailing after them. "Take my car, and while you're at it, get it gassed up and then take your wife out for a nice dinner. Least I can do for keeping you out late tonight. Just meet us back here before ten."

"Okay," Jim Bui said. "In that case, I'm off to see my own wife. See if she remembers who I am."

Tim O'Toole got up and slung his coat over his shoulder. "Me, too," he announced.

"You're not married," I reminded him.

"Yeah, but I'm sure there's someone's wife I can go see," he replied.

"Okay, boys," Mom's voice said. "Just be careful. Oh, and Felix?"

Felix looked up from his desk, as if answering a voice from above. "Yeah?"

"Kindly erase all the copies you've made of Anna Addison's movie. Do it now, and I won't have to hurt you later. Jason? Don't forget to take care of Beowulf. Good-bye, boys."

Felix's glasses slipped down his nose as his eyes bugged out. "How in the hell does she do that?" he said wonderingly.

" 'Cause she's the best, dumb-ass," O'Toole answered him with a grin. Felix frantically typed on his keyboard, no doubt nuking all the file copies he'd made. He then stood up and grabbed his long black trench coat. "I'm outta here," he announced as he took off as if the devil were behind him.

All at once, I had the whole War Room to myself. Not entirely, I corrected myself. I had the projected picture of Anna Addison to keep me company. "So what the hell have you been doing all day?" I asked her frozen image. "You sure haven't been calling me. While we're on the subject, did you really murder Elijah Messenger? And if so, why? Money? Looks like you sure needed seven thousand dollars in a hurry. Who did you give that money to? Or, like Hector suggests, did you keep it? What have you been looking for? Old Bob Hanson said you wanted to look around the house for something. Was it that knife you misplaced? You know, the one that wound up inside Messenger? By the way, kid, it's pretty sloppy form to kill someone and then leave your fingerprints behind. In blood, no less.

"And speaking of Hanson," I continued, "why couldn't he be the murderer? Maybe he found out that Messenger was getting ready to split, and he resented being left behind? Or maybe he knew about all that money Messenger gathered together and wanted it for himself? People have been killed for less. A lot less.

"Then there's Brandon Archimedes. If we're right, then he has a lot more involvement with things than he's letting on about. Did you and Messenger really make that little movie at Club Tantalus? And if so, who shot the video? Let's not forget the fact that Archimedes seems to like sharp, pointy objects like knives and swords. Like the one he admitted he gave to you, Anna. The one that wound up inside Messenger. And for a guy who was found with Messenger's blood literally on his hands, he's been acting pretty damn calm about everything. What about his boy, Stone? Why hasn't he called? Is he just being a butthead, or does he have something to hide?

"And let's not forget that jealous boyfriend of yours, Anna baby. What was his name again? Raven? No, Hanson said you also called him Harold. Was he there at Club Tantalus when I got my ribs kicked in and Detective Banks lost her gun? Is he hiding out with you? Where exactly was he the night Messenger was killed? Somewhere close by?"

My eyes fell on the tape that Felix had made for me, the copy of the audio recording Aurora made during the ritual-turned-homicide. "And that brings us to Aurora/Theodora/Melanie," I said out loud. "There's a woman who has proper motivation to murder. Nothing like a little revenge for a loved one to bring out the worst in people. Not to mention the fact that she tried to cover up her true identity. Let's see what this tape has to offer, shall we?"

I picked up the tape, took it over to Felix's desk, found the stereo system hookup, and fired it up. I cranked the volume, and soon the War Room was filled with the hiss and hum of the tape's background noise. I closed my eyes, trying to picture what the scene at the river would have looked like, placing Messenger, Archimedes, Aurora, Hanson, and Anna in their stations around the fire pit. Messenger's voice appeared, saying, "All are gathered. Spirits of Fire, Spirits of Air, Spirits of Water, Spirits of Earth. I summon thee all. Darksome night and shining moon, I call thee to create the path and open the gate!"

As soon as Messenger said "gate," there was a loud *crack-whomph* sound from the tape, followed by rapid popping noises. Then a scream, a sound echoed by another, possibly from Anna, while a voice that may have been Archimedes shouted "Jesus!" followed by what was surely Hanson calling out, "I can't see!" Then there was some rustling noise, possibly just Aurora's microphone rubbing against cloth. Then the tape went dead.

*Shortly after that, so did Messenger,* I thought. I played the tape a couple of times, but I couldn't glean any new information from it. Either Melanie Barstow was telling the truth when she said that the microphone malfunctioned, or she deliberately shut off the recorder at that point or later erased it.

I sank down in one of the chairs at the round table, causing my side to sharply remind me that I was overdue for some painkilling medication. I was also tired and hungry. I surveyed the table with my notes and reports spread out, thinking I really should be spending the time getting my case notes into some kind of order.

Screw it. I needed a break. I reached for the phone and dialed my favorite telephone number. The sound of Jenny Chance's voice answering did wonders for me. "Hello, beautiful," I said. "How are my two favorite girls doing?"

"Hello, Sherlock," she replied. "I was just asking Angelina why the two of us were sitting here alone on a Saturday night. You going to come over and rescue us?"

"God, I'd love to, but I'm stuck at the office. I lent my car to Hector, and I'm going out later tonight. Besides, I've been left in charge of taking care of the dog."

"Poor Beowulf," Jenny said. "You say you're going out later? Where?"

"Back to Club Tantalus."

"I'm not sure I like the idea of you going back there without me to look out for you," Jenny said seriously. "You didn't do too well the last time you were there."

"Not to worry," I said reassuringly. "I'm taking my own private army with me."

"Your mom's going with you?"

"No. She's still down in Santa Teresa."

"Then I'm worrying."

"Relax. I'll be in the company of three of the most dangerous men I know."

"Dangerous to whom? Yourselves? Look, let me call Uncle

Bruce and see if he can come and sit with Angelina. Then I'll—"

"No way," I interrupted her quickly. "Besides, I've got everything under control."

"I'm sure the captain of the *Titanic* said the very same thing. How much longer do you think you'll be working on this case?"

I sighed. "It looks like I've got a Monday morning deadline, whether I've got my investigation completed or not. So I'm kind of on the clock here."

"Why not do what the good detectives do," Jenny said. "Throw a dinner party and invite all the suspects. Then you cunningly question them until the real murderer reveals himself. It's what Nick Charles would do."

"Who's Nick Charles?"

"He's the detective in *The Thin Man*. He has a beautiful wife named Nora. They solve crimes together."

I laughed despite myself. "Dinner party, you say? Well, seeing as how the prime suspect in my case, who also happens to be the person we're working to clear, has disappeared, I'm afraid a dinner party is out of the question."

"Hmm. Well, then perhaps you should just work on getting the beautiful wife. Speaking of dinner, have you had yours yet?"

"No."

"Men," she said. "Very well, rather than have you endanger yourself, not to mention your mother's kitchen, Angelina and I will come to the rescue."

"You're my heroes," I said, heartfelt.

I hung up the phone, feeling much better and with hopeful anticipation, until I looked up at the frozen image of Anna Addison plastered on the wall.

I gave her a rude gesture and shut off the projector.

# CHAPTER TWENTY-SIX

As Saturday nights go, mine started out exceptionally well.

Jenny and Angelina came over, bearing edible gifts, and for the first two hours I was fed in both body and soul as Beowulf and I enjoyed the company of my favorite ladies. As I watched the pair of them fixing dinner in the kitchen, I found myself thinking, not for the first time, that a man would be fortunate indeed to be part of a family with Jenny and Angelina. It almost made me want to track down Jenny's ex-husband and thank him for being so incredibly stupid as to lose them.

Then the time came for Jenny to take Angelina home, and I was left to prepare for my late-night visit to Club Tantalus. While I waited for the boys to show up, I amused myself by reading parts of Elijah Messenger's book. It was grand entertainment, in its own bizarre way. According to the story, Elijah Messenger was some kind of metaphysical Indiana Jones, traveling all over the world and uncovering ancient secrets. I had just finished the chapter where he single-handedly located a lost tribe of Xinca warriors somewhere in South America and was greeted by them as a kind of god when Hector Morales arrived and I had to reluctantly put the book down. Tim O'Toole and Jim Bui showed up soon after, and the four of us took the Midnight Investigations company van down to Old Town.

We had to park the War Wagon, as Uncle Timmy once dubbed our roving surveillance vehicle, over a block away. The Saturday night crowd was out in force. People were walking into and out of the restaurants and bars while a slow, seemingly endless parade of cars shuddered across the cobblestones, serenaded by the various styles of music, from electric blues guitar to jazz piano to salsa, each vying with the others.

"Which way?" Uncle Jim asked.

"Down to Front Street on the corner of First," I said.

As the four of us crossed the cobblestone street to the plank sidewalks of Old Town, a heady feeling took hold of me. It was a potent mixture: anticipation of the job ahead of us coupled with being in the company of truly dangerous men. Uncle Jim, the Old West history buff, collected statistics on gunfighters and badmen the way some people do on baseball players. While we walked along the creaking wooden planks, I was reminded of the story he told me about the gunfight at the OK Corral, and for a moment I wondered if this was how the Earp brothers and Doc Holliday felt as they walked the mean streets of Tombstone toward their appointment with destiny.

We four must have sent out some kind of subliminal wave ahead of us; people on the covered sidewalk parted to let us pass. Of course, Uncle Jim in his long black coat, suitable for concealing shotguns, and Uncle Tim with his black windbreaker and watch cap over his silver curls looked like stereotypical muggers, so that might have had something to do with it.

I led my crew to the corner of Front Street, stopping them just shy of the turn. "Club Tantalus is just around the corner,"

I said. At this range, I could have found the place with my eyes closed. The raucous sound of industrial heavy metal rock was drowning out the far more melodious music of the other establishments. "One of you guys take a look at the front of the club and see if you can spot the bouncer at the door," I said.

Timmy O'Toole shrugged and stepped around. Standing on tiptoe, he said without taking his eyes away, "I can see a big ugly bald guy at the door. Wearing a dog collar. He a special friend of yours?"

"Stone," I said. "He's a naughty boy. He was supposed to call me today."

Timmy rejoined the gang. "You want to talk to him now? Or do we case the joint first?"

"Let's look around for now," I said. "I just wanted to know if he was here tonight."

"Your call," Jimmy said. "Follow me." He turned and led us back down the sidewalk and around into the first alley we came to. "Tell me what you see," he said to me.

I peered through the alley, seeing that it was wide enough to drive a car through. Across the way, I could see the lights of Second Street. The backsides of the old brick buildings seemed unevenly finished, with odd alcoves here and there. "That's funny," I said. "The alley curves downward, then up again before it gets to the street on the other side."

Jimmy nodded. "Right around the bottom of the curve there is the original ground level. Everything up here at street level has been built up since the 1860s. Come on," he said as he stepped into the darkening alleyway.

The sounds of Old Town faded away rapidly as we trooped downhill on the stone-paved pathway, and the air grew still and somehow even colder. Jimmy and Timmy, taking the lead, lit flashlights and swept the area in front of us. Before setting out on tonight's excursion, I'd equipped myself with an old Maglite I found down in the basement supply cabinet back at the office. It was a dual-utility device; not only would it provide excellent illumination, but it was big enough and sturdy enough to double as an impact weapon. Uncle Timmy had made sure I knew lots of ways to use it.

Clicking on my own light, I saw that the wall to my right showed the outline of what must have once been a window, now sealed off with bricks and mortar of a slightly different color than the rest of the wall. Up ahead I saw a sharp corner.

"Bottom floor," Uncle Timmy said in a whisper. "Now, let's see if there's a back door."

Suddenly a light shot out from around the corner, spearing Jimmy in the face. His right arm was a blur and his coat seemed to whip up like the wing of a giant bird as his hand went for his gun.

"Hold it, cowboy," came a sharp command.

We all froze in our tracks. There was no mistaking that voice.

Stepping from around the corner and into the beam of Timmy's flashlight, Her Royal Majesty Victoria Wilder appeared as if out of nowhere. "Hello, boys. You're late," she chided. "A girl could freeze to death down here."

Hector recovered from the shock first, laughing quietly.

"Not that we're not happy to see you or anything, but jeez!" I said. "What the hell do you think you're doing, scaring us like that?"

"Damn straight," Jimmy grumbled.

"Aren't you supposed to be in Santa Teresa?"

In the reflected glow, Mom smiled her predatory best. "I was, but I decided that I might be needed here, so I arranged to fly back right after our phone conversation. I'll have to head back there before too long and tie up some loose ends, but this little jaunt sounded too good to miss."

I noticed that Her Majesty was ready for trouble and had her custom-made leather shoulder bag with her, the one that put Batman's utility belt to shame.

"We were just looking for the back door," Timmy explained.

"I already found it," Mom said. "Over here." She faded into the darkness, and the rest of us followed her, with Uncle Timmy lighting up the area. "Watch your step," Mom cautioned. The trash obviously didn't get picked up on a regular basis down here. I was watching where I stepped when I heard Uncle Jimmy utter, "Aha."

I looked up and saw a large, dark metal door, somewhat tarnished, set into the wall down a three-step set of stairs. Twinkling back through the light was the reflection off a new-looking dead-bolt lock just above the dark metal door-knob.

"How do we know this is the right spot?" Hector asked.

Mom beckoned me. "Jason, place your ear right to the door. Tell me what you hear."

I did as instructed, gingerly resting the side of my head against the door. The metal was ice cold; I hoped my ear wouldn't freeze solid. I could feel more than hear the deep, driving rhythmic thump and faint wails of the music of Club Tantalus. "I can hear the music from the club," I said. "We've got to be close to it."

Uncle Timmy came down beside me, holding his light close to the lock on the door. "This ain't no emergency exit, neither," he muttered.

"Hopefully your analysis is slightly better than your grammar," Mom said. "Can you get it open?"

"Let's see. You hold the light, Junior," he said. "I'll operate." He handed his flashlight to me and reached into his jacket to produce a flat black leather wallet that held a selection of slim lock picks and associated tools. Tim learned the fine art of breaking and entering when he did a stint as a burglary detective back in his career as a River City policeman, and he later taught the craft to me. I watched as he chose a torsion wrench and a hook pick and set to work.

I'm not certain how many minutes had passed, with Uncle Timmy swearing under his breath as he labored at the lock, when Uncle Jimmy said, "While we're still young, Houdini."

"Too late for that in your case," Timmy grunted, his attention still on the lock. Eventually he stood up and shook out his hands. "Damn. That one was a bear. Okay, who's on first?"

"Hold it," Mom commanded. "Let's secure this area first. Timothy, you'll stay here in the alley. James, you get back up to the street and keep a lookout for anyone that might head our way. I'll take Jason and Hector in with me."

"Huh?" Timmy said. "I think it's better if I go in with you."

"For once, I agree with Tim," Uncle Jimmy said. "You're better off with us coming along."

"Thanks for the offer, boys," Mom said, "but as the woman who signs your paychecks, I get the deciding vote. Get moving."

There was some under-the-breath grumbling from the Terrible Twins, but they didn't delay. Jimmy marched back up the alley as Uncle Timmy stepped aside. Mom nodded to me to open the heavy door, and I obligingly put my shoulder to it and prepared to give it a shove.

Hector said softly, "Uh, I hate to bring this up, but is this legal?"

"Good question, Hector dear," Mom said, "and the answer is, probably not. All the abandoned tunnels and chambers down here are supposed to have been sealed off by the city. On the other hand, our client in this particular case happens to be the mayor of River City. I'd imagine that His Honor certainly wouldn't have a problem with our little nighttime excursion if it can shed any more light on his daughter's activities of late. Does that help?"

"Okay," Hector muttered uncertainly.

With my shoulder to the iron door, I leaned inward, getting a silent reminder from my injured side to take it easy. There was a responding groan and screech from the old metal hinges as the door slowly gave way, venting a gust of foul-smelling air and making me feel like we were breaking into an ancient tomb. I had a sudden regret that I had insisted on being the first one through the door. I held my breath and leaned around the opening for a quick look inside. The beam of my light revealed a narrow corridor with a low, arched ceiling, all made out of old, dark brick. For a moment, it appeared that the corridor came to a dead end, but with a second look I could see what appeared to be a T-shaped intersection at the end of the hall.

"Well, are you going to stand around all night?" Timmy asked impatiently from behind me. I gave the door a final shove and got it open far enough for us to enter one at a time. I crept inside. Cold as it was, I unbuttoned my coat for quick access to my revolver. I heard Mom and Hector coming into the hall behind me. And now I could faintly hear the thumping bass of the music coming from Club Tantalus.

We walked down the tunnel-like hall until we came to the intersection. I shot my light left and right. I could see that the corridor continued in both directions, but where the path to the left seemed to end at a brick wall, the way to the right stopped with what looked like a black curtain about twenty feet away. As I edged my way toward it, I could see a jagged, man-sized opening in the wall at my right, as if someone had broken through it at one time. I aimed my light around the corner, and what I saw made me stop in my tracks.

"What the hell is this place?" Hector whispered.

The area opened to a chamber of horrors. Everywhere my flashlight beam touched, another ugly object was revealed: a rough-looking wooden stockade with a heavy padlock. A black metal frame with handcuffs and chains dangling from it. A table covered with what looked like whips and flails. Something that looked like a wooden bed frame with black leather straps crisscrossing where a mattress would be. Almost against my will, I was drawn into the room, my companions close behind me. I saw that the floor was covered in what appeared to be canvas. Overall there was a musty, sour smell, the composition of which I didn't want to know.

"Jesus Christ," Hector breathed. "What the hell is this place?" he repeated.

"More important," Mom said grimly, "who decked this place out?"

I saw a pair of standing black metal torches, matching the one I'd seen earlier in the garden in Messenger's house. Between the two torches, the canvas on the floor held a dark, uneven stain. Remembering the movie Anna Addison starred in, I wondered if this was the spot where she had posed with the knife. And if so, then where would the camera have been?

I stepped around the dark stain on the floor until I was between the standing torches. Shooting my light at the wall, I raised the beam. It revealed a dark, plastic-looking box affixed to the wall near the ceiling. I could trace a twisted braid of black wires from the box across the ceiling until they disappeared around the corner of the jagged entrance to this room. I put my light back on the box. "That's it, I bet," I whispered. "The camera must be inside that thing. Probably along with a microphone."

Just then I heard the background music from Tantalus get louder—and Mom's urgent whisper. "Someone's coming."

# CHAPTER TWENTY-SEVEN

I clicked off my flashlight. Silently I moved it to my left hand and gripped my revolver with my right.

There was a sudden flapping sound as someone else's light stabbed in, followed instantly by the sight of the light as it went cartwheeling into space. I heard a hollow, metallic clatter that came simultaneously with the liquid grunt of a human body being dropped forcefully to a hard surface. "Lights, please," I heard Her Majesty request.

I flicked my flashlight on; it was followed immediately by illumination from a bare lightbulb overhead. I blinked and saw a black-clad, bald-headed bundle at Mom's feet. She had her prey's arm locked in a pain-inducing hold and a booted foot pressed into his neck. Hector was crouched at the other side of the entrance, sidearm out and ready to go. "Well, now," Mom cooed. "Who do we have here?"

I looked down. Stone's pain-twisted and floor-mashed features greeted me. "Hello there, Stone. Long time no see," I said.

His growl of response suddenly changed to a muted shriek as Mom put more torque in his arm. Along with his flashlight, Stone had also brought an aluminum baseball bat to the party. I picked it up from where it had landed and asked, "Just what were you intending to do with this?"

The heavy rubberized curtain that blocked the far entrance to the chamber revealed Brandon Archimedes. "He was sent to deal with trespassers," he said.

Archimedes was dressed in high style this evening, all in black that looked to be velvet in this harsh light. "Ah, Mr. Archimedes," I said. I tossed the baseball bat behind me. "I was wondering when you'd make an appearance."

"Mr. Archimedes, I don't believe we've been introduced yet," Mom said civilly. She released her hold on Stone and dusted her gloved hands. Hector pulled Stone roughly to his feet, keeping a grip on his arm.

"Who the hell are you?" Archimedes demanded.

"My name is Victoria Wilder. I'm the chief of the Midnight Investigation Agency. By the way, as far as the accusation of trespassing goes, I'd say everyone present is guilty of that."

"What do you mean?" Archimedes demanded. "I own these premises."

"And just what do you call this place?" Mom asked.

Archimedes drew himself up. "This, madam," he said sternly, "is a private area for certain special guests and their entertainment."

Mom made a dismissive wave of her hand. "Oh, I can see how 'special' it is, Mr. Archimedes. Are your guests aware that their little entertainments are being recorded?" Mom took a step closer to Archimedes, and as she did, his tall frame seemed to diminish. "This is where you made that vile little movie of Anna Addison, isn't it?"

Archimedes' eyes flashed. "I had nothing to do with that! That was all Elijah Messenger's doing!"

"Oh, come now," Mom said reasonably. "Surely you must have known all about it? After all, you've already said this is your private playground, and someone had to run the camera, now didn't he?"

For a moment, I thought that Archimedes was going to make a run for it, the way his eyes flicked back and forth as if looking for a way out. Mom was now between him and the exit, though, and she looked as immovable as a marble statue. "It's best if you tell us all you know," Mom said in a voice laden with sweet poison. "Because at this point, it's looking very bad indeed for you."

"What . . . what do you mean?" he stammered.

"Try this on for size," I said. "Messenger and you concoct a scheme to get Anna Addison, the daughter of the mayor of River City, to be filmed in a, shall we say, politically indiscreet way. That movie would be worth a lot of money to either the mayor or his political opponents. Only you get greedy and kill Messenger to keep all the money yourself."

Archimedes' face had gone white. "Kill!" he choked out. "I did no such thing!"

"So how can you explain that Messenger was killed with the knife that showed up in Anna's movie? A knife that you admitted you gave to her? And the fact that you were the only one who had Messenger's blood on your hands when he was killed? Looks pretty convincing from here."

"That's not what happened," Archimedes said in a coarse whisper. "We, Elijah and I, did make the movie. I thought that it might be good insurance, you know? In case I ever needed a, shall we say, political favor? But I didn't do anything with it, I swear."

"Who delivered a copy of the movie to the mayor's office?" Mom asked.

Archimedes' head sank, as if it were suddenly too heavy for his neck to hold up. "I did. I . . . I thought the mayor should know what his daughter's been up to."

"More likely you wanted the mayor to know that someone had the tape," Mom stated. "You didn't have to send any kind of blackmail note just then. That could come later, if you needed it to. For instance, if you wanted the mayor to exert some influence over the police."

"Which still makes you look like a damn good suspect to me," I added.

That drew a baleful look from Archimedes. Mom continued, "You admit to helping Elijah Messenger make that movie of Anna. You admit to delivering a copy of the movie to the mayor. You have admitted previously that the murder weapon used to belong to you. I have to agree with Jason. It looks bad for you."

Archimedes' eyes narrowed. "So you say," he said in a low, dangerous tone.

Mom smiled. "So, here's what you are going to do: You will dismantle your little playground here completely—and believe me when I say I'll send someone to make certain that happens. Second, you will destroy all, and I mean all, tapes of anything that ever went on down here. Consider that your early Christmas present to your 'special friends,' the fact that their little indiscretions won't be shared with others."

"Who are you to dictate to me?" Archimedes said with a flash of anger.

"The woman who would be more than happy to march right out of here and report all of this to the local papers. Just imagine what the *Clarion*'s front page would look like, your picture right there, of course, and the story of River City's Underground Vice King?"

That was my cue. I'd brought along most of the contents of my briefcase for tonight's excursion, including my flat little camera. I slipped it out of my pocket and said, "Smile," as I popped off a quick snapshot of Archimedes. I was pretty sure I caught him with his mouth open. I made a slow turn, shooting half a dozen pictures of all the torture chamber furnishings. In the stark overhead light, what had appeared scary and foreboding by flashlight now just looked tawdry and cheap and somehow sad, in a way I couldn't quite put into words.

When I finished my photo shoot, I looked over to Stone, glaring silently at me as he stood alongside Hector. "And you," I said to him, "I thought you were supposed to call me? Tell me now, what did you see and hear the night Elijah Messenger was killed?"

"I didn't see nuthin'," Stone answered sullenly.

"Tell them about the man with Anna," Archimedes prompted.

Stone's face took on a cast of animal cunning. "Oh, yeah," he said. "That guy."

"What guy is this?" I asked.

"That night," Stone began, "when I got the call from my boss to get my ass out to the river, I passed two people comin' the other way. The first one I think was Anna."

"Okay," I said carefully. "And the second person?"

He shrugged. "It sounded like a big guy. I could hear him huffing loud while he was running. And he was wearing a lot of chains or something. You could hear it jingling."

"He was running with Anna? Not chasing her or running from her?"

Stone just flexed his shoulders again. "I dunno. I just know I passed two people when I ran down to the river. That's all."

I looked to Archimedes. "Any clue as to who this second person might be?"

Archimedes was composed again. He said offhandedly, "No idea. Maybe the real killer?"

Mom had taken out her phone. "Timothy, it's me," she said. "We're coming out now. Give us a light, please." To Archimedes, she said, "Remember what I told you."

"I think you should know," Archimedes said, "that you have made an enemy of me tonight."

Mom laughed like she'd just heard a not particularly funny joke and was trying to be polite. "Oh, be serious," she chided. "You'll have to work a lot harder to even graduate to the level of annoying pest in my book." With that, she turned on her heel and left, taking Hector in tow. I walked past Archimedes, holding his gaze while he silently radiated hatred.

Once back in the narrow tunnel, I followed Mom and Hector to the alleyway exit, resisting the urge to look back. Timothy was lighting our way from ahead, and when I finally got clear of the claustrophobic hallway, I welcomed the slight but cleansing breeze that flowed through the alley. As Timmy pulled the iron door shut behind us, he said, "What the hell went on in there?"

Mom took a deep breath. "Later. Let's get back to the street." We made a procession uphill through the alley, back to the world of lights, music, and people. I stood there and took a moment to enjoy the feeling that I was back in the world of the living.

Jim Bui greeted us, saying, "Anything interesting?"

Mom closed her eyes, seeming to savor the cold night air. "I'll tell you boys about it later. So, Jason, have all the other suspects in this case been as charming as Mr. Archimedes?"

"He's the champion thus far," I said. "Well, he and his boy Stone."

"After that, I need a cold drink and a hot bath," Mom said. "Is there any more trouble to get into tonight?"

The boys and I looked at each other, shaking our heads. "Very well," Mom said. "In that case, as much as I'd like to buy a round of drinks, I think I want to go home and spend some time with Beowulf. After that bath, of course."

Jimmy said, "I'll go back with you. You can fill me in on what went on down there." Timmy piped in with, "Me, too."

"I'll take the van and drop Hector off at his house," I said.

As we were saying our good-byes, I heard Hector tell Uncle Timmy, "You were right."

"About what?" Timmy asked.

"The size of the rats down there," Hector said with a grin.

Mom led Jimmy and Timmy away. Hector and I went across the cobblestone street for the company van, and a short time later, I was navigating slowly through the Saturday night parade of vehicles in Old Town.

"I think I owe you an apology, bro," Hector said.

"What do you mean?"

"I used to think that all you did all day was chase around after cheating spouses and peek in bedroom windows and stuff. But man, you work hard for the money."

"Sometimes," I admitted. "In this business, you work when there's work to do. I get my share of downtime, just not lately." I checked my watch and saw that it was coming up on 11:30, and I wondered if Jenny was asleep yet. Keeping an eye on the slow-moving traffic, I got my phone out and checked my messages. There was only one. It had come in over half an hour ago. It was from Bob Hanson.

"Listen, you told me to let you know if I heard from Anna? Well, she called here a little while ago and said she wanted to come over. I asked her what she was coming over for, and she just said she needed to look for something again. Anyway, I, uh, thought you'd want to know."

"Damn it!"

"What?" Hector asked.

"Anna Addison is supposed to be going to Messenger's house tonight."

"So what are we going to do?"

"As Mom would say, the day ain't over yet, kiddo. I hope that badge of your works if you're not the one driving. As for Anna, she's got a lot of explaining to do."

I made good time on the freeway, but it was still close to midnight when I finally got to Messenger's house, where I was rewarded by the sight of the older black Cadillac I had seen Anna Addison get into a while ago. "Bingo," I said.

Hector and I quietly got out of the van and went to the front door. The closer I got, the more unsettled I felt. We could see now that one of the large doors was open, as if in invitation. We both slowed down, treading carefully. Light was coming from within; at the door, I saw it came from a single naked lightbulb in a lamp lying on the floor of the front room.

Hector and I went in cautiously. The place was in shambles; broken glass littered the carpet, and the furniture, even the large white couch in the living room, was overturned. I did a double take when I saw Bob Hanson lying in the middle of the chaos.

I ran over to him, the glass shards on the thick carpeting popping under my shoes. Hanson's face was a bloody mess, and someone had wrapped silver duct tape around his bearded mouth as well as his wrists and ankles. He was groaning faintly.

*Thump!* The sound came from somewhere above. Hector and I pulled guns out simultaneously.

Hector took to the stairs with me close behind. My heartbeat was surely loud enough to alert people to my presence. As we crept upward, I saw a light coming from the open door of Messenger's room. Someone had smashed his way in. Hector yelled, "Police! Come out with your hands up!"

As if in answer, thunder pounded and lightning flashed in

the hall. Hector threw himself in front of me, and I felt hammering impacts come straight through his body. My hand, the hand that held my gun, spasmed twice. Then Hector became dead weight in my arms, dragging me down to the floor.

# CHAPTER TWENTY-EIGHT

I had blood on my hands.

I'd somehow managed to call 911 on my cell phone. In the eternity it took before the police and ambulance crews showed up, I stayed on the floor of the upper hallway with Hector, telling him over and over to stay down and keep breathing while I kept my eyes on the door to Messenger's room, my gun in my hand and ready to shoot anything that moved. Finally I heard someone call out from below, "Police!" and I yelled back for them to come up. There was a wild, chaotic moment when the first officer up the stairs started shouting to me to drop my gun and I argued back that the real shooter was hiding out in the bedroom down the hall. I finally got it through my scrambled brains that the smart thing to do was drop my revolver and let the officers drag me away.

I was taken downstairs, where another uniformed officer was crouched over Bob Hanson and checking his pulse, and pulled outside into the cold night air, all the time telling anyone and everyone that they had to save Hector. Then the officers put me in the back of a patrol car and seemed to forget all about me.

I watched through the windshield, peering through the flashing haze of the emergency lights that seemed to be everywhere, as paramedics brought out a gurney, shortly followed by another. The ambulances departed, sirens wailing, and then the world went silent as the grave. I leaned back in the seat and closed my eyes against the pulsing red lights. How long they left me there, I have no idea. I was colder than I'd ever been before in my life.

The next thing I knew, the door nearest me opened, and I heard Detective Navarro call my name. I opened my eyes and saw him leaning into the car. "Come inside," he said.

I followed him back into the house, crunching bits of broken glass underfoot again and noticing the reddish stain on the formerly white carpet where Bob Hanson had been lying. I could hear people talking and moving on the upstairs landing, but Navarro gave them as much notice as he gave me; namely, none at all. He led me into the kitchen. Someone must have been through here as well; every cupboard and drawer was opened. But rather than the foodstuffs and utensils you'd expect, the kitchen was littered with typed pages, at least a couple of hundred sheets. On the table was an old-fashioned electric typewriter, but what caught my eye was my revolver, along with two black SIG-Sauer pistols. "Sit down," Navarro said.

I reached for one of the chairs at the table, stopping short as I noticed the red smear of blood on my hand. Hector's blood. Using my wrist, I turned the wooden chair enough to allow me to slide in. I sat down just as I felt my legs quit working on me.

Navarro took a chair next to me. "Is one of these guns yours?"

"Yeah. The revolver."

Navarro nodded his round head, as if I'd given him the right answer to something.

"How's Hector?" I asked.

"He should be fine," Navarro answered. He pointed to one of the SIGs on the table. "Officer Morales took two nine-millimeter bullets in the chest, apparently from that gun there, but his vest stopped them. Good thing he was wearing it. A lot of the younger undercover guys start to develop a bad habit of forgetting. One of the shots he took went through his left arm first, though. He must have brought his arm up before he tried to shoot. The gun that the shooter used is the same gun Detective Banks lost the other night at Club Tantalus."

"Actually," I said, "the first thing Hector did was throw himself in front of me. That's why he got shot instead."

"I see. And then you shot back?"

My mind flashed back to the split second of thunder and lightning in the dark. "Yeah," I heard myself say slowly. "I mean, I think I shot at something. I'm just not sure what."

"There's a body at the end of the hall upstairs. I want you to look and see if you recognize the person."

A cold shock ran through me, as if someone had poured ice water down my spine. "Okay," I managed to say.

Navarro stood, waiting for me. Everything I did seemed to take a strangely long time, as if all my gears were stuck in slow motion. I followed Navarro back though the living room and up the stairs. There were lights at the end of the hall to the right. As we approached, staying clear of the blood-marked spot on the floor where Hector and I had wound up, I could make out four individuals in police jumpsuits and saw the flash of a high-powered camera light. The officers made way for Navarro and me, and I could then see the body displayed just beyond the shattered double bedroom doors.

He was lying on his back, his feet toward me and his arms stretched out wide, making his body into the shape of a cross. He was dressed all in black, from tall leather boots with chrome chains attached to black jeans and a black shirt that looked oddly like something a priest would wear. The shirt had an uneven, darker pattern on the chest, with a pair of small, ragged holes, one near the center of his chest and the other a hand's span away toward his left shoulder. A leather trench coat, open and splayed beneath him like the wings of a large black bird, also had patterns of chrome chain and pointed studs around the sleeves and collar. He was a large man, sheathed in fat, and the face beneath the untidy mop of jet black hair was rounded and pockmarked. I recalled Bob Hanson talking about someone having a face like a full moon.

The dead man's eyes were open and seemed to be staring up toward his eyebrows. His mouth was slack and gaping. I realized that Navarro had said something. "What was that?" I asked.

"I said, do you know this man?"

I shook my head, glad to be able to take my eyes away. Messenger's room was in even more disarray than when Hector and I were here, a time that now felt like it was years ago. On the floor to the right of the body, I saw four shiny brass cartridge casings. Then I saw something else: my small flashlight. The one I gave to Anna Addison. I said, almost automatically, "That's mine, I think."

"What's yours?" Navarro asked.

"That flashlight, on the floor there. I think that might belong to me."

"You said you didn't know this man," Navarro said quickly.

"I don't, but I gave a flashlight just like that one to Anna Addison, and from a description I heard, I think that may be somebody named Raven. Or Harold."

Navarro took my arm. "Come back downstairs." The CSI officers parted and let us back through, returning to their work as we left. Navarro took me back downstairs to the paper-littered kitchen, sat me back in my chair, and asked, "So you admit to firing that revolver tonight?"

"Yeah, but I'm not sure if I hit anything."

Navarro's dark eyes seemed to show a bit of sympathy as he looked down at me and said, "Pending the coroner's review, I think it's quite likely that you were the one who shot that man. Officer Morales's gun has not been fired."

It took a moment for Navarro's words to sink in. Then my brain seemed to go *click* as I entered a dreamlike state. I found myself looking down to my bloodstained hands, suddenly feeling like they belonged to someone else.

"Tell me what happened tonight," Navarro said, sounding like he was standing far away.

In a voice that sounded flat to my ears, I told the detective, "I was taking Hector home when I checked my phone messages. There was a call from Bob Hanson, saying that Anna Addison phoned him and said that she wanted to come over to the house and look for something. What, I don't know. When Hector and I got here, we saw the front door open and found Mr. Hanson on the floor. We heard a noise and went upstairs. That's when . . . that's when somebody started shooting at us."

"So you shot back?"

"Yeah. After Hector got in front of me."

"Did you see or hear anyone else in the house?"

"No. I don't think so. No."

"Are you sure?"

"Yeah. I guess."

"Why didn't you call me?"

Navarro's question didn't register at first. "What?"

"Why didn't you call me when you heard that Anna Addison was coming here tonight?" Navarro asked.

"I don't know . . . I just didn't think of it."

"You didn't think of it," Navarro said flatly. "You didn't

245

think to call me, and now your friend Hector has been shot and there's a dead man upstairs."

"That's enough," said a familiar voice from behind us. I turned my head and saw Mom standing in the doorway to the kitchen. She'd changed out of the Amelia Earhart outfit and now wore an ankle-length, tailored white coat, looking like she'd just come from a night at the opera. Navarro's eyes narrowed suspiciously as he asked, "How long have you been standing there?"

"Long enough to hear that you seem to have run out of pertinent questions to ask my son. Thank you for calling me. May I take Jason home now?"

Detective Navarro bowed his head, thinking. Finally he said, "I will have more questions, I'm sure. And normally we'd have a gunshot residue test performed, but seeing that your son admitted to shooting his gun tonight, I believe we can let him go home for now. We'll have to keep his gun for ballistics tests, of course."

Even in my fuzzy-headed state, I didn't miss the way Navarro said "for now." I stood up, feeling like I was forgetting something. Then it hit me. "You're going to need my ring," I told Navarro.

Navarro looked puzzled. "My ring," I repeated. "It's for the gun. It's got a magnetic trigger lock. It only works if you're wearing the ring."

Navarro seemed to relax a bit. "Oh. All right."

I slipped the ring off my finger. The narrow band of flesh it covered was the only part unstained by Hector's blood. As I handed it to Navarro, who took it as if I were handing him a scorpion, I felt something stir in the back of my mind, like a voice too far away to hear clearly.

"Let's go, Jason," Mom said as she turned toward the kitchen door. I followed her out.

Navarro called from behind us, "I'll be in touch."

Mom didn't say a word to me as she led me outside and past the uniformed officers at the front door. Through the pulsing lights of the police cars, I could make out a sparse crowd at the edge of the semicircular driveway—the neighbors turned out for some late-night entertainment. Mom opened the passenger door of her Jaguar, letting me slide in. I sat there with my hands up, not wanting to touch anything, as she got in the driver's side. She reached into the map box and handed me the industrial-strength waterless skin cleanser we all keep in our cars and a packet of tissues. "Here," she said. "Clean up a bit."

I did as commanded while she drove slowly out past the gawkers and the officers keeping them back. I saw that the big black Cadillac was still where Hector and I saw it when we arrived along with our company van.

"Now, tell me everything," Mom said softly.

And I did, while bouts of uncontrollable shivering kept hitting me. When I reached the end of my story, Mom said, "So you didn't tell Detective Navarro anything about our run-in with Mr. Archimedes tonight? Good. Now, listen to me carefully, Jason. The one thought you need to hold on to tonight is that you didn't do anything wrong. Do you hear me?"

I heard her, all right, but my brain was too fuzzy to appreciate her words. "I shot someone," I heard myself say.

"I know," Mom said gently. "There was nothing else you could do."

I felt too tired and shaky to even make words anymore. We were on the freeway now, and I stared out the windshield toward the city skyline that looked like patterns of stars outshining the full moon sailing overhead until we descended to street level and into the neon-lit canyons. I seemed to be unable to hold on to the concept of passing time and was surprised when I realized that Mom had stopped the car in front of my apartment building. "Go on up," she said. "Turn off your phones and stay in your apartment until I come for you. Go."

I did as I was told, lifting myself out of the car, feeling like I was covered in cold, soft lead. I watched as Mom drove off, leaving me confused but too tired to care. I finally mustered enough sense to go inside and find my way up to my apartment. Just before I reached my door, I was suddenly wrapped up in a firm and blessedly warm hug that carried the scent of jasmine. Jenny.

I started to try to speak, but she put her fingers to my frozen lips. "Your mother called me," she said in an urgent whisper. "Uncle Bruce is with Angelina, so I can stay with you." Her deep blue eyes searched my face. "Tell me what you need," she asked.

All I could think to say was, "I can't get warm."

# CHAPTER TWENTY-NINE

I heard someone call my name.

I opened my eyes and discovered that I was alone in my bed, though the scent of Jenny still lingered. I was trying to decide if I had dreamed hearing someone call me, and then I heard it again as Mom said, "Jason. Get up."

With an effort I raised my head and tried to focus my eyes toward my bedroom door. Mom was standing there, wearing the same long white coat I'd last seen her in. "You have to get up now. Get dressed for the day. Do it!" Then she quietly shut the door.

My thoughts were all jumbled together, like a kaleidoscope that just kept turning. I remembered Jenny, and how she brought me to my room and told me to get into bed, and how she lay down next to me. I remembered holding on to her as if she were the only thing that kept me from drowning in an icy dark ocean . . . I had killed someone.

My head fell back to the pillow as if the realization robbed me of all my strength, and for a while I wasn't sure I could get out of the warm cocoon of the covers. There was no mistaking the sound in my mother's voice, once set on a course, that woman never gives up. I took a breath, threw the covers back, and forced myself into a sitting position. There was a dizzy moment when I was on the verge of falling back into the warm embrace of the bed, but the now too familiar pain from my damaged ribs gave me a focus, spurring me onward rather than luring me back. I lifted myself up, stepped over the ragged pile of discarded clothes, and headed for the bathroom.

I'm not sure how long it took me to shave and shower; I kept forgetting what I was supposed to do next. Eventually I made it through my morning routine. I reached for my bathrobe, then remembered Her Majesty saying something about me getting ready for the day. I dressed in a fresh pair of pants from one of my dark blue suits and a matching turtle-neck sweater. Retrieving my belt from the pants I'd left on the floor, I saw that my revolver holster was still attached. I shook it off the belt and left it where it landed.

I found Mom in my living room. She'd taken off her coat, and I could see that she was dressed in denim jeans and a work shirt, stuff she usually only wore for gardening. She had opened the curtains and was looking out toward the cloud-covered sky visible beyond the city skyline. Without looking at me, she said, "I sent Jenny home. There's food and coffee on the table."

"I'm not hungry."

"Yes, you are," she said in a matter-of-fact tone. "You just don't know it yet. Now have something to eat and drink. Then we'll talk."

I saw that she'd set out a large covered foam coffee cup and a bag that bore the name of one of my favorite bakeries on the table in front of my couch. I knew better than to argue with her, so I sat down and started in. By the time I finished the ham-and-cheese croissant and most of the high-octane coffee, I could feel my body start to come alive again.

Mom must have sensed my partial resurrection. She turned from the window and said, "I had to get you out of that bed.

You're in a state of shock right now, and at a time like this, there's nothing more seductive than the thought of curling up in the covers and hiding from the world. Believe me, I know."

"But that doesn't change the fact that I—"

She cut off my words with the wave of a hand. "You did what needed to be done. What I had you trained to do. You didn't have a choice in the matter."

"But Hector was shot, and that's my fault for certain."

"And he's still alive, probably because of you. I've been to see him in the hospital."

"You have?"

"Oh, yes. I had to bully my way in, but I got to see him. The doctors are keeping him to make sure there are no complications from blunt trauma and shock, but he's expected to fully recover, and there was no significant nerve damage to his arm."

Relief washed over me.

Mom continued, "He gave me a message for you."

"A message?"

"Yes. He said to tell you that he's sorry to leave you on your own now, and to be careful. He also said that because of what you did, he now has to name his first child after you, and because of that he hopes to God it's a boy."

I surprised myself by barking out a laugh.

"If you ever doubt that you did the right thing," Mom said, "all you have to do is talk to Hector's wife, Rebecca. She'll set you straight. And it could have been a lot worse."

"Worse? How?"

"There were almost two deaths last night. Robert Hanson was struck on the head with a pistol, and when the intruder wrapped duct tape around his mouth, he almost died choking on his own blood."

That sobered me up. "Damn. After Hector and I got there,

we heard a noise from upstairs. Then all hell broke loose. We never had a chance to attend to poor old Hanson."

"I know," Mom said sympathetically. "Detective Navarro says the intruder's name was Harold Walters. I take it he was an associate of Anna Addison's?"

"Yeah. He called himself Raven. I think he had a thing for Anna. My guess is she sent him to Messenger's house instead of going herself. So now what?"

"Now you and I are going to get this case of yours in order. We still have an obligation to our client, with a deadline first thing tomorrow morning. I spoke with Detective Navarro again after I brought you home last night, and he's expecting a copy of our complete report as soon as it's ready."

"Sounds like you've been busy," I said. "When did you sleep?"

"I didn't," Mom said simply. "My son needed me. At the moment I'm held together by a gallon of coffee and the miracle of makeup."

Mom walked over to my dining table, and as I followed I saw that she had brought along all the case notes that I'd left at the Midnight Agency, plus the copy of the tape that Aurora/Theodora/Melanie made the night of the murder, and the paperback book Messenger wrote. "Were you able to make sense out of any of this?" I asked.

"Mostly," Mom said. "Believe me, once you've learned how to decipher Timothy O'Toole's handwriting, everyone else's is a breeze. I do have a couple of questions."

"Like what?"

Mom picked up one of my handwritten diagrams. "I see that you made a sketch of where everyone was standing during the ritual, when Mr. Messenger was murdered. So, Mr. Messenger was standing closest to the river. Then his body was found in the water and brought to shore by Mr.

Archimedes, correct? I believe he got rather wet retrieving the body."

"Right. According to what everyone has been saying, anyway."

"How far did he float?"

"What do you mean, float?"

"Mr. Messenger," Mom said. "Do you know how far his body floated in the river?"

It was a damn simple question that had my brain clashing gears. "I have no idea," I admitted.

Mom stared at the diagram. "Judging by this, the two people closest to Mr. Messenger were Anna Addison and Melanie Barstow, also known as Aurora. It appears to me that whoever stabbed Mr. Messenger also wound up pushing him into the river, which means that the person committing the crime may have gotten wet, not to mention bloody."

"True," I said, "and the one person we know who got both wet and bloody was Brandon Archimedes."

"But Anna Addison was the one who ran off," Mom reminded me. "In the dark, and wearing that black robe, she could have been wet or covered in blood and no one would have been the wiser. A question also remains as to what Elijah Messenger was doing the moment before he was killed."

"What do you mean?"

"You said it yourself. From all the evidence, it looks like Elijah Messenger was set to pull off a disappearing act. He changed his appearance, hiding the fact beneath a hooded robe and fake beard, then gathered an audience at a place of his choosing, and there temporarily blinded and deafened them. So what was he going to do for an encore?"

"Beats me. According to the coroner's report, he was wearing street clothes beneath his robes, and he had a pocketknife, and a penlight. Nothing else."

"But he must have been heading somewhere before the murderer cut him off."

I looked at my own diagram. "Well, I can see three possible options: One, he goes around the circle and heads back toward the house. Two, he heads upriver to the trees. Three, he goes the opposite way, downriver."

"Well, if he was killed as quickly as the coroner's report says, he certainly didn't hit the water and swim upstream. We're back to my original question: How far did he float?"

I tapped Anna Addison's spot on the diagram. "The bad news for His Honor the mayor is, if Messenger did head upstream, he moved closest to Anna."

"I need to get a look at the crime scene myself," Her Highness announced. Looking at me with searching eyes, she asked, "You up to it, kiddo?"

"Yeah," I said—and realized I meant it. I went back to my bedroom and grabbed a fresh suit jacket. I hesitated, looking at the ruin that was my topcoat lying on the floor near the bed. I dug my cell phone out of one of the pockets and left the coat crumpled on the floor.

Mom had gathered up all the case materials. I followed her out of my apartment, checking my cell phone for voice mail as I went. I had two messages. The first was from Roland, which I skipped. The second made me stop in my tracks as I heard Brandon Archimedes' voice say, "I have some information concerning a mutual friend. Call me."

Mom must have sensed something was up. She'd stopped in the hallway and was studying me with her sharp gray eyes. "Archimedes called," I said. "Sounds like he wants to give us some info."

"Really? I wonder what it is he's going to want in exchange?"

"One way to find out." As we continued our downward

trek, I replayed the message. Archimedes' call came in at 9:17 A.M. I checked my watch and saw that it was only a little after ten. Once Mom and I were in her Jaguar and under way, I called Archimedes' number. He answered right away.

"This is Jason Wilder. I understand you've got something for me?"

"Well, well, well," Archimedes replied. "Actually, I believe I have something you want. But I want something in return."

"Something in return?" I said aloud for Her Majesty's benefit, noting the I-told-you-so look in her eyes. "Like what?"

Archimedes chuckled. "Let's just say I'll tell you a secret, and in return you keep a secret of mine to yourself, hmm?"

"I don't have time for games."

"No, I suppose you don't. After all, it sounds like you've been a busy boy. What with shooting poor Raven and all."

I felt a spasm in the muscles of my hand. My gun hand. "Who told you that?" I managed to say through gritted teeth.

"The police have already paid me another visit this morning, wanting me to account for my whereabouts last night, etcetera. They told me that oaf Raven got caught breaking into Messenger's house and was shot by a private investigator. That was you, wasn't it? How interesting," he said with relish.

"Get to the point."

"Oh, very well." He sighed. "Little Anna called me just a short while ago, begging me for money. I gave her a definite maybe, and as a result, I know where she's staying."

"Let me get this straight. You want to trade me Anna Addison's location in return for my keeping your perverted playground a secret? Is that it?"

"I like to think of my playground, as you call it, as a public service I offer for those in need. So, what do you say?"

I shot a look of inquiry toward Her Majesty, who slowly nodded. "Fine," I said. "Give it up."

"How do I know I can trust you?"

"You can trust me to come over to your private dungeon with a crowbar if you don't stop screwing around."

"She's at the Econ-O-Mo Lodge in West River, room 47," Archimedes said quickly.

I shut my phone off with a snap, resisting the urge to throw it out the Jaguar's window and instead venting a string of my more imaginative profanity. When I wound down, Mom said, "Deals with the devil are all too common in our business, and if this one serves our clients, then it's good enough."

"I know," I grumbled. "But God, I hate that smug pervert."

"He's not worth it, love," Mom said. "Now, where to?"

I gave Mom the address and she drove expertly through the Sunday morning traffic, taking a right on Mast Street and heading for West River. We crossed the bridge; the same one where Anna Addison and I had our second rendezvous. It didn't take long before we came to the low-price motor lodge where Anna was supposed to be staying. As we pulled into the parking lot, I said to Mom, "Better let me do the approach."

"Agreed. Just don't let her get away."

"Trust me. That girl has got a lot of explaining to do." Mom parked a few stalls down from number 47, and as I got out I noticed how quiet it was. Of course, a place like this does most of its business at night. On an hourly rate.

I eased up to the door, listening for sounds within. I didn't hear any. I knocked on the door, saying, "Anna? It's Jason Wilder. We need to talk."

For what seemed like an eternity, there wasn't the slightest sound. Then I heard the security chain rattle. The door opened an inch or so, and I got a glimpse of one of Anna Addison's dark, almond-shaped eyes.

"Anna, let me in," I said gently.

She didn't say a word; she just stared at me with an eye that didn't blink. Then she moved back, opening the door to the darkened room.

I stepped inside and heard a demonic shriek as something flashed toward my face.

# CHAPTER THIRTY

If Anna Addison hadn't screamed first, she would have gotten me.

My left arm flew up and slammed into her wrist, just below the knife she held. I twisted around, which unfortunately caused me to lose my balance and sent me crashing onto the floor just inside the door. A sharp pain lanced into my right side as a writhing, snarling beast with Anna's face landed on top of me and tried to force a shiny tongue of steel into my throat. I managed to keep my hold on her wrist as she jabbed and thrust until a curtain of her black hair covered my eyes, blinding me. I was holding on for dear life when suddenly there was a slapping sound and Anna's weight collapsed on top of me.

I rolled her off me as if she were a burning log and saw Mom standing over us, just inside the doorway. "Are you all right?" she asked.

I swallowed and nodded. "Yeah. I think so."

"Good. Then get up and help me get this twit over to the bed."

I grabbed the door and lifted myself up. Anna was sprawled on her back, softly moaning, while her eyes desperately tried to focus. Her Highness had come to my rescue and put Anna out of action with an expedient hand strike to a particular spot on the neck that interrupts the blood flow to the brain and causes a mini-blackout. The results only last a few seconds at best, but the recipient is usually stunned for some time thereafter. There was a thumping from the wall to my left, and a muffled voice called out, "Hey! People are trying to sleep here!"

Mom shut the door and yelled back, "Sorry! Broke a nail." She brought out her nine-millimeter Smith and Wesson, scanned the room, and checked out the bathroom and closet to make sure we were alone.

Meanwhile, I picked up the groggy Anna and dropped her on the unmade bed, not doing my injured ribs any favors in the process, and took a look around the room myself. The place was a disaster, awash in discarded fast-food containers and empty bottles and cans that mostly had contained a variety of inexpensive alcohol. The place stank of too many cigarettes and too many bodies.

Anna herself was a reflection of the room. In the dim light leaking from the bathroom, her normally pale complexion looked like old paper, with dark rings encircling her darker eyes. She was dressed in a black T-shirt, way too big for her, over a pair of baggy jeans that she'd stuffed into the ridiculously tall, high-heeled lace-up boots she had worn when I saw her last.

As Her Highness slipped her gun into her overcoat pocket, Anna's eyes focused on my face. "You hit me," she said in a half-awake, accusing tone.

It almost made me laugh. Here the woman tries to stab me, and all of a sudden she's complaining because she got hit instead. Anna's eyes widened as they shifted over to Mom. "Who the fuck are you?"

"Oh, come now, Anna dear," Mom said silkily. "Don't you remember me? As I recall, I took you out of a hotel room very much like this one. Up in Reno."

Anna scrambled back on the bed until she thumped into the headboard. "You! You're that crazy bitch who locked me in the trunk of a car!"

"That's me," Mom said easily. "Now, are you going to behave yourself? Or are we going to do a historical reenactment?"

I was starting to feel jittery from the adrenaline let-down and looked around for a place to sit. That's when I saw the knife on the threadbare carpet.

"No," I heard myself say. "It can't be."

"What?" Mom said sharply. I didn't answer. I reached down and carefully picked up the knife by the guard to avoid disturbing any fingerprints, as if expecting it to disappear. I brought the weapon up to examine it, turning it over slowly.

"Can't be," I said again—but it was. I was looking at an exact duplicate of the knife that killed Elijah Messenger, from the symmetrical blade to the guard in the shape of a pair of twisting snakes to the black handle and silver pommel. Without taking my eyes from the knife, I asked Anna, "Where did you get this?"

"It's mine," she said petulantly.

"But where did you get it? And more important, when?" I demanded.

Anna hugged her knees to her chest. "Archimedes gave it to me. He said you killed Raven!"

Ah. So that's why she tried to do me in. "Let me guess," I said. "You spoke to Archimedes this morning, right? Then I'm betting he called you back and told you that . . . told you about Raven dying."

"He said you did it! And that you were probably going to come after me! And then you did!"

"Listen," I said as gently as I could, "Raven . . . Harold . . . is dead, but only because he shot first. He almost killed a policeman." I paused as Anna's breath hissed, then I said to her, "And he died because you sent him to Messenger's house. Didn't you?"

Anna sat frozen for a moment. A tear slid down her cheek. Then she broke into heaving sobs and threw herself over on her side, burying her face in a pillow. Mom went to Anna and gently cradled her head while she cried. I waited for a small break in the young woman's personal storm, then asked, "Anna? How long have you had this knife?"

Still holding on to Mom, she said in a weary voice, "I don't know. Almost a month, I guess. Why?"

I didn't answer her. I took my phone out instead and called Robin Faye's personal number. "It's me, princess," I said when she answered.

"Jason! Are you all right? I heard about Hector being in the hospital."

"I'm fine, but I really need you to do something for me in a hurry. I need you to check out the murder weapon in the Messenger case."

"Check it out how? That knife has already been examined."

"I know, princess, but I'm telling you now there's something wrong with it. There has to be."

"You're not being very specific," Robin said dubiously. "Besides, it's Sunday. I don't think there's anyone at the lab right now."

"I need this. Truly. Do whatever you have to do. Use that letter from the mayor I gave you if need be, but check that knife out. Please?"

"Okay," she said after a pause. "I'll do it for you, but it

would help if you told me what I'm supposed to be looking for."

"I'm thinking someone may have switched knives or something like that. Concentrate on the fingerprint. I don't know how or why, but I'm telling you there must be something that was missed. And thanks, princess. I owe you one." I clicked off the phone.

Anna had quieted down, and the two women were sitting on the bed side by side. I said to Anna, "You really didn't kill Messenger, did you?"

"I told you that," she said, rolling her eyes.

"You told me a lot of things," I said. "You also kept a lot of things to yourself."

Mom was looking at me with intense scrutiny. "You're on to something," she stated.

I just nodded, not wanting to speak in front of Anna. For the first time since this whole case began, I thought I might be on to something in Anna's favor. One thing, at least—and it centered on the knife.

There are two ways to hold a knife: underhand, so the blade is pointing up, in the fencer's grip; or overhand, blade down, in what's called the ice pick grip. People don't tend to be switch-hitters in this department. When Anna had attempted to perforate me just now, she had used the overhand ice pick grip, so it was likely that she would have used the same type of attack on Messenger. But whoever killed Elijah Messenger used a straight-on thrust into the abdomen, a very awkward thing to do if you're holding the knife pointing down.

"Anna," I said. "It's time for the truth. All of it."

Her shoulders sagged. "All right. What do you want to know?"

"Why have you been avoiding the police?"

"I can't tell you that," she mumbled.

Mom leaned in closer to her. "Does it have anything to do with the movie?"

Anna jerked as if Mom had touched her with a live wire. "What! Oh, Christ!"

"Your father already knows," Mom told her.

For a moment, I thought Anna was going to curl back up in a ball, but she simply said, "Oh, God," in a childlike voice.

"Tell us about it," Mom urged gently. "Everything."

Anna stared reciting like a kid in Sunday school. "It was supposed to be a private thing. Elijah was going to initiate me, teach me. He said I was ready to evolve to a deeper under-standing of my own psychic abilities, you know?"

"Yes, dear," Mom said. "Go on."

"So he took me to a place. I can't really remember much. Elijah said I needed to have some help to attain a higher con-sciousness, so he gave me something shortly before the ritual."

He got her stoned out of her gourd, I mentally translated. "Where'd he take you, Anna?" I asked.

"I don't know. He said it was a secret place. I don't re-member how I got there. But I remembered the knife, and how beautiful it was. Later, I asked Elijah where he got it, and he told me that Archimedes gave it to him. When I asked Eli-jah if I could have it, he said yes, then later told me that he must have misplaced it somewhere. The next time I saw Archimedes, I told him I wanted a knife just like the one he gave Elijah, and he got me one. That one."

"What about the movie?" I asked.

Anna's lip twisted as if she had bitten into something bitter. "Elijah came to me about two weeks ago and said something terrible had happened. He said that someone was spying on us. They filmed my ritual, and now they wanted money. Otherwise, they were going to send the movie to the press. I couldn't let that happen. It would have ruined Daddy."

Mom and I traded looks over Anna's head; evidently she didn't realize that Brandon Archimedes was the one doing the videotaping, with Elijah Messenger's active cooperation. "Did Messenger ever tell you who was trying to blackmail you?"

"No, he said he didn't know, but I'm pretty sure that bitch Aurora had something to do with it, the way she was always snooping around. But Elijah told me that someone anonymously sent him a copy of the movie, you know, to prove they had it, and they asked for ten thousand dollars. I told Elijah all I could come up with was a little over seven thousand. He said he'd take that and find the rest himself and get the movie for me. He promised. Then, before he died, he told me he had the original tape of the movie and that he'd hidden it somewhere safe. He told me that he'd give it to me later, when we were alone. Only he never got the chance."

"Why did you run off when Messenger was killed?" I asked.

She shivered. "At first, I wasn't sure what happened, then when I heard Messenger was dead, and I could see the hilt of the Atheme sticking up out of his chest through the moonlight, I just freaked. I thought the blackmailers were out to get both of us, so I ran. That's when I saw Raven. He'd followed me to Messenger's that night and was waiting out by the trail to the river. He got me out of there before the police showed up. Later, I knew I had to get the tape of the movie before anyone else found it. If it got into the wrong hands, I don't know what Daddy would do. I tried to go and see Archimedes later, to see if he'd help me. That's when I found out that the cops thought I killed Elijah."

"So last night, you sent Raven to Messenger's house to try

to find the movie," I said. "Did you know he had a gun with him?"

Anna's eyes were desperate, pleading; then she closed them as she whispered, "I swear, I didn't think he'd use it. I didn't want anyone else to be hurt. I swear to God." She fell silent, then asked, "So now what?"

Mom stood up from the bed. "The first thing we do is get you out of here. You realize that you do have to speak to the police, and soon, don't you?"

Anna swallowed, then nodded.

Mom continued, "Very well. Jason and I will do all we can for you in the meantime."

"Actually," I said, "I think it'd be best if we all go and get a look at the crime scene. Mom and I were on our way there when we found out you were here. Do you think you're up to going with us? It would help a lot to have you there."

Anna's gaze was bouncing back and forth between Her Majesty and me. "This woman is your mother?" she asked incredulously.

"Ah, well," Mom said warmly, "we all have our familial misfortunes. Now, let's get you out of here, shall we?"

# CHAPTER THIRTY-ONE

We got Anna Addison wrapped up in her oversized black trench coat and got ready to leave. I held up the knife, asking, "Do you have a sheath or something for this?" She nodded and rummaged around a pile of discarded clothes heaped on a chair, coming up with an ornate black scabbard with entwined metal snakes running down the length of it.

We pulled out of the parking lot with the girls in the back and me getting to drive the Jag for a change. I was almost to the bridge when I had to pull over to make way for a River City police car zooming in the opposite direction, lights flashing but running silent. I watched in my rearview mirror until I saw it sweep into the motel parking lot we'd just exited. "Looks like someone tipped off the constabulary," I commented.

I drove on toward Messenger's place and had made it onto the freeway when my cell phone buzzed. "Wilder here," I answered.

"This is Detective Navarro. Do you know where Anna Addison is?" he asked tersely.

I handed my phone back over my shoulder. "It's for you," I said.

Mom took the phone. "Hello, Detective, this is Victoria Wilder. Yes, I have Ms. Addison here with me . . . Please calm down, Detective, and there's no call for that sort of language . . . As I recall, there is no official arrest warrant active for Ms. Addison, and we have until tomorrow morning before the district attorney reviews your evidence. Until that time, Ms. Addison will be in my custody. Yes, Detective, I'm quite aware that I am no longer a policewoman. I work for a living now . . . Then I suggest you take that up with the mayor . . . and good morning to you, too." Mom snapped my phone shut and tossed it onto the front passenger seat. "Well, I must say, Nicholas sounds a little tense this morning."

"How'd the cops know where I was?" Anna asked.

"I'm betting Brandon Archimedes isn't the good friend you thought he was," I said. "He was the one who told us where you were. My guess is he's also trying to curry favor with the police by snitching on you."

I heard Anna sigh, then say, "So Daddy knows about the movie?"

"Yes," Mom said. "He does. I think we'll be able to see that the tape doesn't get out to the public, though."

"But that means Raven died for nothing," Anna said hoarsely. There was silence, then she said, "Raven always had kind of a thing for me, you know? I think all he really wanted to do was protect me. And now he's dead. Like Elijah."

"There's nothing anyone can do about that now," Mom said, not unkindly. "All we can try to do is to see that no one else comes to harm now."

As I drove down the freeway, I glanced toward the collection of notes and other material I'd collected in this case. Keeping an eye on the road, I picked up the tape Melanie Barstow had recorded when Messenger was killed. I slipped it into the Jag's stereo system. "Anna? I want you to listen to this, see if it helps your memory any."

The tape ran its course, and I heard Anna's surprised gasp. "Oh, my God! Where did you get that?"

"Where it came from doesn't matter," Mom said quickly. "The important thing is, can you tell if it's an accurate recording of what happened when Elijah Messenger was killed?"

"I . . . I think so. I mean, that sounds about right."

"Did anything sound odd or out of place?" I asked.

"What? No. I don't think so. Christ, did I really scream like that? I can't remember."

I resisted my own impulse to curse as my hopes of Anna Addison being able to shed some light on this situation started to fade. I kept my thoughts to myself until I got us off the freeway and into the high-rent residential neighborhood where Elijah Messenger had recently lived and died. I approached the house cautiously, on the lookout for lurking police vehicles, but unless the River City Police Department had recently purchased some luxury sedans and SUVs, I didn't spot any likely candidates. I pulled into the wide semicircular driveway of the rose-colored mansion, seeing the Midnight Investigations van right where Hector and I had left it, along with Robert Hanson's beat-up old truck. I briefly wondered how Bob was doing after getting pistol-whipped and nearly asphyxiated last night.

We got out of the Jaguar under a darkening sky, and I hoped that it wouldn't start raining while we were down by the river. I led the way along the high walls of the house back to the trail that led over the levee and through the tangled woods to the stone-strewn clearing by the water. We had to take our time on the walk; Anna couldn't move very fast in her high-heeled boots. From what I could tell, everything was just as I had seen it last.

I took Mom and Anna over to the water's edge, close to where Elijah Messenger had stood before all hell broke loose the night he was killed. "Anna," I asked, "is this the spot where Messenger was?"

She nodded glumly. Mom's attention seemed focused on the dark water. "Where was Mr. Messenger when he was first seen in the river?" Mom asked.

Anna walked a few paces downstream, close to where Melanie Barstow and Brandon Archimedes were supposed to have been standing, I noticed. "About here, I guess," Anna said.

"How far out was he?" Mom inquired.

Anna just shrugged, and I said, "Did you see how far Archimedes had to go in to get him?"

Anna looked upward in thought. "He was in almost up to his waist."

"Archimedes is over six feet tall," I added. "So, say Messenger was in at least two and a half feet of water. Enough that he'd be floating, anyway."

Mom nodded, then started looking on the ground. She picked up a branch and tossed it into the water from the spot where Messenger had last stood. The branch floated past Melanie Barstow's spot before I could count to four.

"I think if Mr. Messenger landed in the water from here," Mom said, "he would have been long gone by the time anyone noticed."

I eyed the dark, moving water. "That's not exactly a scientific experiment. A human body might move differently."

"Well, unless you're willing to jump in and do the dead man's float, it'll have to do for now."

"Good enough for me," I said quickly. "So, chances are he went into the water somewhere upstream?"

Without taking her eyes off the river, Mom nodded agreement. Unfortunately, I realized, that also meant that Messenger had moved closer to Anna. I looked upriver from the water's edge. From where I was standing, it looked like there was a narrow trail separating the trees from the river. "He wasn't equipped for a hike," I said, "judging by what the coroner's office found on him."

Her Majesty pointed to the trail. "Go and see if that leads anywhere," she commanded. I nodded and trudged off. Once into the trees, the going was a bit tricky until the trail veered off away from the water. I took my time along the gently twisting path through the tangled woods and was almost surprised when I suddenly emerged from the obscuring branches and found myself staring at the levee again. I hiked up to the half-buried railroad tracks at the top. I could look to my left and see the back of Messenger's house and the top of the trail leading to the clearing by the river. Almost directly ahead was a path that led between two other large houses set on a cul-de-sac, and I wondered if this was Elijah Messenger's planned escape route for his disappearing act.

I retraced my steps—and because I was watching where I put my feet along the uneven ground, I almost missed it. Back in the woods I caught a glimpse of white out of the corner of my eye, standing out from the earthy browns and woodsy greens surrounding me. I traced the thin white line that almost disappeared into the branches of a tree, stopping above what looked like a giant piece of rotting fruit hanging in the air.

My mind flashed back to the open box of green plastic garbage bags Hector had found in Elijah Messenger's room. In front of me was a bag like that, suspended by a white cord that had been thrown over a high branch and tied off on a lower one. When I had come the other way, it had been hidden behind the tree. I remembered the two items Messenger had in his pockets when he died: a small knife and a flashlight. All you'd need to find and retrieve the bag hanging there.

I used the blade on my key-ring tool to cut the cord, dropping the bag to the ground with a muted thump. I opened it, revealing a medium-sized black nylon zippered suitcase. Inside the case, I found a woolen jacket stuffed on top, and under that, more stacks of money than I could count at a glance.

It was hard not to laugh as I pictured Messenger's plan. Once he'd blinded his audience, he would have disappeared, no doubt aided by the black cloak he wore. He'd already changed his appearance, concealed beneath the hood. He would have made his way here, retrieved the bag of money, taken off the cloak, and off he'd go. If the police were called to investigate, they'd spend their time looking downriver, in the event Messenger had fallen in. All in all, a pretty cunning plan.

But the thought that Messenger was killed prior to his escape sobered me. As did the thought that if Messenger was heading this way, he'd have passed closer to Anna than to any of the others. And there was still that inconvenient problem of her fingerprint being found on the murder weapon. I took my cell phone out and clicked on Robin Faye's personal phone.

She must have seen my number on her display, because she answered, "How did you know?"

"Uh, I give up. How did I know what?"

"Jason Wilder, don't play games with me. How did you know about the fingerprint?"

"You found something?"

"I'm at the lab right now. It's easy to see how it was missed the first time."

"How what was missed? What have you got?"

"Well, you know that the knife was still in place when Messenger's body arrived at the lab, right?"

"Yeah. So?"

"The fingerprint was examined for a comparison, but no one bothered with an analysis. No point, right?"

"Speaking of points, could you get to this one?"

"What made you harangue me into checking this out for you?"

271

I clamped down on my impatience, saying as calmly as I could, "I found a second knife, an exact match for the first. The primary suspect swears that she's had her knife all this time. So, either she's lying, or maybe someone tried to set her up. Also, it occurred to me, if the deed was done with one quick blow, then how could the blood have worked its way between the hilt and the hand that held it?" That had trickled into my mind after I saw how Hector's blood didn't get to the part of my finger covered by my ring. "So, come on, girl, give!" I implored.

"The blood on the fingerprint isn't human."

"Say what now?"

"In fact, it's not even real blood. It's some kind of carbohydrate-based compound that shows traces of a red vegetable dye. Whatever this stuff is, when the real blood hit it, the blood stuck to it like glue."

"Damn," I whispered as I remembered the film of Anna's ritual with the knife. In my mind's eye, I saw the reddish, viscous stuff that was smeared on the blade. Suddenly, it made perfect sense: fake blood for a fake ritual "Robin," I said. "Did I ever mention how much I love you?"

"So I take it this helps?"

"Maybe. If I'm smart enough to figure out how it all fits together. Gotta go, 'bye." I snapped my phone shut, staring at the bag of money. I looked around, seeing that I was still alone, then stuffed the jacket back in the case and wrapped it up in the garbage bag. I tossed the cord back over the branch and hoisted it up, tying it off the way I found it and pocketing the cut piece. I hurried back down the trail.

I found Mom and Anna over by the circle in the clearing. "I was wondering if I should call for a search party," Her Majesty greeted me. Then she gave me a quizzical look. "You found something," she stated.

"Maybe," I said. Going over to Anna, I said to her, "Look, can you remember anything else about the night Messenger was killed? Anything you haven't told me yet?"

"No," she said petulantly. "I told you everything!"

I resisted the urge to reach out and shake her in the hopes that something useful would rattle loose. Instead, I went and stood at the head of the circle, the spot where Messenger had been. I took a slow look around, noting where everyone else was supposed to be. I closed my eyes, replaying in my head the tape Melanie Barstow made. The tape—

"The tape!"

"What about it?" Mom asked sharply. "Did you hear something on it?"

"No," I said. "It's what I didn't hear." I pulled Anna's knife out of my jacket pocket. "Mom, take Anna back to the car. Wait for me. I'll be along in a second."

Anna opened her mouth, but Mom shut it with a look. "Come along," Mom said. With a last I-hope-you-know-what-you're-doing-kiddo look over her shoulder, Her Majesty took Anna away out of the circle. I watched them go, remembering Jenny telling me that if I were a real detective, I'd arrange a dinner party and reveal the murderer that way.

*No, not a dinner party,* I thought—*but maybe a picnic.* I hefted the knife in my hand. Now I had to see if I could make the pieces of the puzzle fit together.

# CHAPTER THIRTY-TWO

I'd been out by the river for over two hours since Mom took Anna back to the car. In that time, I'd damned near drained the battery of my phone, making calls. The first one was the most difficult: Detective Navarro. "Let me get this straight," he said. "You want me to get all the witnesses together and bring them down to the crime scene. Did it occur to you that some of the people are possible suspects?"

"Yeah," I said. "In fact, I'm counting on that."

"And in return, you say you'll produce Anna Addison."

"Yes. But you've got to promise me that you'll let her stay and do the reenactment."

"I have one last question. Are you out of your mind?"

I finally managed to verbally wrestle Detective Navarro into going along with my idiotic scheme, as he referred to it, mainly on the grounds that he could have Anna Addison when the whole thing was over. Navarro said, though, that he could only ask all the players to show up, and if they refused, there was nothing he could do. I figured Bob Hanson and Melanie Barstow would probably cooperate, and I told Navarro that if he had any problems with Brandon Archimedes, he should mention to the club owner that his deal with me was dependent on his civic-minded cooperation.

"Deal?" Navarro asked sharply. "What deal?"

"That's between him and me," I said as smoothly as I could, "but I'm betting that Archimedes ends up coming along."

I then called Mom and advised her that we'd be having Detective Navarro's company in the near future and that I was hoping that he'd gather all the suspects together. Her Majesty also inquired if I was out of my mind, and I reminded her that if I was, the cause was probably genetic.

Then I waited and paced, driven by the excitement that I was about to be proved right, coupled with my fear that I could be completely wrong.

Finally I saw Mom and Anna coming toward me in the company of Detective Navarro. The three of them together resembled chess pieces. Her Majesty was the white queen, with short and squat Navarro a black rook. That made Anna Addison a black pawn, or so I hoped.

I asked Navarro, "Did you make all the calls?"

He nodded, his face half hidden beneath his wide-brimmed black rain hat. "I did. And to my surprise everyone agreed to come."

"Did Archimedes give you a hard time?"

Navarro gave me a suspicious look. "At first, but when I mentioned your name, he got cooperative."

I looked over at Anna. "You doing okay?"

The look I got from her was pure contempt. "I hope you know what the hell you're doing," she growled.

Mom patted her arm. "Of course he does, dear," she said reassuringly. I was glad Anna missed Mom's look heavenward after her statement of confidence.

I was saved from having to explain myself to the mayor's daughter by the appearance of Robert Hanson. Even from a distance, I could see that his face had been really messed up; he had a white bandage attached to his left cheek and not quite covering the makings of a colossal black eye. He was wearing another plaid flannel shirt with a faded denim jacket and jeans, and he was wearing his prescription sunglasses again. "Mr. Hanson, I'm glad you could make it," I said to him.

As he came up and shook my hand, Hanson said, "Guess I wouldn't be here at all if it wasn't for you. The doctor told me that if you hadn't come along when you did, I'd have likely died. I was just real sorry to hear about your partner getting shot."

"Thanks," I said. "He's doing fine, from what I've heard." Bob Hanson seemed to notice Anna for the first time, his gray eyebrows popping up from behind the dark lenses, but he didn't say anything to her. Instead, he said to me, "Well, like I said, I owe you. So whatever I can do to help is fine."

Next into the clearing came Melanie Barstow, buttoned up in a blue ski jacket with her wavy red hair pulled back into a thick ponytail. She was looking around the area as if she were waiting for something to leap out of the trees at her. She and Anna narrowed their eyes at each other, and I almost expected to hear the sound of hissing.

Bob Hanson nodded. "Aurora. How you doing?"

"Hi, Bob," she replied. "God, what happened to your face?"

Hanson shifted uncomfortably. "Long story," he mumbled.

Coming in last, of course, was Brandon Archimedes, strolling along as if he had all the time in the world. He came attired in a long, expensive overcoat that looked like it belonged on an Edwardian prince. In the light of the overcast day, his neatly trimmed black hair and beard with the white accents looked as phony as he was.

I addressed the gathering. "Thank you all for coming. I'll try to make this brief."

Melanie Barstow spoke up. "Detective Navarro? Why are we here? Is this necessary?"

"Really," Archimedes added dryly. "I'm certain most of us have better things to do."

With a sidelong glance at me, Navarro said, "All I can say officially is that the River City Police Department appreciates everyone's cooperation in this matter."

Mom chimed in. "Let's get the show on the road, shall we?"

As Archimedes vented a theatrical sigh, I said, "This should take just a few minutes. What I want is to have you take the same places you did the night Elijah Messenger gathered you all here. So, if you would be so kind?"

There was some shrugging and a bit of grumbling from Melanie and Archimedes, but they all did as they were asked. Once everyone was moving into position, I said, "Now, Melanie? If you'd pick up the broom there, and Bob, as I recall, you were holding the torch. We don't have the chalice that Anna was holding, so we'll have to do without."

As I was speaking, I went over to the bushes behind Archimedes and picked up the long knife that everyone referred to as the Atheme. Holding it out blade first, I handed it to Archimedes. "I believe you were holding on to this?"

Archimedes smiled as he took the knife from me, and I noticed that his grip on the hilt was professionally adept. He hefted the weapon in his hand, smiling at me the whole time, looking like a cobra contemplating a mouse.

"Now," I said. "I'll take the place where Elijah Messenger was, right about here, I believe." I scanned the circle from left to right. Archimedes held the Atheme like a man hoping to put it to use in the very near future. Melanie held the broomstick, looking sullen and suspicious. Bob Hanson stood in his spot with the metal torch pole, waiting patiently. Anna Addison just stood there, flanked by Mom and Detective Navarro, looking miserable.

Showtime.

"Now," I said, keeping a wary eye on Archimedes, "when I say 'go,' try to do what you did when the explosion went off. Ready? Go!"

There was a moment of confusion, with everyone looking around at everyone else, then Archimedes shrugged and stepped back while Melanie started to crouch. Anna just stood where she was.

Then everyone's head turned toward a sound that rang out like a gong.

Bob Hanson stood stock-still. The metal torch pole was bouncing on the flat stones by his feet, ringing like an out-of-tune bell. "Ah," I said. "Now there's a sound that no one heard before."

Fixing my eyes on Hanson, I went toward him, saying, "Elijah Messenger wasn't doing a ritual that night, he was planning to do a disappearing act. You knew that, didn't you, Mr. Hanson? Someone here called you one of Messenger's acolytes, but you were more of a magician's assistant, weren't you?"

I couldn't read the look in Hanson's eyes, masked as they were behind his dark lenses, but I could see his face pale until it almost matched the white of his bandage. "You helped Messenger set the stage here," I said, still moving toward him, "and you knew exactly what was going to happen. While you had your head bowed during Messenger's opening speech, you must have had your eyes shut tight, waiting for the explosion. When the flash hit, blinding everyone else, you shouted out that you were blind, too. Only that wasn't true, now was it?"

Hanson had backed up a couple of steps. I picked up the metal pole he'd dropped and said, "And why didn't anyone hear the sound of the torch dropping and hitting the rocks? Because you didn't drop it. You needed it. You needed it for this."

I pulled the knife Anna Addison tried to use on me earlier from my jacket pocket, shoving the hilt into the round open end of the torch and pulling the scabbard off.

Just like that, I was holding a spear.

"This is how you did it, isn't it? You knew which way Messenger was going to go, so all you had to do was run to the trail ahead of him. One quick stab, then all you had to do was twist him around and shove him into the water. The knife stayed in his body, and the pole kept you from getting your own hands bloody. You probably even had time to dip the end of the shaft into the water and wash it off. Then all you had to do was sneak back toward the circle, take off your glasses, and lay the pole down quietly."

Hanson was trembling as I said, "The question is, why? Was it for all that money I found hidden up a tree in the woods there?"

Hanson's voice cracked as he roared and dug his hands into his jacket, ripping out a blur of dark metal. I let the makeshift spear drop and yelled the word "Gun!" as I went for him.

# CHAPTER THIRTY-THREE

No doubt about it, it'd been one hell of a day.

It was early Sunday evening as I sat half melted into one of Her Majesty's guest chairs. Mom and I were writing up my case notes. I was dictating my report and scratching the supine Beowulf behind his ears while Mom translated my nearly incoherent ramblings, typing on the wireless keyboard on her ornate desk. We were on the verge of wrapping up when we had a visitor arrive. I pried myself out of the chair and answered the door, finding Detective Navarro on the front porch, soaking wet from the rain.

I took his hat and coat, then escorted him back to Her Majesty's Throne Room and seated him in the other guest chair. He settled in, exuding the quiet satisfaction of a man who's done a good, hard day's work. "I thought you'd want to know what Robert Hanson had to say for himself," Navarro said.

"I'd say we're entitled to that," Mom agreed.

"Yes," Navarro said easily. "Although it was a bit difficult, having to interview the man on the way to the hospital. I almost got carsick in the ambulance."

"Sorry," I said, "but when Hanson went for the gun, I didn't have any choice." In fact, I'd been trained in a couple of ways to disarm people in a frontal attack. One method removes the gun from your opponent with minimal contact. The other way really hurts. When Hanson pulled the gun, I automatically went through the motions I'd practiced countless times, making him release the cheap-looking .32 revolver he pulled out and breaking his arm in the process. Why my subconscious chose that particular move, I had no idea.

Navarro gave me a look. "You know, I've seen that technique you used taught at our police academies, but I've never known anyone who's used it. Kind of ironic when you think that just the night before, you wound up saving Hanson's life."

"Jason saved his life twice," Mom said matter-of-factly. "I was prepared to shoot that man the moment he pulled a gun."

"Still," Navarro countered, "it made my interview a little difficult. But he talked, just the same. Tell me, how did you figure out he was the one who killed Elijah Messenger?"

"You first, Detective," I insisted.

Navarro shrugged. "Very well. First of all, there's Elijah Messenger. He was a man who never was."

"Care to elucidate?" I asked.

"Elijah Messenger began life as a character in a story. A story written by Robert Hanson."

"Ah." I sighed. "I think I see. According to the coroner's report, the Elijah Messenger who showed up at the lab appeared to be too young to have done all that world traveling thirty years ago or so. According to the book, anyway. So Hanson actually wrote *The Illuminated Traveler?*"

Navarro nodded. "Oh, yes. Under the pen name Elijah Messenger. It was the only story he ever got published, by a company that changed the story from fiction to a supposed real-life adventure. Well, apparently Hanson made a bad deal and signed away all the rights, and the company that published it went out of business not too long after. He never even got paid for it."

"Where does the flesh-and-blood Messenger come in?" I asked.

"Ah, you mean the man pretending to be Messenger? His name was Maxwell Caulder. From what Hanson told me, he was a semitalented stage magician who decided that there was better money in using his abilities to convince gullible people that he was a real psychic. He found Hanson's book in a secondhand bookstore and just stole the identity, whitening his hair to appear older. The scam worked pretty well up until the scandal in Arizona with Melanie Barstow's friend. When Theodora Carlyle died and her family sued Messenger, his name wound up in the news. Our friend Hanson heard about it, packed up his truck, and went to Arizona to find the imposter. Hanson tracked the false Messenger down and later forced him into a partnership. It was either that, or Hanson would go to the dead girl's family and reveal everything, branding Caulder as a cold-blooded opportunist and opening him up to greater fraud charges."

"So then they had to flee for other pastures," Mom said.

"Right," Navarro agreed. "It was our bad luck they chose River City. For a while they did pretty well for themselves— Caulder passing himself off as the psychic Elijah Messenger, Hanson posing as the faithful follower. Then Melanie Barstow came looking for the man she felt caused the death of her friend Theodora Carlyle. She managed to insinuate herself with Messenger, posing as another true believer. Then she started sending the threats, just to rattle Messenger, she thought. It worked, too. According to Hanson, Max Caulder freaked out and wanted to take off right away, afraid that his past was catching up with him. He was losing his nerve, too, and wanted to quit the scam outright. So Hanson told him he had a better idea."

"Let me guess," I said. "This is where the disappearing act comes in."

"Right again," Navarro said. "Hanson convinced Caulder that if he was going to disappear, then he needed to do it in such a way that no one would look for him. Hanson hatched the scheme where Messenger would foretell his own death. Then the two of them planned the big disappearing act. Poor Caulder thought that the idea was for him to vanish in a puff of smoke, so to speak, and most people would assume that he fell into the water and his body was never found, while others would start to believe that the mysterious Messenger met an equally mysterious fate. What the poor guy didn't know was that Hanson planned to kill him and keep the money Caulder had squeezed out of his followers, figuring it'd be safe there in the woods until the coast was clear. Hanson was going to make more money by writing a book about Elijah Messenger, the man who foretold his own death."

"But why did Mr. Caulder go to the police and then later come to us?" Mom asked.

"Ah, that was Hanson's idea, too," Navarro said. "He figured that by having Messenger go to the police to predict his own death, there'd be extra credibility to the story. And when Lori Banks thought it'd be funny to send an obvious crackpot, or so she believed, to your door, that's how you became involved. Now it's your turn. How did you know Hanson was the murderer?"

When Navarro had his notebook ready, I said, "Well, I admit that for almost the entire time, I thought Anna Addison was the best and most logical suspect. Especially since she's so crazy. It wasn't until we caught up with her today and found that knife in her possession that I started to believe her. That's what got me started thinking about the bloody fingerprint on the blade that wound up in Messenger. It didn't stand to reason that if the culprit stabbed Messenger once, that blood could have worked its way in between the hilt and the hand that held the knife.

"Anyway, when I thought there might have been something about the knife that was overlooked, I called my friend Robin Faye over at the coroner's office. She's the one who deserves the credit for finding out that the blood that the fingerprint was left in wasn't human. Sometime prior to the night of the murder, Anna Addison was involved in some kind of weird 'blood ritual' with Messenger that involved the use of the same knife that later became the murder weapon. Turns out that the blood used in the ritual was as fake as the rest of Messenger's so-called magic. Anna wouldn't have noticed that, seeing how she was stoned out of her mind at the time. But afterward, Hanson must have gotten ahold of that knife, a knife that now had a great set of Anna Addison's fingerprints attached to it."

"How did you know that he used the pole from the lantern to kill him?" Navarro asked. "Which, I confess, was a pretty cunning move on his part. It allowed Hanson to stab Caulder and stay far enough away to avoid getting blood on himself."

"That must have been Hanson's biggest problem," I said. "Here he had a murder weapon that was connected to the perfect patsy, crazy Anna Addison. He had to think of a way to kill Messenger with the knife without getting any blood evidence on himself. Hanson, a former machinist, by the way, figured out that with the knife slipped on to the end of the metal torch pole, he'd have all the distance he needed. He just had to be careful after killing Messenger to lay the pole down quietly. You heard what an ungodly racket that thing made when dropped on the stones. On my first daylight trip to the crime scene, I picked up that pole myself and then let it fall. It didn't hit me until later that when Melanie Barstow tape-recorded the murder the sound of the pole hitting the ground should have been on the tape, only it wasn't. By the time I figured it out, I had a twin copy of the knife, courtesy of Ms. Addison, and the metal pole at hand. I just put them together."

I let Navarro jot down a few more notes before I added, "There may be another connecting piece of evidence as well. My friend Robin Faye told me that Messenger's hands had traces of iron oxide on them. At the time, I just assumed that it was residue from Messenger's pyrotechnic display. But if I remember my high school chemistry, iron oxide is a fancy term for rust. When Messenger was stabbed, he probably grabbed on to the rusty pole, and when Hanson pulled the pole free, it transferred the stuff to Messenger's hands."

Navarro shook his head, smiling. "I like to think that I'd have figured all this out myself. I've got to give you credit, you put it all together first. But what was that talk about money in the woods? That was the remark that seemed to send Hanson over the edge today."

It was Mom's turn. "My son also found a great deal of money that Maxwell Caulder, alias Elijah Messenger, took from a number of our good citizens under false pretenses. Money that we believe Robert Hanson was going to collect when the coast was clear. We also have a list of the people that the money belongs to, and we will happily return it to them."

Navarro frowned. "But that money is evidence!"

"It would have been," Mom said, "had you found it first, and then it would languish in a police evidence locker. We'll give you a complete accounting of the money and the names of the victims, of course, but I intend to see that the money goes back to the rightful owners as soon as possible. No one is going to suffer needlessly on my watch," she said with finality.

I thought for a moment that Navarro was going to explode, but he surprised me by simply having a short, quiet fit of laughter. Throwing up his hands, he said, "I concede. It's too small a point to argue, and I doubt it would do me any good anyway."

"Quite right," Her Majesty said graciously. "Now, if there's nothing else we can do for you?"

Navarro sighed and rose from his chair. "No, thank you. You've both done more than enough. I do expect a copy of your report."

"You'll have it tomorrow," Mom promised. *Minus all the juicy parts about Anna Addison and her performance in Archimedes' personal dungeon,* I thought.

"Very good." Navarro looked down at me. "See me out?" he asked.

I got up and took Navarro out to the front porch. The rain was really coming down now. As he buttoned up his raincoat, Navarro said, "I just wanted to say again what an excellent job you've done."

I suppose I should have been happy or relived or something at Navarro's words, but I just felt numb, disconnected, as if my capacity for emotion were a battery that had been drained dry.

When I didn't speak, Navarro said, "Although, as I told you before, there were a few people who would have been happy to see the daughter of the mayor come to grief, so don't be surprised to find that you've made some enemies in this town."

I thought of Brandon Archimedes and his less than veiled

threats. "Thanks," I said. "I guess that's getting to be a habit with me."

Navarro touched my shoulder, turning me to face him. "You've also made some friends," he said seriously. "Me, for one."

"Say what?"

"You saved the life of a River City police officer, and you helped prevent a possible miscarriage of justice. I will never forget that." Navarro hunched his shoulders and walked out into the rain.

I reentered Mom's office just as she was putting her computer keyboard away in her desk. She'd stacked the loose papers of my case notes neatly under the gold bug-shaped paperweight that's been on her desk as long as I can remember. She looked up as I came in. "He's right, you know."

She'd obviously been listening in via the hidden microphone on the porch. "About what?" I asked.

Mom came from around her desk and took a guest chair, letting her hand find Beowulf's head. "About the job you've done. The question now is, how do you feel?"

"I don't know. Maybe I'm just too burned-out, but right now it feels like it's all something that happened to someone else. But it didn't. I killed a man."

"Yes," Mom said. "You did. Because you had no choice in the matter. If anyone's to blame, it would be the man who died. He had a choice, though I believe his judgment must have been clouded by his feelings for Anna Addison. Where his choice to shoot at you and Hector began, yours ended."

"What do you mean?"

"Jason," Mom said gently, "why do you think I subjected you to all those years of training? It was so that in a moment like that, you'd react without thinking, and do the one thing

I needed you to do: survive. When that moment came, you didn't get to make a choice. You did the only thing you could do."

"Great. So you programmed me to be a killing machine. Not to mention an arm-breaking one."

"It's a dangerous world, my love, and it's full of dangerous people. Having you trained the way I did was the best way I knew to keep you safe. Short of locking you up in the cellar for the rest of your life. Now it's up to you."

"What is?"

"What you're going to do now. There's no point in staying alive if you're not going to continue living, if you know what I mean. You also need to decide if you can stay in this line of work. You've shown me that you have a definite talent for the job, but that doesn't really matter. What matters is if you're happy doing this, and that's something only you can decide for yourself. In the meantime, I suggest you start getting your head together. Jenny and Angelina can help in that department until I get back."

"Get back? From where?"

"Santa Teresa," Mom said. "Remember? I said I had to leave a few loose ends down there in my rush to get back home and see how you were doing. I'm flying back there tonight."

"Tonight? But you haven't slept in over twenty-four hours!"

"I intend to get back there and crash tonight, so I can finish up my case first thing tomorrow. James and Timothy can hold down the fort here. In the meantime, consider yourself temporarily fired. You can afford it for now, with the massive bill I'm going to hit His Honor the mayor with for saving his idiot daughter. I figure you're good for at least a week off. In the meantime, call Jenny. And remember, there are precious few second chances in this world. You might not get one with a woman like her. You got that?"

"Yeah. I do."

Mom's lip twisted in a little smile. "Now there's a phrase your poor old mother has been waiting to hear you say. Preferably in a church. Now get going."

"Yes, Your Highness."

"And don't forget to take care of Beowulf while I'm gone."

I saluted and got my suit jacket. As I was walking through the front reception area, my mind was on calling Jenny and hoping it wasn't too late to see Angelina as well. I was so lost in the thought of where I wanted to be that I ran right into the woman who was standing in front of the door. "Oh, excuse me!" she gasped.

I was too startled to speak. The woman before me was wrapped in a beige raincoat, with long dark hair that was plastered to her face and shoulders. Her eyes were concealed behind a large pair of glasses, occluded with raindrops. "Oh, I'm sorry!" she said.

"No, that's okay," I replied. "Uh, what are you doing here?"

The woman seemed to hold her breath for a moment, and then her words came pouring out. "Oh, I'm really sorry. I mean, I know it's late and all, but, you see, I was told that this office can help me. I don't know why I came out tonight. I should have realized that you'd be closed and all, and . . . and I mean, I don't really think my husband wants to kill me. Not really. I mean, that's silly, right?"

As she spoke, I remembered when the man who called himself Elijah Messenger came to our door—and how I let him go off into the night, only to get himself killed. I thought of all the things I might have done differently. If only I'd had a second chance.

I looked at the soaked and disheveled woman in front of me, her lips half parted, as if she were silently in the midst of some kind of prayer.

"My name is Jason Wilder," I said, not just to her but to myself as well. "I'm a private detective here at the Midnight Investigation Agency. Why don't you come inside and tell me all about it?"